IRISH BLOOD

1

The return of The Troubles.
The return of Alex Green.

2nd April 2027

Chavash Varmane Bor National Park, Russia

Grigorii Belov glanced at his favourite watch, a Tag Heuer Aquaracer that he'd bought years ago while passing through Dubai. Fourteen minutes to seven in the morning. He'd been watching the house in front of him for four days now, and the man had left it for his early morning swim in the lake between seven and seven-oh-five on each one of them. A creature of habit, he surmised.

Today was going to be different though. Today, the man would not be going back in to his house in the woods.

Lying on the ground in front of him, protected from the earth by a heavy canvas sheet, was his hunting rifle. Others probably wouldn't consider it a hunting rifle, but he did, as did many hunters in the United States he'd been reliably informed. At over a hundred years old, his Mosin-Nagant was the most reliable weapon he'd ever owned, roughly on par with the Kalashnikov AK-47 or it's replacement the AKM from his military days. It would still operate when crusted with desert sand, after a month underwater, or caked in mud. It had been the weapon of choice for the Russian military from around 1890 until the end of the Second World War when the AK-47 was initially introduced. It took a five-round clip and operated with a bolt action. One round was now ready and waiting in the chamber, ready for him to execute his plan.

Grigorii had been in the forest for almost ten months now and he thought that it was time to return to the real world, to be with people again. One winter living out there had been more than enough. From what little news he picked up on his pocket radio – it often tuned-in to nothing out in the wilderness, the signal useless – COVID was now more or less under control, a vaccine now being produced locally in almost every country on the planet.

The serum had been discovered in South Africa by a small Special Air Service team. Thinking about this made him squeeze his eyes tightly shut, anger rising in his chest. He could have been a part of that discovery, but he'd fucked-up. There had been two teams on the mission, the SAS from the UK, and his own Spetsnaz team from the Motherland. Due to personal failings that he still found difficult to accept, his own team had been obliterated, himself the only survivor.

He took off a black woollen hat and ran a hand over his bald head, an attempt to brush away the anger and frustration. He wasn't bitter that the English team had found the answer to COVID: he was just bitterly disappointed that he had bombed-out so badly, especially as the cost had been the lives of his team members.

He looked at the Tag once again, noting that it was now only a minute before the hour. It was a time to clear his mind, to prioritise the task at hand, to focus hard on the here and now.

This would be his last hit. He needed to get it right.

He looked again towards the cabin door, aware that the man inside would be up and about, pulling on his swimming shorts, preparing to shock his body into life with his daily plunge, never realising that this one would be his last.

Grigorii lifted the Mosin-Nagant, almost caressing the rifle, his baby. He was already in the prone position, the most stable for the shot, the barrel of the weapon just protruding out of the cover of the bushes where he hid, a full one hundred metres from the target. At this range and with his skills, it was a no-miss shot, a hundred-and-fifty percenter. No trained soldier could fail from here, and as an ex-Spetsnaz man, Grigorii was much more than a trained soldier. He was a highly trained killer.

The door of the cabin opened, a man of about sixty strolling down the wooden porch, stretching a little, then beating his chest with his fists, a routine to psyche himself up for the cold waters of the lake. He'd done this each day before leaping into the water, swimming a fast front crawl for maybe twenty metres, then turning around and doing a slow breaststroke back to the jetty.

It made the shot all the simpler for Grigorii, and he'd already taken the decision of just when to end the target's life. He'd let him have his swim, let him have that final pleasure, then take him down as he hauled himself from the water.

The man dived into the lake, the splash echoing from the trees that surrounded the water. His front crawl was sloppy, too much splash, not enough forward progress in Grigorii's mind, but it was clear to the soldier that the man was going through his routine as usual. Running out of air, he stopped and turned, the slower breaststroke silent after the wild thrashing about of his freestyle.

Grigorii pulled the weapon into his shoulder, finding the spot where it felt just right. He took a deep breath, exhaled, took another, fully filling his lungs as he waited for the moment. It would be soon.

The man reached the bottom of a set of steps mounted on the end of the short wooden jetty, pausing as he grabbed them with his right hand. He looked around the lake, breathing in the tranquillity of the place, trying to be one with nature. His gaze seemed to stop right where Grigorii lay, but the ex-soldier knew that he couldn't be seen, that his camouflage was perfect.

The man ducked his head under the water, then exploded upwards, starting to climb the steps.

Grigorii took a last breath, expanding his lungs to the full, held it for a second then slowly released it, eye now close to the weapon, capturing his target in the cross hairs of the telescopic sight.

Almost in slow motion, the ex-politician stepped on to the jetty's deck, bending to pick-up a large towel that he'd left there. He pulled it around his shoulders, pausing to again look at the silent world around him.

The centre of his forehead was fixed in the cross hairs, the air from Grigorii's lungs almost all gone. He had taken-up the slack from the trigger, his left hand comfortably holding the stock of the rifle. His right index finger tightened slightly, the final ounce of pressure that was needed to initiate the shot.

BOOM!

The gunshot echoed around the lake, but this didn't matter in the slightest; there were no other dwellings anywhere in the vicinity, no one to hear the sound of death.

Grigorii didn't move, letting the rifle settle in his grasp, right eye still close to the scope. He watched the man collapse in a heap, a small twitch from his right leg the final movement. Grigorii could see the blood where the bullet had entered his skull, couldn't see the exit wound because of the way the man had fallen, but could see the open eyes, a surprised expression obvious in them.

He lowered the weapon, drawing back from the cover of the bushes, taking his gear with him.

It was time for breakfast.

The cabin was well stocked, warm, the interior more than comfortable. The only thing missing was a cute female, Grigorii decided.

A pan of scrambled eggs slowly thickened on the stove and the kettle bubbled on the worktop. He flicked on the TV, a chance to really catch-up with the goings-on in the rest of the world. His Mosin-Nagant stood by the door, it's duty done for the day. He'd already rolled the body into the water. A treat for the fish.

His toast popped, and he found the cupboard with plates. A breakfast bar with fur-topped chairs completed his return to normality. The forest floor had been his home for long enough.

Fed, he decided that a couple of hours in a real bed and then a shower were in order. Perhaps stay for the night. And then it was time to return back to civilisation.

The red BMW X3 didn't seem to fit the rustic surroundings of the cabin, woods and lake. That seemed a good enough reason for Grigorii to make use of it, to take it back to the world where it belonged, along with himself.

Of course he knew it was theft, but he couldn't imagine that anyone out here would be too bothered by that. It probably wasn't even registered – the owner had chosen obscurity all by himself, along with a number of other politicians who'd done a runner when COVID had got out of control. Guilty consciences, Grigorii surmised; starting a pandemic was one thing, losing control of your little toy quite another. They'd fucked-up the world, and now he had fucked them up. An eye for an eye. Tooth for a tooth.

The keys were in a large crystal bowl by the door. He took them, had a last look around the cabin, then headed out to the car.

2nd April 2027

Umhlanga Rocks, Durban, South Africa

Alex Green could hardly believe the changes to the suburb since he'd first visited the place a year back. Shops were again open, the hotels were doing a roaring trade, and even the golden sand of the beach was busy. He knew that COVID wasn't fully beaten yet, but having a cure was enough to give the world confidence to start over again, to go out there and live once more. If you were unfortunate enough to catch it, the serum was available, and a lot of that had been down to his team.

"Are you really going back to Hereford?" Nkosi Sithole asked him, a frown on his dark face. "Surely you don't want to give up all of this?"

A dolphin leapt out of the water, probably less than fifty metres from the beach, splashed back into the Indian Ocean. It was a good question, Alex knew. The place was absolutely gorgeous, but it was time to get back home, to earn his keep. The job here in Africa was done, the locals now back in control of their country, teams of home-grown men trained by Alex and his Special Air Service troops. Some of his team would stay, but for him it was time to move on.

"It is a great place mate, but I need to get back to the Regiment." He looked past the young Zulu, to where the man's new wife Kaya and her sister Andile sat at the bar sipping cocktails. "It's different for you; this is your home."

Nkosi had been a part of the first team of SAS men to return to South Africa, helping protect Andile from the lawless land that the country had become. Andile was the doctor who had discovered something in the venom of toads, taken the stuff to cure herself of the virus, then helped the British scientists to develop an industrial scale solution that had then been rolled out to the rest of the world. It was still difficult to believe that the fun-loving Zulu girl sat at the bar had possibly saved the planet.

He picked up his beer, saluted his comrade. "We'll keep in touch Nkosi, don't worry about that." He sipped the cold beer, the warm sun on his back also reminding him that England wouldn't be so pleasant. "When is the baby due?"

Nkosi's face split into a wide grin, glancing across at Kaya. "Two months still, but that'll be soon enough." He put his pint back on the table, leaning forward. "Thanks for all of your support Alex," he said. "Maybe we'd have made it anyway, but you sending me back down here was a Godsend. Kaya wouldn't have stayed in the UK too long without her sis. You know how close they are now."

Alex nodded in agreement, watching the girls sharing a moment. If he was honest with himself, he'd have liked to see where a relationship with Andile might have gone. She had a quick mind, great humour, and she was stunning to look at. He sighed.

"Penny for your thoughts," Nkosi murmured. "I might have a wild guess about what they were, if you like." He grinned, following Alex's gaze.

"Probably better that you don't," Alex countered. He slapped his thigh, getting up. "Sitting here and reminiscing isn't getting anything done," he said. "I'll meet you all for dinner at eight, but first I need to get a few things out of the way." He waved to the girls, high-fived Nkosi. "Have fun."

Back in his room, Alex took out his mobile phone, something that hadn't worked when he'd first returned to South Africa, but operational again now that the cell phone towers were reinstated. The only thing that had worked when he'd initially been down there looking for a solution to the virus had been his army issue satellite phone.

He'd been back in the country for nine months this time, initially basing himself in Cape Town and working north, training locals along the way. Nkosi had begun his own trip from the northern end of Kwa-Zulu Natal, a place called Jozini, the place where Andile had extracted what later turned out to be the 'COVID-cure' from large toads that lived in the lake there. Another team had been based in Port Elizabeth, with two more in Johannesburg and Pretoria. They'd searched out a highly nervous local population that had lived in hiding for the last years, given them weapons and military training, boosting their confidence and allowing some sort of rule of law to return to the land.

It hadn't all been fun; one thing Alex would never forget was the beauty of the country, but he'd also remember the harshness of the place. There was little middle-ground to be found in South Africa – things were extreme, fantastically nice, or horribly bad. Life was cheap, and he had seen incredibly ugly scenes on the route to freedom. Rape, murder, burning tyres placed over a living soul's head, mutilation… It had been a terribly harsh journey.

On the opposite side of the coin, he had seen how friendly the people could be if you gave something back in return. And the land was outstanding, vistas the like of which he had never seen in all of his travels, wild animals so close to hand that you could almost touch them, sunsets over the Indian Ocean.

No, he decided to himself, you simply couldn't imagine Africa without living in it. It was too intense, too perfect and yet so imperfect, all at the same time.

He did a ring around the other three teams, just a daily check-in that was all part of his routine. No surprises. The country was running, the politicians slowly reappearing, coming back from wherever they had run off to during the pandemic. When their country had been in dire straits, they had fled, but now that things were recovering, they wanted their piece of the pie. That was Africa.

He sat on his hotel room balcony, looking at the deep blue sea ahead of him. It was time for the main call. He pressed the quick dial, waiting for the connection.

"Mike Sanders," the voice answered. "That you Alex?"

Alex waited half a second, wondering what the commanding officer of the SAS regiment was doing back at home. He'd come down to Africa twice during the last months, not intruding, just letting his people see that he hadn't forgotten them.

"Yes boss, it's me," he finally sighed in to the handset. "I think it's time to come home."

There was a short silence from the UK end of the connection. "I guessed that was what you were going to say," the colonel replied. "The job is over, and that means that you're probably getting bored again."

Alex was nodding to the phone, knowing that his leader couldn't see this. "You're right boss," he finally said. "I think I'm ready for a change of scene, otherwise I might never come back."

"And we couldn't have that Mister Green," Sanders retorted. Alex could almost see him grinning. "It's a good time to come home Alex," the officer added. "We have a few things happening over here and I could use someone who can think outside of the box. Someone like you."

Alex joined Nkosi and the girls in a bar opposite the Beverly Hills Hotel, now fully restored to its former glory. He could hardly believe that he'd been a part of a firefight there only ten months before, a battle in which two Russian soldiers had died. He pushed the thought to the back of his mind, not willing to let the evening be ruined by the past.

At seven months pregnant, Kaya was still quite thin, especially from behind. The bump was all frontal, and she still seemed to get herself into the same clothes as she had months back. Andile was of a similar build; a slim lady of around five-and-half foot, with curves in all of the right places. She wore her hair short, her dark eyes now searching out Alex's, trying to read his thoughts.

"You're leaving, aren't you?" she asked quietly. Her face was still, not showing any emotions, but Alex knew that they had grown quite close over the last months. She did not turn away, wiping her right eye with the back of her hand.

"Yes," Alex said apologetically. "My job here's over. The boss has stuff for me to do back at home."

She forced a smile, nodding as if understanding. "I'll miss you," she said simply.

"You need a drink?" Alex asked, an excuse to get away from them all for a second. Andile wasn't the only one who had feelings.

"I'll join you," she said. "I can help carry."

The two of them moved up to the bar to order, Kaya and Nkosi watching. "She will miss him badly," the Zulu girl told the SAS soldier. "I wish he would stay."

Nkosi nodded agreement. "He's the best boss I've ever had," he told her. "But he feels he has to go back, that he must do his duty. You know Alex," he said, as if this explained everything.

"She'll still miss him."

It was the end of the evening, Nkosi and Kaya already retired for the night. Alex and Andile sat again at the bar, two of the last ten or so that had hung around after their meals. The music was low, the mood sleepy.

"I don't know how I'll get by without you," Andile said softly. "You've become a part of my life." Her eyes were damp, perhaps partially from the booze, but Alex didn't think that was all.

"You'll be fine," he told her bravely. He exhaled loudly, a sad sounding sigh. "I'll miss you too Andile," he added.

"Then don't go," she told him. "We can make a life together here."

A massive part of Alex wanted to agree with her, to take a chance, to give it all up. But an equally large part of him wanted to get back home, back to the Regiment, the SAS. Maybe one day he would stop, but he didn't think he could do that yet. There were so many things in the world that needed putting right and he wanted to be a part of it. "Maybe one day we will," he said. "I just need to get something out of my system, otherwise it's going to bug me forever."

She took his hands into her own, her big eyes locking on his. "I understand. You are a good soldier, I am a good doctor. These are our vocations. But the link we have is more than a job." She paused, released one hand, took a sip of her wine, drawing strength from it. "Go and do what you must, but please come back. And don't take too long."

Alex opened his eyes, the first rays of sunshine finding their way into his room, the poorly pulled curtains not able to hold onto the darkness.

He looked at the beautiful women who lay on her side on the far edge of the king-sized bed. He could recall almost everything from the previous night, the beauty of it all, the one drink too many that had led them both to dropping their defences. It was what they'd both wanted, but now he felt that it had been a bad decision; he was returning to Hereford the following morning. This was no time to start a relationship.

He watched Andile's shoulders rise and fall, the sheet covering her lower body, her back facing him. God, she was gorgeous.

He slipped silently out of bed, headed for the bathroom. He didn't want to hurt her, and he knew that leaving would do that, no doubt about it.

"We are adults Alex, and adults have choices," she informed him. "I chose to be with you, and I would make that choice all over again if it came to it." They walked along the Umhlanga promenade, just the two of them, a chance to talk things through, better understand what last night had meant to them both. "Don't feel bad. I don't."

"I'm leaving tomorrow morning Andile," he reminded her. "It would have been better just parting as friends. I have no idea when I might see you again, no clue as to where the Regiment may want me to go." He looked over at her, angry and disappointed with himself. It wasn't that he didn't care for her, it was just that he couldn't walk away from his job, a profession that he loved. And a dangerous profession to boot. He could be in another theatre of war next week, hardly a great way to start a long-term relationship.

She shook her head, trying to shake out the anger that blazed in it. "I know what you do, and I still wanted to be with you." She walked a little faster, burning off angry energy and trying to remain calm. "You must do what you must, and then we will see what the future will bring. For good or for bad," she concluded.

He didn't know how to reply to that. She was giving him a way out, but she was also making it hard.

"Cat got your tongue?" she snapped after a minute of walking in silence.

He glanced at her, a wicked grin on her face. He stopped, now also grinning, and pulled her into a hug.

"How will we manage apart?" he whispered.

"We will manage," she said softly. "If it is meant to be. Remember; I'm a Sangoma, a witchdoctor," she finished with a smile.

Andile watched the Emirates Boeing 777 climb out of King Shaka International Airport, turning on to its course for Dubai. Alex would then route onwards to London and to whatever his powers-that-be wished upon him. It was a worrying thought, but not as bad as it would have been a few years back if she'd known him then. Coronavirus had slowed down many conflicts around the globe, made people realise how fragile their lease on life really was. Less war meant less risk. The world was a slightly safer place for now.

"Damn!" she cursed herself. Why had she not made a move on the man months ago? They'd been good friends for over a year now, her sister was his best mate's wife, the opportunities had been right there. Why did these things always happen too late, like just when there was no time left?

She walked to her car, wondering what to do next. No Alex. No distractions.

She did what she always did when frustrated and left to her own devices, pointing the car into the city of Durban and her home there, the hospital. Research, research and more research. COVID was gone, but there was always another challenge for her. Another solution to seek out and conquer.

2nd April 2027

Just outside Antrim, Northern Ireland

The house was just off Castle Road, close to the northern shores of the giant Lough Neagh, and only about fifteen minutes ride outside of Antrim, not long past the golf course. It was a very nice area, the sort of place you wanted to live, close enough to work, but far enough away to avoid the city bustle. Belfast could be a horrible traffic jam in the morning, just like any major metropolis anywhere in the world.

It was a two storey ex-farmhouse, refurbished in recent years, set nicely in two acres of green grass. There again, where except the towns and cities were not set in lush green grass in Northern Ireland, Declan wondered? His late father had always told him, 'if it's not raining now, then it soon will be'. It made for rolling hills of pure emerald, but it really didn't do anything for suntans or arthritis. He'd learned that later in life from others with joints that had failed too soon.

He'd stopped the car at the end of the driveway, had turned his headlights off a few hundred metres before that. He checked his watch, already very aware of the time. Three in the morning, and not a star in the sky. He thought about taking a cigarette but decided there was no point pushing it.

"Shall we get on with this Declan?" Paddy Murphy asked from the seat beside him. Paddy had always been an impatient bastard, had nearly dropped them all in it a few times in the past through not taking his time, checking that all was as it appeared.

"Hold your horses boy," old Frank said from the back seat. "This wouldn't be the first time that the police have set someone up for a surprise."

Declan nodded agreement, his eyes roaming over the property, onwards to the detached garage block, looking for a reason to cancel the show. He was almost forty years of age now and had no intention of not making that number.

"We've been here more than five minutes now and…"

"Shut-up Paddy!" Declan snapped. He rounded on the man. "Frank's right. If we charge in there and the police are waiting for us, then we're truly fucked."

"And not in a pleasant way," Frank added quietly.

Chastised, Paddy looked through the window, wondering to himself why these old men couldn't just make a decision. At twenty-one, he was far more alert than these two and could see that their way was clear, the target asleep. He decided, not for the first time, that Declan was a bit of a chicken, watching his own arse and not giving his all for the cause. Frank was just an old git.

An awkward silence filled the car.

"Alright, it's time," Declan told them after another three minutes of tense watching and no words. "We all know what we should find here, we all know our jobs, so let's not make a mess of it," he ordered. "Check your weapons."

Another useless instruction Paddy thought. He'd checked his about a thousand times already this evening, couldn't see things changing from it having been sat under the front seat for the last half-an-hour. He kept his gob shut though. Behind him, Frank opened his door, the hinges oiled earlier to avoid any unwanted surprises. Paddy and Declan followed suit, the men slowly stepping out of the car.

Declan put a finger to his lips, motioned them forward, all sticking to the grass, avoiding the gravel of the driveway. The dark was their friend tonight, but the gravel could also be a giveaway, the slight crunch of it at this early hour could wake the man inside of the building.

The front door was alarmed, that they knew for sure. Probably also the other downstairs doors and windows, but the tradesman who had a leaning to their cause hadn't been able to confirm that. Politicians were always well protected, and his job in the house had been supervised throughout. One trip to the toilet had been the only real chance to dig about a bit, and that's when he'd discovered the bathroom had no trip on the window. Maybe the only unalarmed point of entry in the whole place, and sods law had it right next to the main bedroom.

That's how it was. No point cursing.

The bonus was that it was directly above the porch, so at least something to use for access, no need for ladders or drainpipes. Always some good with the bad.

He gave Frank a sign to return to the vehicle, pointed out the window above the front door, the trellis beside it.

Denis McAvoy rolled over in bed, his mind only half awake. Had he heard something? He looked to where his wife Jenny slept across the bed, feet sticking out from under the covers, out like a light.

Probably nothing, but he'd check. Even as a low-level political figure in Northern Ireland, it was always worth checking. Things that went 'bump' in the night over there often made extra loud 'bumps'.

He rolled off the side of the bed, thought about the pistol he kept in the bedside cabinet. Probably a good idea. He moved towards the cabinet, Jenny now stirring, disturbed by his own motions. He paused, keeping quiet, hoping that she'd drift off again.

A sound of something falling – sounded like from the bathroom – a muttered curse, and he was no longer concerned about waking his wife, only in getting to the dresser ASAP. He needed that gun, and he needed it yesterday. This was about as bad as it got.

Behind his back the bedroom door burst open, a torch splitting the darkness of the room. He had the drawer open, his right hand closing on the weapon, remembering that he didn't have a magazine inserted, knowing that this would cost him another couple of seconds at the best. Out of the corner of his eye he saw that the torch had captured Jenny, half-sitting up in her bed, shock all over her pale features, bedcover up to her neck.

BOOM! The report of the gun filled the whole room, spinning him around, his fingers losing their hold on the loaded magazine, his body locking-up, expecting the pain of the impact to follow. Jenny gave a yelp to his side, the torch still on her, a single red hole on the front of her face, more blood and grey matter on the pillow behind her head.

"NO!" he screamed, dropping to his knees and trying to find the magazine of bullets, his left hand searching back and forth across the floor. More noise behind him, at least another man he guessed, two beams of light searching him out.

BANG!

He hardly heard the second report, hardly felt anything, his hand finding the magazine and trying desperately to fit it to the weapon, his grip on it now loose, his head turning again towards his wife.

BANG!

The next shot impacted with the back of his skull, exiting through the right eye.

All systems went black and red, the lights failing, the room spinning into oblivion…

"Okay, let's get the feck out of here!" Declan ordered unnecessarily. He shepherded Paddy ahead of him, Frank already bringing the car along the driveway, turning it around to get them away as soon as humanly possible.

Paddy stopped in the doorway, looked back, astounded by what he'd just done. He'd killed a man, a member of the enemy, wished he'd killed the woman too. It was his first kill, the first time that he'd taken another human being's life, and now he was flying on a wave of adrenalin. At that moment in time he felt incredibly strong, invulnerable, bullet proof.

"Get the fuck out of here!" Declan yelled in his ear, pushing him in the back. Paddy considered what it would be like to kill Declan too, maybe even Frank. That would be the end of them giving him bloody orders. He'd be the boss, make his own decisions.

Instead he turned, followed the older man back out of the bathroom window, back out into the night.

So far no audible or visual alarms. With the house so far from any others, perhaps they would even leave unnoticed. Declan searched for problems, found none.

Back at the vehicle Frank was already making his way into the back seat, knowing his role and also his limitations. Declan leapt behind the wheel, putting the car into gear and driving carefully back towards the road, headlights still off.

"Fuck, that was a gas!" Paddy said far too loud and too enthusiastically, ears still booming from the roar of the guns.

Declan looked at the boy, then back to Frank. They had a real loose cannon on their hands here. One of those crackerjacks that would end up dropping them all in it one day. He could see from the expression on the face of the old man that he thought the same.

He shook his head, focussing his attentions on getting them far away from the crime scene, back towards Armagh where they would find more like-minded people.

They would have to sort out Paddy another day.

5th April 2027

Heathrow Airport, London, UK

The overnight flight had given Alex a lot of time to think, but he still couldn't organise his thoughts into a decision that both his head and his heart could agree on. Andile had been at the forefront of his brain the whole way home, and where he would normally have managed to sleep for at least half of the flight, he knew he'd be lucky if he'd actually had two hours during the full journey.

He knew that the job in South Africa was essentially over and that meant that his special skills needed to be applied elsewhere. That's what he had trained for, that's why he'd volunteered to join the SAS. He was a soldier with a difference, as were all of the team that made up 22 Special Air Service Regiment. They had to be used wisely, not just to carry out duties that could easily be assigned to normal troops. If not, then why bother spending all of the tax payers cash to train them so well?

Then there was Andile. This is where his heart took over, questioning his need to risk his life yet again, when everything he needed seemed to be in this perfect woman. Add to this that he was also in love with Africa itself, and it was hard to argue that he could have – should have? – made a life there.

His soul was being ripped in two.

He crossed the airbridge to the terminal, trying to force his private thoughts out of his mind, switching on his cell phone. It took a few minutes to power-up and find a network, then another couple before beeping a few times to let him know that he had messages.

As he strolled through the terminal he noticed how much the country had changed in the months he'd been away, something he'd partially picked-up on while passing through Dubai. It was almost back to normal again, almost the same old UK that had been there before COVID. The serum had made the difference, that much was more than obvious. He hoped the same changes were as positive in the city itself. It would make it so much easier to be home.

Reaching the baggage carousel, he decided to see what was what on his cell, whether anything of use was waiting for his attention. The first message was just to welcome him back to the network, the standard blurb that the network provider pushed out. He pressed delete, not at all interested in the offers for top-ups and texts. The company paid anyway.

The next was from Mike Sanders, booking him in for a meeting in Hereford the following morning. Nothing to worry about, just a chat about a potential project. Vague as usual from the boss, phone and software security one of his bugbears nowadays.

Next message was from Andile, hoping that he'd had a good journey and reminding him to call. He considered doing so right away but decided to first check the last message.

An alert for a voicemail. He called the number wondering how old the message was and if it was still relevant, who it might be from.

"Hi Alex," the message started. Alex noticed that the bags were just starting to appear through the black rubber strips at the start of the conveyor. "It's me, Derek 'Flipflop' Johnson, your old mucker from South Africa." The recording laughed. "I'm your local taxi today, compliments of the boss. He's had a change of plan and wants you at a meeting tomorrow in London. I'm your driver, just like old times." He went on to explain where Alex should find him, the car a standard black Range Rover still favoured by the SAS crews.

Alex frowned. It seemed like he wouldn't be getting much time to himself, but perhaps this was for the better. He needed to get his teeth into something. It was either that or get back on a plane to South Africa and a certain Zulu witchdoctor.

Flipflop had been on the initial mission to Africa, a major part of Alex's six man team, and one of those people who could make you smile even when times were desperate. He found the car easily enough, and soon Flipflop's infectious good humour had Alex in a better frame of mind. They talked about old times, making the traffic jam that was the route back into the capital pass quickly.

"Do you ever hear from that Russian guy who was with us down there?" Flipflop asked. "He fucked-up quite badly during the op, but you seemed to be getting along with him quite well on the route home."

Alex thought about Grigorii and the military flights back from Africa, the phone call he'd had from him several weeks later. He still didn't have all the facts, but his reading was that the Russian blamed senior people for the beginnings of the coronavirus, and that he'd taken it on himself to correct things. How he'd do this was anyone's guess, but Alex knew that an ex-Spetsnaz soldier could achieve many things that others only dreamt about.

"Yeah, he made a mess of things down there, but I think he was honestly unhappy with how things turned out, and about his own influence on them. He was a soldier, just like us, and he was concerned about how the hierarchy would handle things when he got home," Alex replied. "We've all been there."

"That's where having a boss like Mike Sanders makes such a big difference," Flipflop said, serious for a change. "He'd back us to the hilt, of that I'm certain."

Alex nodded, knowing it was true. Mike had pushed through the latest training program in South Africa, used his social skills to get the Prime Minister onside, even backed Alex on his promotion of Nkosi to lead the Natal contingent. "You're right, but I think in Russia things work a little differently," he said.

Flipflop thought about this, and you could almost hear the wheels whirling in his head. Alex waited for the punchline that he was certain would follow.

"I guess in England, we'd get a debrief, a slap on the wrist for any cock-ups, and perhaps some additional training to put them right," he began, his eyes on the traffic ahead that had again started to roll. "In Russia if things go well you probably get a bottle of vodka, and perhaps a blond to keep you warm at night. That's if things actually went well, that is." He glanced across, a flicker of a grin starting at the corner of his lips. "And if it all went tits-up, then I guess that you get Stalag 19."

Alex smiled, realising that he hadn't heard much dark squaddie humour for several months. It was good to be back. "We didn't even get our wrists slapped," he told the trooper. "Must have been really bad." He glanced over at Flipflop, surprised that he wasn't also smiling. He frowned. "What's up?"

The other man was focused on the traffic, his face serious. "I shouldn't have said that really," he eventually responded. "What if they did put Grigorii away somewhere?"

Alex thought about this for a short while, himself unsure as to where the Russian was now, only remembering his last call with the man, the call from somewhere in the middle of nowhere.

"I haven't spoken to him in months, but I know he was okay back then," he said thoughtfully. "I think he'll be okay mate, but I also think some other people may not be. He was an angry man and wanted to somehow put right the mistakes he'd made in Africa. He wanted to punish the people who he felt had helped cause them."

Flipflop concentrated on the driving, a silence descending briefly in the vehicle. "Good luck to him with that," he eventually replied. "I just hope he does nothing too stupid."

Mike Sanders had requested a breakfast meet at a coffeehouse close to Westminster at eight-thirty, so Alex had allowed himself the luxury of a couple of beers with Flipflop the evening before. He'd also spent twenty short minutes on the phone to Andile; it had been a tough call, both uncertain of what to say, confused as to whether they had a future together, neither of them wishing to say the wrong thing. The call had ended up in a stalemate, both promising to keep in touch, but the pair of them knowing that a long distance relationship could soon fade and die.

Alex felt that he was at a T-junction, and that if he turned in the wrong direction he would probably screw-up the rest of his life. He would either end up hating the Regiment for keeping him apart from his lover; or he'd hate Andile for pulling him away from his band of brothers.

The conundrum was still taxing his brain while he sat waiting for his boss to turn up, a sparkling water sat in front of him at his window seat.

"Hey Alex, how's it going?" a cheery voice broke into his reverie, a hand clapping his shoulder. He turned to see the boss already there. He'd been so deep in his own musings that he had totally missed him entering the café. "Will bacon sandwiches do the trick? Maybe a coffee?"

He nodded to both, trying to get up from his seat to help collect things from the counter, but Mike just waved him away. It gave him a chance to adjust his focus, to join the here and now. Andile versus the job would have to wait until later.

Mike was back a few minutes later, a tray with two coffees, a bacon bap for Alex, and toast for himself.

"Good to be back?"

"Still adjusting boss," he replied, wondering if he should tell more. He decided to can it for now; it was probably just a bit of 'reverse homesickness' caused by too long away. As if Africa had become his home, England just the holiday destination.

Sanders frowned. "Yeah, I'm sorry not to give you a little time out but something's come up, and with you routing through London it was a chance I decided to capitalise on."

Alex looked at the head of the SAS, still young and fit, looking more like an adult-entry university student than a trained killer. He had no idea how the man handled the stress that must have been a standard part of his job description. It wasn't as if the African project was the only thing happening in the world, and nowadays a large part of his remit was meetings with the political hierarchy in an advisory role, attending both ad-hoc and planned get-togethers, a regular on the COBRA meetings.

"No bother," he responded, knowing he'd taken a second longer than he should have. 'Must stop thinking, just click on the soldiering button again', he thought. "What sort of thing is it? The thing that's come up," he clarified.

Mike sipped his coffee, first swallowing a bite of toast. "We have a meeting with the PM at nine," he said, slurping a little more of the dark liquid. "God, that coffee's shit!" He pulled a face, put down the cup. "There have been three political shootings in Northern Ireland in the past month. The PM wants my take on it. I thought I might drag you along in case they want to get us more involved, sort of a project for you." He grinned. "Can't have one of my star players sat around the Lines with bugger all to do. You might get bored, go back to Africa," he said with a wink.

Alex wondered what he was getting dragged into here, but also puzzled over how much the boss knew about his present dilemma. Had Nkosi said something?

He looked at the boss, thinking of a suitable reply. Mike Sanders had a grin on his face as wide as the Mississippi, and Alex knew then that the man had had the full brief already. And he'd not been back twenty-four hours yet.

The Special Air Service was a tight unit. Too tight sometimes, he thought.

He wouldn't have had it any other way though.

"I'm not really dressed for the job", he finally replied.

"I don't think that Dominic will be too pissed-off about that," Sanders said lightly. "His favourite SAS man, the answer to the COVID crisis?" He smirked before continuing. "It'll keep the rest of the attendees quiet. Nobody likes to speak when there's a spy in the room."

The meeting was being hosted by the Prime Minister, Dominic Wild, in an overheated wood panelled room in the Palace of Westminster, the radiators ancient and massive. Apart from the PM himself, the Northern Ireland Secretary, Nicholas Thomas, the Home Secretary, Ruth Maybank, and the Chief Constable of the Police Service of Northern Ireland, one Colin Shankly were all in attendance. Alex not only felt out of place because of the jeans and casual shirt that he was wearing but also because these people all sat well above his pay grade. It made him wonder if Mike Sanders had only dragged him along for a bit of moral support.

Though well out of his depth, Alex had been pressganged into this type of situation before, with the boss insisting that he attend a meeting in Moscow about a year earlier. That meeting had included both the PM and the Russian President and had eventually led to the mission in South Africa that had discovered the COVID cure. It had been an embarrassing meeting for Alex, not one that he would ever forget. He had spoken out of turn, but the PM had saved the day for him. The success of the mission had then kept him in the PM's line-of-sight, making him a household name in the Wild residence.

"Hi Alex", the PM greeted him on entering. "Good to see you back in our country." Alex blushed as the PM shook his hand warmly, the other high-ups looking on and deliberating as to whom he might be.

"Thank you sir," he replied politely, hoping that he'd addressed the man correctly. "Great to be back."

"So Mike's bullying you into another 'Mission Impossible' is he?" Dominic continued with a grin. He turned towards the others, waving his arm towards the SAS man. "Sorry, but I should introduce you all to Alex Green, the man who volunteered to lead the mission down south, the man who brought back the magic toad juice." He laughed a little at his own joke, the others joining in.

"He's here to support me sir," Mike interrupted, drawing the attention from Alex. "He arrived back in London from Africa yesterday evening, so I thought that it might be convenient for him to come along and assist me today."

The room sort of nodded in agreement, the PSNI man grunting something that may have been "nice to meet you," his ginger moustache bobbing along with the words.

"And of course, we can have our debrief in the car on the return to Hereford," Mike said with a small grin. "Sort of saving taxpayers money."

"I think we're all in support of that one," Dominic said with a grin, still shuffling papers and effectively closing the topic. "Now, on to today's meeting." He sat down, signalling the others to follow suit, finished assembling some paperwork and a notepad in front of him. "Subject is Northern Ireland," he said. "Hence the audience."

Everyone else pulled out pads and files, preparing themselves for business. Alex suddenly felt even more naked; he wasn't at all prepared for this. Mike shoved a notepad and biro in front of him, adding a tiny nod of support. Alex gave him a thumbs-up below the table. He leant forward, taking the pen, eyes on the PM.

"Now most of us will have guessed why we are all here today, but please allow me to give some background for Alex as he's been out of the country for a good while now." The PM glanced to the young soldier, remembering the meeting in Moscow, now so long ago. "You probably know most of it anyway, so if I just repeat things, forgive me. It means that we all start out on the same page at least."

Alex nodded agreement, pen poised.

"Two nights ago the Democratic Unionist MP for Antrim and his wife were shot dead in their beds. Denis McAvoy." The PM paused partially for effect, but largely because he'd met the man on a few occasions and had actually had high hopes for him. He had seen a young politician who was still grounded, cared about his constituency, and didn't just spout drivel. Some rare qualities in a politician these days, he'd decided. He pushed the thought aside, continued with his story. "Two weeks back the Unionist MP for Portrush met the same fate, but in his case the gunmen also killed his wife and two children, twelve and fourteen year-old girls." He let that one hang. Being a member of parliament and being a target of sorts was part of the job; your family also being legitimate targets was despicable.

He again moved on. "Three weeks ago, a Sinn Fein MP from Armagh was also shot. He was single, so no family to target, thank God."

Alex had heard about the killings in the news but being so far away from their source meant that he had given them little notice. Hearing it like this brought it much closer to home.

The others waited silently, the PM considering his next words.

"No group has claimed any of these murders," he said shortly. "Which is strange in itself, but the other strange thing is that we have had no real sectarian violence in the Province since COVID first struck, and we now have three incidents in three weeks." He passed his gaze over his audience, one by one, making his point.

"The other striking thing is that though two of the politicians were Unionists, the other was a Republican. Does this indicate a tit-for-tat spree of killings? Is this the beginning of something bigger? And if it is, how do we nip it in the bud?"

Dominic Wild let the questions hang in the room, then spread his arms, an invitation for anyone to comment. Initially, no-one took the bait, all of them mentally framing replies and checking that they stacked up.

"I think that you could be right," Nicholas Thomas finally spat out, probably anxious to show he had a good understanding of his bailiwick. "If the first hit was to silence a Catholic man, then it would make sense for the Republicans to want to do something a little more shocking." His voice was all public school, and Alex wondered why people like that were put in positions of power in places like Northern Ireland. Although things hadn't been bad there for years, this was probably only due to the restrictions brought about by COVID, just as the PM had implied. Putting an English public schoolboy in charge of the Province was hardly going to be a winner of hearts and minds, an SAS goal anywhere in the world. Alex considered saying as much but bit his tongue.

The policeman – Colin Shankly – was shaking his head, his eyes fixed on the desk. He gave the impression that he'd sat in many meetings like this over the years, and though he was not afraid of putting his head over the parapet, it wasn't something he greatly enjoyed. He was more a 'doing' man than a 'talking' man. Now was the time to speak though. He cleared his throat, eyes swivelling towards the PM.

"All of the killings have had the same MO – modus operandi for those not in the know, but I'm sure everybody here has watched too many crime thrillers by now." He raised a slight grin from most of the audience here, notable exception being Nicholas Thomas. Alex pondered briefly on how the two men worked together, both having their permanent base over the other side of the Irish Sea.

"These killings have been carried out at night, two of the three targets living in the countryside, far from watching eyes and wagging ears. All have been shootings, with one weapon being present in the first two killings according to our ballistics people. We still haven't finished working over the McAvoy scene yet, but it looks to be the same set-up, a break-in, a shooting with nine-millimetre handguns, and then an escape by road." He took a drink from a bottle of water that stood before his seat. "That means that on the face of it, the same people are killing both Protestants and Catholics."

"But you couldn't call that conclusive proof, could you," Ruth Maybank challenged. Alex watched her, knowing from something he'd once read that she had some sort of legal background. This statement itself proved that, he decided.

"And that's why I said, 'on the face of it', Ruth," Shankly said tightly. He hated lawyers, the bane of all good policemen, possibly only slightly better than politicians in many of his people's eyes.

"Of course," she hurried back, trying to atone a little. "But we should keep open minds, shouldn't we?"

Alex noticed that she looked to the PM with this, trying to find a little moral support.

"Which actually brings us no further forward," Dominic replied, avoiding her gaze. "So now I would like to pose another question." He directed his gaze to Mike Sanders, letting it stray to also include Alex. "What would my wonderful Special Air Service do about such a situation? How would you stop more killings before they start?"

Mike Sanders had attended thousands of these high level get-togethers over the years, knew roughly how to handle anything that was thrown his way, but wasn't enjoying the latest meeting any more than his first one. And now the curveball…

He bent down and rummaged in his bag for a pen – he already had one on the desk, but he needed to buy a little breathing space, a chance to think. Bloody politicians, he thought. They always seemed to find problems all by themselves, but always picked someone else to try and find ways to solve them. And then of course they would claim the glory for themselves and bank the brownie points ready for the next election. He was pleased he didn't have to operate like this.

He took a long breath and raised his eyes from his blank notebook.

"Before I start trying to give you an answer, I think I have two questions that I need to clarify with yourselves," he told the assembled group. "First question would be – what sort of security presence do you want to have in Ireland? I mean, do you want to go back to the old days, to get the army on the streets again? Or could you do that with the PSNI alone?" He directed the last part of the question towards the head of police, but the rest was really just a sticky political decision. He was certain no-one wanted the army back on the streets, but he needed these people to say it, to own the fact.

No-one spoke, so he went on with his second question. "The second point would be to try and determine the scale of the problem," he told them. "Who are you wanting to protect? Just the politicians? Ministers? Perhaps even serving and ex-police and military? In the past, all of these people have become targets. Do you try and defend them all?"

You could have heard a pin drop when Mike stopped speaking, no-one appearing to be happy to take up the gauntlet, to try and answer any of his queries. Mike let an uncomfortable silence hang for a few seconds then stepped back in, happier now that he had a better feel for the situation, had the political types on the backfoot.

"I'm afraid that there is no easy answer to this. You should be pushing the intelligence community, perhaps MI5 or MI6 have something going on in the rumour mill. Try old snitches in Belfast and Dublin, maybe they are hearing something, but I guess that you are already doing most of this." He glanced across at Alex, deciding to let him have his tuppence worth. "Do you feel the same Alex?" he asked.

"Full agreement boss, but perhaps one other point needs a bit of research too," he said, nervously tapping his biro on the pad. "I think you need to look at who can gain from all of this, and what might be their motivation." He wanted to stop, already having said more words than he was usually comfortable with in such company, but there was one more point that he needed to make. "I've been away for a while, so I might be out of touch, but the one thing I noticed in the news quite often was the reintroduction of the hard border, a result of the Brexit deal collapsing. Could this be why they are hitting both sides of the political divide? Weren't all of these people supporters of the new border, the checkpoints, the general separation again between north and south?"

Dominic Wild was nodding, staring at the young soldier. "Sometimes you just can't see the wood for the trees," he muttered. "You might have something there Alex. We are all so stuck in our ways, we may have missed the blatantly obvious." He looked around at the others. "Comments?" he asked.

Only Shankly offered anything. "I will add this to the mix in the investigation," he told them. "It might just connect some of the dots, but it still doesn't give us anyone in particular to chase."

Mike Sanders spoke quietly. "You need someone to claim responsibility, someone to go after." He glanced at Alex, directing his question towards him. "We need to draw them out, make them show their hands. Any suggestions?"

Alex was back on the spot, the man of the moment, not something he craved, but he did have an idea and decided to put it out there. "Fake news," he said simply.

The others all looked at him as if he was mad, but Mike Sanders face split into a broad grin. "Explain to them Alex."

Alex wiped a hand across his jaw, let his breath hiss out. "I'm not a big Trump fan, but his idea of fake news was brilliant. It meant no-one knew what to believe, what to trust, and that's a bad thing. But it can have its uses." He looked from Mike to Dominic, the two people in the room that he felt comfortable with. "I think you have to twist these killings and attribute them to someone that couldn't possibly have done them. That will make the real killers – perhaps not all of them, but you only need one of them to bite – show their hand. No-one likes doing all of the work, then letting someone else claim all of the glory."

Alex finished there, sure he would put his foot in it if he continued any longer.

Mike Sanders reflected on his earlier thoughts about politicians and their riding along on the achievements of others. He would share a joke in the car later with Alex about that one.

"I think we all have enough to do without dragging this on any longer," Dominic Wild said, standing at his place. "Colin, could you start checking out the rumour mill, both official and unofficial sources," he tasked the Chief Constable. "Ruth and Nick, can you have a think on the fake news angle, then bounce ideas off both Colin and myself tomorrow." He shuffled his papers together. "Mike and Alex, could you hang on for a minute. I need to talk about Africa."

"Could you shut the door please Alex," Dominic requested once the other three had left. Alex had noticed the petulant glance that Ruth Maybank had tossed his way on departure, clearly a lady not accustomed to being dismissed from the PM's meetings. He did as bid, returned to the table, suddenly noticing that the PM had visibly aged since their last encounter. Not a job for the faint hearted, Alex thought.

"What is it that you need to know about South Africa?" Alex asked.

Both Mike and Dominic glanced knowingly at one another, a private joke perhaps thought the younger man.

"Nothing about Africa," the PM responded softly. "Just wanted to get rid of waggling ears." The comment caused him to smile, something he didn't get to do often enough. "Now COVID is done, the country doesn't need a doctor as a PM anymore, so now it's back to normal politics, dog-eat-dog. Not something I love, so it helps to have a normal conversation from time-to-time. Like now."

"But I think you do have something else in mind," Mike added. To Alex, this was all a bit staged, something that the two of them must have agreed earlier.

"Mike told me that you were returning from the south, and I thought it sort of just fit in nicely with this Irish problem that we are now experiencing," the PM said. "I need someone with a grounded view to use as a sounding board occasionally, otherwise whatever is done over there will be done for all of the wrong reasons. I thought perhaps you might be the man for the job, and your leader agreed."

Alex looked at the boss, checking that what he was hearing was on the level. It appeared it was.

"Would you be okay to spend a part of each week in the city, be available for me, let's say, every Wednesday or Thursday, perhaps both?"

Alex was a bit flummoxed now. He'd hardly got back home, and already he was being dropped into another high profile frying pan. "It's not my call really," he replied. "Boss?"

Mike shrugged, hands coming from his sides, palms pointing upwards.

"Who am I to make a decision like that?" he asked with a smirk. "This man here is the one who foots all of the bills, and if he's willing to pay for your services, then the SAS are willing to loan you out for a little while."

"So that's it decided," Dominic Wild concluded. "I'd advise that you return to Hereford and have a few days to sort yourself out. Then I'll see you back here next week." He picked up his papers and phone, glancing at a couple of flashing messages on it. "And have a few more thoughts on the fake news idea that you suggested. Your input might be useful. And anything else on the Ireland topic please," he added before leaving.

7th April 2027

Moscow, Russia

It had taken two full days and nights to reach the capital, two days of hard driving, much of it on roads that were barely tracks, potholed and rutted. The Beemer had performed fairly well, but the X3 wasn't what Grigorii would call a 'real' off-roader. It was more of a ladies posing machine for the city, something you could easily get the two-and-a-half standard kids into for the school run.

He'd slept in the back of the car, folding the seats down to give him more room, using the sleeping bag he'd used in the woods for the last months, it's next stop likely to be a trash can. Now that he had reached Moscow he was unsure of what to do next, this despite running a million scenarios through his bored mind during the drive. When he'd left the capital he'd been a persona non grata; three of a four man team he'd once been a part of during a job in China had disappeared. He'd got out of there before he did the same, and now he wasn't certain that he would be welcomed back, or simply 'disappeared' himself.

He pulled into a petrol station, not intending to fill up with fuel, just to allow himself a little more time to think through the options. Who was running the show now? Was there someone he could count on, someone safe who could sound out the authorities without effectively handing himself in?

In Russia, the safest way to get help was to get it from someone that owed you something. Someone you had some sort of a hold over. Friends could be bought, even when they really were friends. If the authorities could also make your family 'disappear', then most people would trade a friend for a wife, a comrade for a child.

Sitting in the car he ran through his contacts list, mentally crossing off the ones that he thought could be bribed or pressurised into talking. Then he also crossed off the ones that he thought may no longer be available, maybe already removed from circulation by the authorities. It didn't leave him too much choice.

He would have to call his old boss, the man who'd said too much all of those months back, the man who'd assisted him in escaping from the system.

There was no-one else.

Odyssey Popov was almost twenty-eight years of age and had already attained the rank of colonel in the country's military intelligence service. Having been a part of the President's team during the operation to find the cure for COVID had done him no damage at all, even though the operational unit that had left for South Africa had been mainly wiped out. He'd covered his bases, tied up loose ends, and stayed close to the main man. Because of this, the President himself trusted him, used him to monitor others that he didn't have the same faith in.

He now had a staff of forty, all based in the Kremlin, a place where all of the main military control functions had been moved to during the worst days of the virus. Some had now drifted back out to other buildings in the city, but the President had taken the decision that the intelligence community should be kept close to hand.

For Odyssey, this was a great decision. It kept him close to the seat of power, kept his career rising like a shooting star. Where would his comet stop? Could he even make President himself one day?

His desk phone buzzed, dragging him back into the here and now, away from the grandiose daydream of leading Russia.

"Popov," he answered simply, giving away as little as possible.

The earpiece stayed silent, but he could hear someone there, background noises that indicated the call was probably coming from a payphone. He waited a few seconds, contemplated putting the phone back in the cradle, tracing the call. Quite probably a wrong number; not many had his direct line.

"Hello Odyssey," a voice finally said, a voice that seemed to be familiar, but one he couldn't quite put a name to.

"Hello," he responded, careful not to give anything away, but also careful not to be impolite. The voice could be anyone, and maybe not someone that he would wish to offend. "Who's speaking please?" he enquired.

"I'd prefer not to give you my name just yet, but I would like to ask you for a little information," the man at the other end said. "Let's just say that we once worked together, and that you helped me out once. I'm hoping that you may be able to do that again."

Odyssey still couldn't place the man, but the tone and cadence seemed more familiar with each word. He would need to keep the man talking. "What sort of help?" he asked.

The silence again, a man deciding whether to talk or not. "Who do you answer to nowadays?"

This was a strange question, and not one that Odyssey wanted to answer. "Why do you ask?" he replied. "It isn't something that is normally for public consumption."

"I think that you can tell me, but maybe first I should tell you something," the voice told him. "You flew with the President to London last year. Then you had a meeting with the British Prime Minister here in Moscow. I know many things that you have done and telling me who you answer to nowadays would not be betraying anything I can't find out through other channels." The man stopped for a second, then continued. "So perhaps now you can guess who I am and answer my question."

Odyssey could feel the man in his mind, but the name was still evading him. "I report directly to the President," he finally admitted. "Why is that important to you?"

The man sighed into the mouthpiece, and Odyssey thought he could hear something in his voice, a release of tension from within. "I need to know if I am safe to reappear," the man told him. "And if you have access to the President, then you can make sure that I am safe to do so or not."

"Who are you?"

The man was silent again, but his mind was now made-up. He had to take a chance. He needed someone who would support him, otherwise he may as well drive back to the woods that he'd left behind just days previously.

"Grigorii Belov," he announced.

They met in small café only five minutes' walk from Red Square, a place with plenty of shoppers but in all probability no-one that would recognise either of them. It was better to do this than meet officially, at least until Odyssey had had a chance to run things by the President. To do that, he first needed to check his facts, not just run on a gut instinct. He believed that he knew what Grigorii had been up to for the last ten months, but he needed to be certain.

The two sat at a corner table, backs to the wall, allowing them both a good view of the entrance. It was a conditioned reflex for them, not a display of distrust, though both were testing the water here, feeling their way.

"You look well Grigorii," Odyssey started. "Looks as if you've been keeping fit."

"I was living the outdoor life for quite a while now. Lots of walking, not too much food, and very little alcohol. You should try it," he said with a smirk.

Odyssey automatically pulled in his stomach. His office job didn't exactly keep him in shape, his youth helped, but he knew he'd piled a few pounds on in the last six months. "Perhaps I will," he countered. "One day."

They stopped the small talk when their coffees arrived, thanking the waitress and waiting for her to get out of earshot.

"Was it you down at Chavash Varmane Bor, 'tidying-up'", the Russian colonel asked. He'd decided that he needed answers and the direct approach would be the fastest, while also avoiding later misunderstandings. Straight question, straight answer.

Grigorii was smiling at him now, something that was a rarity in itself. "'Tidying-up'", he replied. "I like that." He picked up his coffee, took a tiny sip, the liquid still too hot to enjoy. "And the answer is yes," he added.

Odyssey nodded, eyes flicking around the room. "I guessed it was probably you when the first one happened. I thought that would be it, but then the rest…" He trailed off, thinking. "One I could explain away, but I think it must be six now."

"Seven. You probably haven't discovered the last one yet."

Seven bodies. Seven senior figures, business or politics all. Not too easy to just sweep under the mat.

"Would you consider them 'friends' of the President, or enemies? The first four could certainly fall into the latter category, perhaps the other two, or at least close enough to it."

"Number seven won't fall outside of it either." He leant in, his lips close the Odyssey's ear and whispered a name. The colonel jerked away as if electrocuted.

"Shit Grigorii," he exclaimed. "The President might even pay you for that one." He stared at the ex-Spetsnaz man, clearly shocked by how much he'd managed to achieve in a relatively short period of time. "What do you want?"

"I guess you could say that I want to come back in to the fold, in from the cold," Grigorii replied. "Is it possible?"

Odyssey rubbed his chin, his morning shave already turning to stubble. "For me, it is possible," he said. "I could use you somewhere, probably far away from Moscow, at least initially. It's whether our leader would accept you back."

"You could persuade him," the Spetsnaz man responded. "I keep my mouth shut about what you told me in a moment of weakness, and you send me off to somewhere that will not worry you or the boss." He took his cup again, managing a little more of the hot drink this time. "I just want to be given a real task again, and anywhere will do." He sipped more coffee, almost done now.

The intelligence officer suddenly stood-up, coffee untouched. "Call me tomorrow, nine o'clock. I'll do what I can, but no promises." With that he turned and left the café.

Grigorii looked at his untouched coffee, lifted the cup and drank it.

"Waste not, want not," he told himself. After months of living rough in the forest he wasn't going to waste a good cup of coffee.

Nikolai Ignatov looked up from the papers that he was in the process of signing, his signature barely recognisable from what it had been prior to becoming President of all Russia. Back then he'd been proud of his moniker, something that he had completed with a flourish, with zest. Nowadays he just scrawled a mark, anything really, doing it so often it meant little to him. He barely even read what he was signing for, trusting his aids to ensure that all was well.

"Odyssey, how nice to see you!" The young intelligence officer was guided into the room by Nikolai's PA, the girl waiting to see if the men needed refreshments. "Two coffees please Tanja," the President requested, taking the decision for the younger man. "You said that you needed a meeting. Something up?" He motioned towards the chair next to his desk.

Odyssey sat down, a pen and pad in hand, always prepared to receive instructions. He'd rehearsed his presentation but knew that the President was inclined to change the course of the conversation, to throw in something from left field.

"I have some information that will be of interest to you sir. Some you know, some you don't." He paused while coffees were delivered, thanked the girl as she turned to leave. Once the door was shut he began again. "You know about the six assassinations in Chavash Varmane Bor in recent months, but I believe that you are not yet aware of the latest one, the killing of Viktor Yevseyev. I only learned of this one yesterday, hence the request to meet with you." He hesitated, letting the information sink in, also trying to gauge the reaction to the news. The surprise on the President's face made it clear that he had not been aware of this fact, but it was a pleasantly surprised look, not a 'shock-horror' one. "I also now know who has been carrying out the killings." He stopped again, enjoying himself.

Nikolai slapped the desk with his right hand. "Come on man!" he yelled. "Don't tease me. Out with it."

"Do you remember our man Grigorii Belov, the one we sent down to South Africa last year? The one who went a little off the rails down there, lost all of his men?"

"Of course I remember," the President said, his voice thoughtful. "Did he do this? Did he take out all of those people?"

"He did sir."

Nikolai ran his fingers through his thinning hair, his eyes on the desk as he ran the dead men's names through his mind. They had all been difficult people, and all had been involved with the Chinese in hatching the idea of starting a virus, a virus that they'd eventually lost control of. They all had blood on their hands, blood of Russians, but also blood from every other country on the planet. By taking them out, Belov had done the world a favour. And kept Russia's involvement in COVID a secret.

"Where is he now?" he enquired.

"He's in Moscow. I have a call with him at nine, that's why I needed the early meeting with you." Odyssey leant forward, elbows on knees. "He wants to work for us again."

Nikolai scratched his chin, mulling over the request. He shouldn't really approve the killing of seven Russian citizens, but they weren't the kind of people that he had any love for. They were people that he would have liked to die, and now they had. But to publicly allow the killer to come back and work for him…

"I thought that we could possibly use him on operations that are outside of the country." Odyssey spoke again, breaking his chain of thoughts. "Base him somewhere well away from here, keep his actions quiet for the time being."

Nikolai nodded. This was a good idea. They kept their man, used him where and when they liked, but put him somewhere where he was out of the public eye. "Do it," he said, decision taken. "But first I want to see him. It would be interesting to know how he did what he managed."

8th April 2027
London, UK

The trip back up to Hereford with the boss had been illuminating, bringing Alex up-to-date with the various operations running around the globe with the Regiment at that time. With a cure for the virus now readily available, it meant that the SAS was once again fully deployed, with only a standby squadron holding in the country ready to engage in an antiterrorist role. Soldiers were deployed in a variety of training functions in the UAE, Egypt and Jordan; another team were involved in developing potential new warfare roles using single-person flight packs over in the States; whilst an undercover team from the boat troop was working with Border Force to combat a new wave of illegal immigration from across the Channel.

"What do these people see in our country?" Alex had asked. "You would understand it if they tried to stay in Italy, or the South of France, but the UK?" He shook his head, no longer a big fan of the UK's weather.

"We have a very understanding benefits system," Mike answered. "Or another way of putting it would be that we're too bloody soft. All talk and no trousers, as they say."

Alex nodded agreement, exhaling noisily. "You're right," he confirmed. "We are a soft touch nowadays, and that's no lie. The politicians always promise the world, but rarely deliver, even if we are out of the European Union now."

"Out, but still seemingly having to answer to far too many of their rules. COVID really slowed things up on us standing alone."

Once back in Hereford, Alex had returned to his own room, the barracks largely deserted. He wondered what role the boss might have had for him if the PM hadn't called on his skills. He also wondered how much of that had already been agreed between the two men prior to the meeting. Probably all of it, he decided. Mike Sanders and Dominic Wild had been forced to work closely together during the COVID crisis, and that relationship had appeared to be even better during the latest meeting. It was most likely no 'chance' that the 'get together' had happened to occur on Alex's return.

It took two full days to get his kit sorted out and his head back in order, and then he was on the verge of total boredom. It was hard to switch from a hundred miles an hour to zero in a couple of days. His mind was still racing, thinking about all of the things that needed to be done in South Africa, all the time knowing he had to take his hands off the operation, to leave it to the new leadership.

It was time to call Andile again, but first he wanted to think through what he was going to say. He wanted her but he also wanted the job, especially with the new challenge of working so close to the decision makers. For them to be together meant that one of them had to give something up; Andile had to give up her beloved country, and possibly her job as a doctor; or he had to give up the SAS. It was one or the other, otherwise the relationship had only a limited shelf life, this much he knew.

"So why am I taking so long on making a choice," he mumbled to himself.

The answer was clear. He wanted both the job and the girl but didn't want to pressurise Andile into making a choice herself in case it turned out to be the wrong one for him. He was procrastinating, delaying the inevitable.

The boss dropped Alex at Hereford Railway Station on the Monday morning, partly as a favour but also to read the rules of engagement to him when dealing with the PM.

"You're there to advise, to be used to give a military angle on their problems, but not to commit to operations. I'm afraid that that has to come through me, though I know that the people down there will try and rope you in to stuff. They like scapegoats, and I don't want you to become one."

Though it sounded a little harsh, Alex knew that Mike Sanders was only trying to protect him, to cover his arse from political manoeuvring. And in the end it was fair enough for him; Mike was the colonel, he was a sergeant. Operations cost money, and spending it was above his pay grade, not his call.

"I'll handle it boss," he replied, pointing towards a car that looked to be in the process of leaving. "How often do you want me to report in?"

Mike shrugged, still looking for a better place to pull-in and drop-off, the front of the station busier than he'd expected. "Just call if you have anything important. Your discretion," he added.

Now on the first part of the journey to Newport in South Wales, Alex decided that he had to talk to Andile. It had been four days since they'd last spoken, and he knew that waiting any longer would look like he was avoiding her. He'd do it that evening, no more excuses.

First though he would call-up Nkosi. It was normal military practice; prior planning prevented poor performance, with at least one more 'P' thrown in during a lecture to the lads.

"Hi Andile, how's things down there?" he asked, his stomach feeling tight. He could hear the tension in his own voice, was sure that she could too, but it was time to get on with it, to see whereabouts this conversation drifted to.

"Oh my God, if it isn't Alex Green!" she exclaimed, mock surprise and a touch of sarcasm oozing out of the words. "I'm good, and you?" she added. "I thought that you might have been on a secret mission or something, at least until Nkosi said that you'd called."

"I told him to keep that quiet."

"Some chance of that, my man," she retorted. "He's married to my sister, so he does whatever big sis tells him, and that includes reporting on you." There was a short silence on the phone, then she continued. "He tells me you have quite a good job going right now?"

"I can confirm that or otherwise next time we talk I guess. Tomorrow's the first day, so let's see how it goes."

"Alex," she sounded serious now. "I know you have a lot to concentrate on, and I know you love your job as much as I love mine, so don't feel pressure to call me all of the time. What happened, happened, and I'm more than comfortable with that." She sighed, then silence. She'd voiced the hard words, now the ball was firmly back in his court.

He paused, running his words through his head before speaking. "I'm comfortable too Andile," he said. "I was just horribly shocked at how much I missed you when I left, but at the same time I enjoyed being back with the Regiment." He frowned, looking for the next words to say. "It was like I was being torn two ways, and I wanted to go in both of them."

She giggled at the other end of the phone, quickly stopping, worried. "I'm sorry!" she gasped. "I wasn't laughing at you, it's just that I felt the same. I thought of quitting my job and moving to England. That's how I feel."

A long silence followed, neither sure how to go on. Finally Andile spoke.

"Let's leave things for a month, maybe only two weeks. Then let's talk again, see if we still have the same feelings."

Alex felt his throat closing-up, cleared it with a soft grunt, trying to regain control of his emotions. This was no way for a hard SAS man to behave, he thought. But he knew that was just how most of his comrades were, balancing their love-lives with the dangers of belonging to an elite force. "You're so bloody good at putting things into words," he told her. "So practical about it all. I wish I could do that."

"I'm not Alex, don't believe otherwise. I get ripped-up inside just the same as you, but we have to be honest about it all. I need you, but I need my work. You are the same." She took a breath, easing it out slowly, then went on. "We give it a few weeks, then let's talk again. Maybe this puppy-love is over by then," she said, the smile in her voice apparent.

"I somehow don't think so Andile," Alex spoke softly into the phone, barely a whisper.

"Me neither," the young Zulu girl agreed.

"Hi, is that Alex Green speaking?" a female voice echoed over Alex's mobile phone.

He glanced at the number, not recognizing who it was, only knowing it was a local London code. "It is," he answered carefully. "Can I ask who is calling?"

"My name's Nicole. We met last year on the trip to Moscow," she hesitated a second. "Not sure that you'll remember me, but I'm the PA for the PM."

"Of course I remember you," Alex confirmed, thinking that 'PA for the PM' was a hell of a job title. "Does this mean that the Prime Minister wants to talk to me?" The only thing Alex knew about the arrangement was from the brief meeting he'd had with his country's leader, but then that had not been at all specific. Perhaps it would be a phone call, perhaps a short get together again in Westminster. He had little or no experience in the day-to-day dealings with senior politicians, had no idea how their schedules ran. "The agreement was all a little vague up to now."

A short laugh from the other end of the connection, then Nicole came back on. "That's our Dominic," she told him. "I've worked for a few senior politicians over the years, and I can't remember one of them being as informal as he is. I guess it's his background, coming from the medical profession. It kept him grounded."

Alex found himself nodding to the receiver, stopping himself and replying. "Yes, I believe that to be true. I was briefed by my boss, so I understand a little." He grinned, comfortable with the lady. "So where and when?"

"Unconventional though it might be, he'd like you to join him and his wife Trish for dinner this evening. She's as easy going as he is, more so perhaps."

This was a surprise, not anything close to what the SAS soldier had expected. "Where do I need to be, and what time?" he asked. Then another thought struck him. "And what should I wear? I don't usually eat with the PM," he added.

Nicole gave another tinkle of laughter, clearly enjoying herself. "The venue is here at number ten, and let's say seven. Most business should be done by then." She paused, ticking off his questions in her head. "Oh, and they'll probably change into casual clothes, so anything you'd like to wear," she added.

A couple of minutes later she'd explained how to get into the tradesmen's entrance to number Ten Downing Street, saying she could meet him there before she left the office for the evening. "Some of us have a home to go to," she finished.

If he wasn't actually doing it, he would never have believed it, but here he was in the PMs London offices sharing pizzas with him and his wife. A bottle of Italian red – a very nice Amarone – shared the table with the food, a small salad on the side. Even more shocking was the fact that the only people present apart from the security dotted around the place was the three of them, Trish, Dominic and Alex. It was nothing like what he would have dreamt up, and he wondered how much of it he could repeat. It would certainly be a great one to dine out on.

The food was basic, the company relaxed, and the conversation low-key. Alex later realised that the latter was for his benefit, an attempt by the hosts to calm him, make him feel a part of the setting. They worked well together, and he knew that this magic must also work beautifully on foreign leaders and their wives during official visits. He knew that at some stage the discussions would have to become more serious, but when they finally did he'd become so comfortable that it almost shocked him.

"So Alex," Dominic said, biting into another triangle of spicy meat pizza. "Did you have any thoughts on how to get these Irish buggers to expose themselves? Your 'fake news' idea?" Trish had sat back, studying something on her phone, knowing clearly that this was a time for the boys to talk, the serious part of the evening. She made an excuse, stood and moved away from the table, a good wife who'd seen this sort of thing many times previously.

Alex swallowed what he was chewing, took a sip of the wine. "I had a few thoughts on it over the last days, even had a bit of a session with the boss to include his opinions," he said. "I know that you mentioned that two of the politicians were Protestants and one was a Catholic, so this confuses the whole thing a little, but if all of the hits were effectively the same, and some of the weapons were the same in all three murders, then I believe it has to be the same people doing the killing." Dominic was nodding agreement, giving Alex a bit more confidence. "Without someone claiming the deaths it is all a bit of a stab in the dark, but I would guess that the killers are probably from the Catholic community." He paused, counting on the fingers of his right hand. "One, the greater number of people killed are Protestants. Two, the hits look more like those of the Irish Republican Army back in the day," he said this in full as he knew many people didn't have much knowledge of the IRA nowadays.

"Understood Alex, but that's all a little flimsy isn't it?"

"It is sir, but we don't have much else to go on. Anyway, a third point is based on some research from my side into the Catholic man who was killed." He hesitated, Dominic now putting down his food and leaning forward. "He was a strong Brexit supporter, as were the two Protestants, and he also agreed that the country needed to have the hard border back."

"You're right," the PM agreed.

"So effectively he was agreeing to splitting Ireland in two once again, siding with the Brits as they'd say over there."

Dominic Wild thought about the implications of what Alex had just presented, the view of others on a once more split island of Ireland. With COVID now gone, people felt safe enough to come out of their shells once more, to take up the fight. That was what they were seeing. And it had taken a sergeant in the SAS to see it and say it.

"More wine?" he asked Alex. "You bloody well deserve it." He poured for both of them, then stood-up. "Perhaps this needs something stronger," he said, but Trish had out manoeuvred him, coming back to the table with a good bottle of Scotch whisky.

"Tomorrow we will meet again with the Northern Ireland Secretary and the Chief of the PSNI. Perhaps I also invite Ruth along." He poured a good measure for each of them. "One last thing before we enjoy a deserved break. What about the 'fake news?'"

"I think that's simple," Alex answered, trying hard not to sound too big-headed. "We need to find a believable argument for a Protestant group to have done all three of the killings. We put it out there with the press, get some coverage, then wait for the real owners to come forward and claim their work."

In Alex's mind, simple was usually best. Less could go wrong.

The PM considered the suggestion for a full minute, his eyes fixed on a portrait on the far wall of one Sir Winston Churchill. He'd found that looking at the picture often helped him to make hard decisions.

"Let's drink to that," he eventually said, raising his glass. "Probably the best and most straightforward idea I've heard in months. Bound to work." The three of them took a sip of the harsh liquor, the PM's eyes again drifting back to the portrait. He finally had a good feeling about where things were headed.

11th April 2027

Armagh, Northern Ireland

They met in a pub at the edge of the city limits, almost in the countryside, close to the border but not too close. Though the army were not deployed nowadays, the police on both sides of the invisible line conducted extra patrols there, an attempt to discourage illegal activity, though crossing the border was still quite simple. Back lanes, farm tracks, walking and cycling routes all existed from the old days, and permanently manned crossing points only existed on major roads, mainly to control the flow of lorries and trade.

They were sat in a quiet corner of the pub, old Frank and Declan with a pint of Guinness apiece – 'the black stuff' as they liked to call it – and Paddy with a bottle of something called Red Stripe, a beer that appealed more to the younger generation.

"So they're blaming the Proddies for all three hits," Paddy was saying, in Declan's eyes just a little too loudly. Frank stared into his beer, ignoring the young hothead.

Declan glanced around the bar, making sure that no-one was eavesdropping on them, his right hand on the table, waving it gently to indicate that Paddy should be more careful. The place was no longer riddled with informers, but in this game you couldn't be too careful. "Keep it down a bit Paddy," he said softly.

"But how do we get our message across if people don't know who the feck we are?" the youth asked. "This way no-one knows who we are or what we want." He put a hand up, knowing what was coming from Declan. "I know we have to stay anonymous, I'm not saying go and hand out our names to the press or anything, but if they don't know why we're killing people, then they won't do anything to put it right, that's for sure."

Declan let him fizzle out, sipping on his porter. "We will let them know," he finally said. "That's why we're here now, not just to talk about the next target." This seemed to placate Paddy for a second at least. "But first we need a name to give to the press."

"That's easy," Paddy said, enthusiastic again. "The Armagh IRA. Sounds great, doesn't it?"

Frank looked at the lad as if he belonged in a hospital, and not a normal one either. He lifted his beer, looking to Declan for help.

"Do you not think that's a bit 'old school' on one hand, and sort of makes it easy for the Brits to track us down on the other?" Declan asked, trying hard not to just tell the boy that he was a total eejit. He again wondered if they should have ever invited him to join them, but his dad had been a local rebel back in the day, and even now, no-one really had the balls to cross him. "We need something new, something that shows what we stand for."

Paddy now noticed that Frank had lost all interest in the discussion. The old boy was just like his dad; too old to get involved in the dangerous side of the work, but still wanting to be a part of the cause. The man had no interest in subjects such as choosing a name, but would no doubt come alive again when they were talking about the next target, probably aided by another Guinness or two. He decided to follow the man's example and keep out of things for now.

Declan was still considering his own last words, thinking about what their label should be. "How about 'Men of Ireland?'" he asked. "That's what we are."

Frank leant back, his leg swinging out and catching the table. "Sorry," he said. "Was getting a bit of cramp. Lucky that the beers aren't full."

"'Men of Ireland'. I like it." Paddy took a swig from his bottle. Agreeing was easier than arguing, at least for now. He needed another beer.

Frank was thinking, actually considering joining in the conversation. "I don't like it," he finally offered. "What if we end up with a woman in the group? That happens nowadays, you know."

Declan nodded agreement, though he was a little shocked at such an observation from the older generation. He knew a few ladies who'd do a better job than both of these blokes, that went without saying. "What about something that simply says what we want?" There were no comments, but also no arguments to this. "What about 'One Ireland.' It sort of says it all."

"'One Ireland'", Frank repeated thoughtfully. He lifted his glass, toasting the two of them. "I kind of like the ring of that."

The two half empty glasses of Guinness clashed with the now empty bottle of Red Stripe. The group had a name.

The target was a member of the Ulster Unionist Party, a woman who'd won the seat for North Antrim in the COVID-delayed elections. It had been one of the few things that the Province had all agreed on for a change; no way to fight an election when you had to observe social distancing. No pressing the flesh, kissing babies, opening new schools.

She'd lived on the outskirts of Ballymoney, a pleasant enough place to live and not too far from the Antrim coast. Also a hop-skip-and-jump from Belfast, the place where all of the action really happened. And now she was dead, her husband a lucky man who'd just happened to be away on a business trip. Fate.

On the route back to Armagh, they had made a very short detour into Belfast, just a short loop off the motorway really to Clarendon Dock. There they found a spot where they saw no surveillance cameras, and no-one to witness their ever being there. At three in the morning this was easy enough, and the only worry they actually had was possibly meeting a nosy policeman, which they didn't. The rain helped.

Declan left the other two in the car, pulled a woolly hat low on his brow and turned up the collar of his Barbour jacket. He made his way from the car, keeping in the shadows. It was a short walk.

At the offices of the Belfast Telegraph he paused and had a final look around him. The place was deserted, just as he'd expected.

He took a padded envelope from his poachers pocket, slipped it through the letterbox.

Two minutes later he was back in the car, as usual, the driver. They would be back in Armagh within the hour and now their intentions were no longer a secret.

21st April 2027

London, UK

It was Alex's second week in the capital and already he couldn't believe how senior politicians behaved in public. They were just like kids he decided. No, it was worse than being back at school, with people talking over one another, ignoring the questions that they were posed and just putting out their own message, everyone seemingly only in it for themselves. He decided that he wouldn't want a single one of them on his team back in Hereford, with the possible exception of Dominic Wild. The man was a good negotiator, didn't get sucked into petty squabbles, and added to all of that he would also bring along his medical knowledge.

"One Ireland," the Northern Ireland Secretary was saying, sarcasm oozing. "These idiots don't care about one Ireland, two Irelands or three! They just use this as an excuse to kill people. Probably also running drugs or something similar."

The Chief Constable was shaking his head, his face showing little emotion. Alex wondered what he really thought of all of this. He was now aware that Colin had also come from a military background, was used to calling a spade a spade.

"What are you thinking Colin?" the PM asked, noting that the man wasn't happy with things. "What are you hearing from the coalface?"

Shankly faced the PM, glanced briefly at Alex, froze out the rest. "That's just it, sir," he started. "We aren't hearing anything from our informants, no boasting, no threats, nothing. It seems that these people must be a small and tight group, not known to many. Even the pictures that we gained of their man delivering their message in Belfast are inconclusive. No sign of their car, face covered, aware of the security cameras and generally avoiding them."

"That doesn't mean that they're not just a bunch of murderers," Nicholas Thomas spat out. "That's four families that they've destroyed now, and we're no closer to knowing who they are!"

Dominic placed his hands flat down on the table, fingers spread and tense. He needed to calm things down, to make an attempt at some brainstorming, not in-fighting. "Gentlemen," he said clearly, an edge to his

49

voice. "We are on the same side here, so let's act like it." He turned to Alex, an outsider who he hoped would bring some direction to the conversation. "What do you think about it Alex?" he asked.

Ruth Maybank allowed herself a tight grin, sensing that the soldier didn't enjoy these moments. He was a doer, not a talker, she could see that. Would never make it in politics.

Alex caught the smirk out of the corner of his eye, decided to ignore it. The PM had called, he'd do his best to summarise how he saw things.

"They do roughly the same thing every time, nothing too complex, just in, do their business, and out again," he started. "To me that indicates a small group, just as Colin mentioned. That's partially good, but also bad. With few members, they probably can't target more than one person at a time, most likely couldn't take the fight to the mainland, but it also means it will be harder to infiltrate them. If numbers are small, maybe no-one outside of their team knows them, so less chance of a leak."

"But now that they've become 'official', my bet would be that they will want to expand their numbers," the policeman added. "If they were happy to just keep killing the odd politician, then why bother announcing who they are? It's just another risk."

Alex nodded his agreement. "But if they expand, there will be a greater opportunity for someone to say something out of place. It might not just be on the recruitment side. Don't forget that with more people, they also need more equipment, especially weapons."

"Good point," Colin Shankly said. "We will monitor that side of things too." He scribbled a note on his pad.

"So what do we do now?" Nicholas Thomas asked. "Wait for the next hit?"

Colin continued to exercise his poker face, but Alex could again sense the tension between the two men. Not a great situation, he thought. The two at the table with the greatest responsibility for the Province, and they were almost tearing strips of each other.

"Calm down Nick," the PM interjected. "We have to find ways to solve problems, not invent them for each other."

A momentary silence enveloped the room, and just for a second Alex thought that Ruth Maybank was about to intervene. She leant forward in her seat, drew in a breath, then exhaled and sat back.

"What is it Ruth?" Dominic asked.

"The 'fake news' idea worked to draw them out," she started, a brief nod to Alex. "Couldn't we do the same again? Some other tease to get them to bite?"

"Ideas?" the PM asked.

Alex's mind was racing, part of him wondering if he should say nothing yet and bounce his ideas off Mike Sanders before offering them out here. The problem was that would mean another delay, perhaps another death.

"Let's just assume that they are in the market for people and equipment," he said. "With people I'm fairly sure that they will be ultra-careful, only recruiting their own. You could try and use an Irishman, maybe a copper," he continued, looking towards Colin. "But if it went wrong, then I don't need to explain how wrong it could go."

"I have people who would risk it," the police officer said. "But it wouldn't be a preferred route."

"So let's take the second point, equipment." Alex had been scribbling on his pad, trying to write down his ideas before he verbalised them. "The main thing that they will need would be weapons, probably handguns, but perhaps also rifles, shotguns. Where would they get them?"

"There's a lot of weapons within Ireland, both north and south of the border," Colin informed them. "Back from the days of the Troubles, many of them old, pretty unreliable." He hesitated. "But you can easily buy them on the black market, from Russia, Albania, Europe generally really. It wouldn't be too tough to source something."

Alex had a plan forming in his mind, but it needed a little more thinking through, some research on his part.

"What about if we were to set-up a 'fake' dealership?" he asked. "Give me a day or two, but I may have an idea. Is that okay?"

Dominic Wild considered the request for a second, expecting Nicholas Thomas to complain about the delayed decision. He decided not to give him a chance. "I need an outline of your idea for tomorrow Alex. We can't risk these people striking again, and every day lost could possibly be another life."

The intervention shut-up the minister, at least temporarily. "That's fine sir," Alex answered. "I just want to run an idea past Mike Sanders."

The PM nodded. "Same time, same place tomorrow."

As soon as he reached his room, Alex called Hereford. He was told that Sanders was in a meeting but should be able to return the call within the hour. That was as good as it would get, so he popped down to the local Marks & Spencer's store and grabbed a sandwich and a coke.

Back in his room, he started scribbling down the thoughts he'd begun to assemble while on the underground transfer from the meeting.

He wanted to get all of his ducks in line before bouncing his plan off Mike Sanders.

The plan was still live and loose, ambitious enough that the boss had offered to join the meeting if needed, not something that Alex had wanted. It was his idea, and this was the time for him to stand alone and be counted.

The attendance of the meeting was the same, with the PM, Ruth Maybank, Nicholas Thomas and the Chief Constable all waiting for him to say his piece. Allies two, axis two, he thought to himself. He'd have preferred it if the initial brief had been just with the PM but he now felt that he could trust Colin Shankly too. Thomas and Maybank... Well, that was another story, but Sanders had told him not to worry, just to put his thoughts out there.

The PM and Ruth Maybank were exchanging a few whispered words, the others sitting silently, waiting. Alex's nerves were on edge, again centre-stage, a place he hated but seemed to keep coming back to. He glanced at his note pad, really just a list of bullet points that he'd assembled back at the hotel.

"Sorry about that Alex," the PM interrupted his thoughts. "Just had to clear that one up with Ruth." He sat down at his place, Maybank doing the same, carefully checking that her business suit jacket was just so. "Lead on, young man."

"This shouldn't take too long," he started, trying to control the speed of his speech. "Most of it we covered yesterday, but if you're okay with it, I'll just swiftly summarise." He positioned the tip of his pen next to the first bullet point, then looked at Dominic. "Most of what we have right now is guesswork. The only facts we can be sure of is that the four killings were all similar, and that at least one weapon has been matched to all four by the PSNI logistics people. With most of the killings having more than one victim, we can almost certainly agree that there was more than one terrorist involved in each operation. We also know from the PSNI investigations that it looks like only one car was used at each scene, so we can guess that the number of gunmen involved was four or less." He paused, giving the others a chance to challenge any of this. "Agreed so far?"

Colin Shankly nodded agreement, the others indicating nothing either way. Alex looked at the next point on the list.

"We know that they have reacted to our misinformation once, this leading to them giving us their title, a sort of 'nom de guerre.' So we have a label for them now – 'One Ireland.'" He moved the pen further along his notes, quickly reading the next heading. "It's not much to go on, but if they took the bait last time, I think they might take it again."

"It often works that way," Colin Shankly agreed. It was the first real support that had come from any of them, and Alex appreciated it.

"The next point is really sheer conjecture, purely based on our discussions yesterday," Alex went on. "Why would they reveal themselves – even just with a group name – if they didn't want to grow? Let's say it's just a couple of lunatics who get off on topping politicians." That got a grimace from Maybank and Thomas, but actually a grin from the PM and a cough into the palm from Shankly. 'Careful Alex,' he thought. 'Don't need to make any enemies here.'

He took a sip of water, his throat dry. "What I'm trying to say is that if you didn't have a goal, then why advertise? You just keep quiet, no-one has a clue as to who you are, and you either continue your private war or you fade out of sight." He put his glass down, watching for reaction. "Based on this, I think that these people are looking to get bigger, just as we discussed at yesterday's meeting."

Dominic held up a hand, stopping Alex continuing. "I understand that all of this is recap, and I know it is probably necessary to build-up your case but do you have something new?"

Alex felt his cheeks flush, decided it was time to cut to the chase. "Sir, I discussed all of this with Mike Sanders, and he said I should fill in the background before leaping in, but here we go." He pushed his pad away, not needing the notes anymore. "We said yesterday that if they intend to grow their organisation, they need equipment, especially weaponry. The Chief also mentioned that this could be secured within Europe, but I think all of us are well aware that Russia has a tendency to get involved in dealings like this. There are plenty of firearms available in the system there."

"That was also my thinking," Colin agreed, again showing visible support.

"So I believe we could use this as the bait for our 'fake news'. We let it be known that the PSNI has become aware of arms coming into the Province, and that the source is Russian. We can even pass the information on to the press to grow the story."

"And then we set-up a military or police sting operation?" the PM said. "That is, if they take the bait."

Alex slowly shook his head. The next part was why he'd needed to speak with the boss first. "I think that the army or PSNI is too risky. One slip and these people will fade away out of sight, or worse, someone could get killed. They will be nervous, covering their backs."

"So what else can we do?" Dominic asked.

"We set-up a real Russian sting operation," Alex replied with a smile. "But we need you to help with that one, sir."

14th April 2027

The Kremlin, Moscow, Russia

"I've been asked for some help by Dominic Wild, the British Prime Minister. I'm sure you remember him well, Odyssey," Nikolai Ignatov said, his intelligence chief and himself sitting alone in his office. The President had a milky coffee – decaffeinated nowadays at his doctor's insistence – whilst Odyssey drank black herb flavoured tea. It was a longshot from the old days when both of them would probably have sipped on cold and rough vodka, no mixers required.

The intelligence man considered whether a response was needed, but as the silence extended out he guessed that he was expected to say something. Though he looked older, his face now more lined with the stress from his position, his leader was still an old soldier at heart, also originating from the intelligence community. The man would probably never lose his knack for interrogation.

"Can I ask what sort of a favour?" he offered, breaking the silent deadlock.

The President smiled, happy that the junior man had played along with him. "You may have read that they have some problems on their home front, Northern Ireland, to be exact. A few murdered politicians, some tensions once again about border issues. Was always on the cards with their rather messy Brexit, just took a little while to show up because of the COVID situation taking so long to resolve." He lifted his cup, took a sip on the now lukewarm liquid.

"I've read about it in the news," Odyssey replied. "But how can we assist there?"

"Dominic has no idea who is behind the murders. The old suspects have largely disappeared, and a new group calling themselves 'One Ireland' have emerged. There's very little data on them, no known membership." He raised his hands in a sort of 'over to you' gesture. "He thinks that maybe we can help to draw them out of the woodwork."

Odyssey frowned, still not sure where the conversation was going or how he could be any part of it. "And how should we do that sir?" he asked.

Instead of answering the question directly, the President decided to give the colonel a few more teasers. "The PM has assembled a mini taskforce to deal with the problem, just a few key players, including a military advisor."

Aha, this is where I fit in Odyssey thought. They want to see what we know on the subject, if we have any links to the problem. "I can put word out and see if any of our contacts have heard anything," he offered, making a note.

"It's not quite what they want, but a good idea anyway. Might even speed things up for them," Nikolai responded. "What they want is more about smoke and mirrors," he added.

The colonel grinned. "They learn to be more like us every day," he said. "How do I assist them?"

"They believe that the new group is in the process of expanding, and this means both recruiting and equipping. By equipping, they mainly mean arming up, getting weapons. They'd like us to be the supplier."

"But not a true supplier," Odyssey said slowly, seeing the bigger picture now. "Just lending the scheme a little credence really, then reeling in the bad guys." He raised an eyebrow. A plan was starting to run together in his head. "Do we know the military link in their taskforce?" he asked.

The President was beaming now. "I thought that you'd never ask."

Nikolai had instructed him to contact Mike Sanders, the SAS link he had from the African COVID project, and now also his point-of-contact for the new operation in Northern Ireland. Odyssey remembered the SAS commander well from their meetings in both London and Moscow the previous year, recalling that he'd initially been nervous of cooperating with the British Forces but had eventually warmed to the man. For a Special Forces colonel the man had been extremely grounded.

He assembled his thoughts, made a few notes, then dialled the number that he had been given.

"Is that you Odyssey?" the Englishman answered, obviously expecting the call.

"It is. Good to speak to you again Mike," he replied immediately, pleased to have the chance to practice his English again. "I guess you know why I'm calling."

Mike laughed, a pleasant sound, friendly. "Yes, I know our two leaders have been plotting again, and now we have to make things happen. The usual story I suppose."

They talked through the outline of the plot that had been hatched, Odyssey asking questions and taking notes as they progressed. It sounded simple enough to him and didn't mean too much exposure for any of his people. The whole thing could possibly be done by phone and email, no boots on the ground even.

"I'm not so sure about that," Mike said when he raised this point. "The Irish will be quite thorough I think. They have a lot at risk, and as a newly formed organisation will probably be a little nervy." He hesitated, wondering whether he should ask more about the Russian's commitment, or whether to leave it for the PM to convince the President. "I think that you will need a man on the ground, at least for a meeting or two. Confidence builders more than anything, plus it might be our only way to actually see who's involved."

"I see," Odyssey replied, wondering if Nikolai had already been approached on this.

"I think we both know that mails can be routed to be untraceable. Even teenagers know how to use the Dark Web nowadays, so without a physical contact we probably don't get any nearer to the targets."

"We were very good on that side of things prior to the COVID crisis, but our systems are still being upgraded right now, playing catch-up. You're probably right." The Russian was thinking back to their hacking of the accounts of the US presidential hopefuls in 2017. It was sad that in the interim ten years they hadn't improved much. Coronavirus had much to answer for, not only the human toll.

"Can you commit to a man on the ground?" Mike Sanders asked, deciding to push things forward.

Odyssey considered his options before answering. "I think that I can, and I think that I know who I would use," he said. "But putting an agent on foreign soil always needs the support of a higher authority over here, as I'm sure it does for you in the UK too."

Mike sighed in to the receiver. "So it looks like we are both in similar situations here." He paused. "Let's do our research and talk again in the morning."

"So what are your thoughts Nikolai?" Odyssey asked, his face running with sweat as the temperature inside the sauna began to get serious. The President liked them hot and had been ladling eucalyptus infused water onto the hot coals while he had summarised his conversation with the SAS colonel. The sauna had been the only opportunity to squeeze in a meeting before tomorrow's phone call and he could have lived without it. A freezing cold vodka would have been preferable, a great way to free his mind from the daily chores. At least things were less formal in the sauna; it's hard to be prim and proper when you're both sat there with nothing more than a towel to cover up your vanity.

The President slowly poured another measure of water over the burner, gasping as he breathed in the hot vapours. "Who would you consider using?" he asked. "If we get caught out putting agents into the UK, would it not be difficult if it came out? I'm thinking of the Novichok operation in Salisbury a few years ago. We could make ourselves unpopular all over again if it got out that we sold arms to Irish terrorists," he finished.

"We could make it a deniable operation, but with some sort of clandestine side-agreement with the Brits to get our man out if he's found out. Nothing official, but not just hanging the man out to dry either."

Nikolai thought about that for a few seconds. "I'm sure that Dom would go with that if I made it a condition of assisting them. And it would only be there for a 'worst case' scenario anyway."

Odyssey wiped sweat from his eyes, now finding it difficult to breath. The only thing keeping him in there was pride. "I think it would only need one man, any back-up would have to come from the English, tying them into the whole thing in any case. No chance of total denial on their part."

"Good idea." It was now Nikolai's turn to mop his brow, a pleasing sign for the younger Russian officer. "How soon could we set it up? I'm guessing that the Brits will want to see action, not just talk."

"Quickly, if needed," Odyssey replied, hoping to end the discussion soon. "I think I have the right man for the job. Someone you know, so I hope that we can agree on it now."

The President let that one run through his brain for a second, puzzled as to where this was going. "And of whom do we speak?" he finally asked.

Despite the heat of the sauna, the intelligence officer managed a smile. "Someone we discussed quite recently Mister President," he answered. "Somebody that we agreed could be useful but would be better employed away from home soil."

"Grigorii Belov," Nikolai responded. He gave a nod of agreement then stood. "Time for a cold shower," he said. "I think that you are also about ready for one." He moved towards the door, a grin on his face, Odyssey following immediately behind. "It sounds like a good plan."

Mike Sanders was silent for a full thirty seconds after Odyssey had finished describing the outcome of his meeting with Nikolai. He was especially thinking about the name of the operative that had been suggested. Grigorii and Alex had operated together on the South African operation a year earlier, and though the operation had ended in success, they had crossed swords more than once during it. The two men had totally different thinking on how soldiering worked, especially when it came to actually practicing the art.

"What are you thinking Mike?" the Russian finally asked.

Mike considered how to answer, knowing that it was a possible solution, but it was one that left the British holding at least some of the blame if things went awry. "The plan sounds reasonable, and also in my eyes fair. Whether the politicians will go along with it is another question. I'm just thinking about throwing Alex and Grigorii back together again..."

"Alex? The same Alex from the South African job?" Odyssey questioned.

"The same," Mike confirmed. "He's acting as a sort of military advisor on the project, meeting with the PM and his team on a weekly basis. He's my man for the job."

It was the Russian colonel's turn to ponder the circumstances that he found himself in. "Do you think they could work together?" he finally asked. "From the debrief on their return, I felt that they had built bridges, maybe even had found some respect for one another."

Mike was nodding gently at the other end of the secure connection, an action of course unseen by the other man. "I believe that you're right," he verbally acknowledged. "And Alex is really a consummate professional, so if I order that he works with Grigorii, I know that he would give it his all."

"Then I suggest that we only have one way forward," was the reply. "You talk to your man, I talk to mine. But I believe that we can both present an agreement on the operational side of things to our leaders and agree personnel at a later date."

Mike looked out of the office window, running scenarios through his mind. What could go wrong, he thought? The PM wanted to stop the killings, and he'd been tasked to look into it. Even if the plan wasn't the best, that was for Dominic to decide. At least it was a proposal. "Agreed," he finally said. "Let's move things forward and talk detail if the powers-that-be give us the go ahead."

The two men exchanged goodbyes and broke the connection. Each had other work to do, but now both needed to prepare a short briefing paper for their respective bosses. A paper that would not only outline the plan, but also include as many potential pitfalls as they could envisage.

'Covering your arse' as Mike liked to call it.

"I have no problem working again with Grigorii," Alex replied to his boss. The request had been unexpected; the last he'd heard of the ex-Spetsnaz man, he'd been heading out into the Russian wilderness on a personal vendetta. Then nothing until now. "Is he still in the military over there?" he asked. He still hadn't told Mike about his private calls with the man, nor about a conversation they'd had a year before on the Hercules aircraft back from Africa.

"I'm not sure, to tell the truth," his boss replied. "The impression I got was that he worked 'for' the military, not 'with' their army. Sort of a contractor. They want him to be a semi-deniable asset, that was the way the conversation was going," he added. "Still just an outline plan, Alex, just wanted to sound you out before I took it to the PM."

Alex was pleased that this was a phone conversation so that Mike couldn't see his expression right now. He remembered the problems that the two men had when working together in South Africa, how the Russian and his team had operated alone, that finally resulting in five of them dying. He had sort of made his peace with the man after saving him in a final firefight, but also knew that he had then 'gone rogue', taking out senior Russians in some forested area far east of Moscow. Some of it had reached the papers in London. How would you support a man like that in a hostile environment like Northern Ireland? Would he stick to the rules, or become a loose cannon once again?

"I think that we can work together," he said, trying to sound as positive as possible. "But I guess that someone also has to ask the same question to Grigorii. It's a two way decision."

"Odyssey will be on to him as we speak I believe. It seems that the PM is anxious to get this one rolling, so Nikolai Ignatov is pushing his man too."

Alex hesitated, thinking about his answer carefully. "I'm in," he finally stated. "Let's see what we get back from Russia."

It was another coffeeshop get together, a quiet corner where they wouldn't stand out, wouldn't attract unnecessary attention. Odyssey wore jeans, jacket and a baseball cap, feeling as if he was some sort of American tourist. Nothing military, nothing official.

"Alex Green?" Grigorii was asking as the colonel finished his summary of the various discussions to date.

"Yes, the same Alex Green of the SAS that you worked with in South Africa," the intelligence man responded. "He would be your back-up over there if you took the job. You'd effectively be a part of his team, answer to him." That caused him to smile. "But of course, reporting to me." The Soviets would never stop spying on the West the Russian officer had decided years before. There'd always be some sort of mistrust, some wariness of the other's intentions. They were wired differently.

Grigorii pondered his options before answering. He wanted to be working again for the State, but he had become accustomed to being his own boss in the woods of Chavash Varmane Bor. Working for the British SAS man to whom he owed his life? When he thought of it that way, there was really only one answer. He 'owed'.

"I'm in," he concluded.

16th April 2027

Lakeview Road, Craigavon, Northern Ireland

Declan's day job was in the county offices for the Borough, based in the nearby town of Craigavon. It meant a twenty mile round trip every day, but the money was pretty good, the hours flexible, and being their main man for Information Technology also meant that nobody else there really knew whether he was actually doing anything productive or not. He couldn't recall how many times he'd told his management that he needed to fix a 'glitch in the system', or 'complete IT updates' on the council's software.

It also gave him access to a fairly high-end computer system, and a fairly anonymous search engine that became even more confusing for anyone trying to track back to a single user, especially once it linked into the mass of employee addresses. Being the system administrator, Declan could tunnel in to the rest of the world as any person that worked there. He could also cancel complete histories, and not only the cursory 'delete' that was available on a normal computer. Effectively, he could do whatever he wanted with the system, do it incognito, and wipe out any record of ever doing it.

It meant that he was able to do things that they definitely hadn't taught him back at Queens University in Belfast.

Right now he was manoeuvring around on the Dark Web, his office door closed, a back-up screen ready to flick-on should anyone walk in. He wasn't the most sociable person in the offices there – most people just put it down to him being a computer nerd – so he didn't actually expect any company, but you couldn't be too careful.

He was looking for two things right now; he wanted to raise the subject of linking their little organisation to someone in the south, a first step in coordinating their campaign with becoming a united Ireland; and he was also looking for locally based people who appeared disillusioned with the way that things were going, people who indicated that they may have an interest in correcting Irish history. Neither were subjects that you could just Google.

The first topic wasn't going too well. It didn't surprise him really. You didn't advertise your terror group, not even on the Dark Web, and everyone was well aware that the police also had specialists in Cyber Crime nowadays. He'd need to think of another way to break into that one.

The search for prospective members to add to his so far tiny group did go better though. Again this was no big surprise, and he was certain that some people probably just posted their thoughts on Facebook and Instagram if he bothered to look there, but they weren't really the sort of folk that you wanted in a secret group. Your secret wouldn't last too long with the social media freaks.

His thought was to go for someone a little older, but not as old as Frank for example. Someone who perhaps already had experience with weapons, maybe had been involved with the IRA back in the day, had maybe even done a little prison time for their activities back then. The breeding zones for these people seemed to be West Belfast, Londonderry, possibly Warrenpoint, to name but a few. The ones that he was most interested in didn't post their names, just links to other pages, and even these didn't give many more details, just asked for a contact number and they'd 'get back to you'.

Did he really want to give them his contact details? What if this was a trap from the authorities? He considered his options. On one side he was pretty much a ghost in the system, anyone hunting him down could really only trace him as far as the council's IT system, not even a specific office. Another layer of protection was his use of the Dark Web and browsers associated with it. And a third layer was that the people he was looking for should be just as cautious as he was. But that was not something that he could verify. Yet.

The weak link was giving up his phone number. That was something that he wasn't so far willing to do.

He needed to think about it some more. There had to be another way.

He found the solution in the most obvious of places, something that a man with his training should have thought of immediately.

Lying in bed that evening, a Bushmills Whiskey and a bar of chocolate on the bedside table, a James Patterson book in his hand, he was escaping both the world and the cold of the house without costing himself a packet in gas bills. A blanket covered the quilt, an extra layer against the elements. It was a clear sky outside, the heat of the day long gone, the mercury dropping like a stone. Springtime in Ireland.

It was actually James Patterson that gave him the answer. A burner phone. The bad guy in the book had just bought one.

With this he would have an unknown number, he could keep it for as long or short a time as he wished, and he could chuck the thing into Lough Neagh one lunchtime at work when he did want to dispose of it. It definitely seemed to fit the bill.

He said a silent 'Slainte' to his favourite author right now, had a sip of the malt, and carried on reading the novel. Perhaps it could give him even more inspiration.

A cheap phone, a SIM card with limited credit, and he was ready to rock-and-roll.

It had taken him only a few minutes of his lunch break to walk to the nearby Tesco Extra and find what he needed. The whole package had cost less than fifty quid and left him wishing that he could have got the points on his Clubcard into the bargain, knowing this couldn't be as it would be traceable back to him.

He had a new spring in his step walking back to the office. He still hadn't told Paddy and Frank about his plans, but he thought that it would be a great way to start their meeting off that evening. He could then move on to more important things, such as their next target. That was something else that had come to him in his bed the night before.

"Some people must pay," he almost sang to himself.

It was now all about setting-up the phone and leaving his contact details with a few of the interested parties. Contact details and a cut-off time, a limited window. This phone wasn't anything like a puppy – it definitely wasn't for life.

And the game he was now in was also not for life. He grinned at his own private joke. It was all about death.

20th April 2027

London Heathrow, Arrivals

"So we meet once again Mister Green," said the smiling ex-Spetsnaz man. Alex looked at Grigorii closely, wondering how much the man had changed since their African adventure together. Or perhaps more to the point, apart. The only real time 'together' had been in the aircraft home, and that was when the Russian had let things slip about his country's involvement in the beginnings of the coronavirus. That was when he'd let his true self show through, when he'd finally displayed some sort of remorse for getting his whole team wiped out.

'Keep your guard up Alex', he thought to himself.

"A pleasant surprise for me too Grigorii," he responded, his own smile at least fifty percent real. In his eyes this man was dangerous but showing even some sort of remorse warranted some respect. Perhaps even leopards could change their spots, or at least rearrange them a little. And he looked fit – the time in the forests had surely not done him any harm at all.

Their time together was limited, Grigorii only in the country for three hours before returning back to Moscow. It was something that the SAS man had insisted on before the plan got any more detailed. Talking on the phone, video-conferencing and all the rest, just didn't make-up for good old human-to-human interaction. Looking into a man's eyes told you much more than a million meaningless words separated by thousands of miles.

"Shall we grab a 'cuppa' as you Brits say?" the Russian asked. He nodded towards a nearby Starbucks.

Alex shook his head, pointing back towards the Arrivals sign. "I've booked a room to allow us to speak privately," he told the man. "I also have a flask of coffee ordered, so we shouldn't die of thirst."

The two men moved towards a bright blue door marked 'Staff Only', Alex taking a key-card from his pocket and letting them enter. Inside was fairly barren, just a small, round table, two chairs and a tall silver flask. And two mugs. It looked like what it was: somewhere to interview suspicious individuals. It would do.

"So I assume that Odyssey has filled you in with the details of what we are proposing?" Alex asked, getting straight to the point. He took the seat closest to the door, pulled the two cups to him and started unscrewing the top of the thermos flask. "Did you have any thoughts?"

Grigorii took the other chair, pulling himself close to the table.

"He did, but can I hear it from you please?" he asked, ignoring the second question. "Sometimes the small details can be lost in the translation," he added. "Sometimes they are intentionally lost, especially if it suits the teller."

Alex smiled at this, knowing that it was more than true. Half stories were often worse than none at all.

For the next ten minutes he ran through where things stood and his ideas on how to try and catch the killers. Grigorii asked few questions, mainly just listening to the Englishman. To Alex, this was in itself a change of character. The Russian he'd met before the South African venture would have talked over him, trying to be the most important part of the show. The man had changed.

"Another coffee?" Alex asked, the brief outline of his plan over. He poured two more cups, pushed one across the table to the Russian. "What do you think?" he asked.

Grigorii cupped his hands together behind his neck, tilted his head back and closed his eyes. "I think it's a long shot," he finally said. "But the way I see it, it's probably the only shot that you're going to get. If this is a new group and they keep it tight, you can do something like this, or just sit and wait for them to make a mistake. And while you wait, they keep killing people," he added.

"That's exactly how I see it," Alex agreed. "And no-one is happy to just sit and wait and count up the dead."

"Would you want me to go into Ireland, put myself about a bit?"

"That's pretty much how I see it playing out, but it's also up to you. It's one of the reasons that I wanted this meeting, even if it was a lot of travel for you. I just wanted to be straight with you, face-to-face, no bullshit. We wouldn't be in a position to give you lots of support, no real back-up. That would just warn off the bad guys, send them right back under cover."

"So I'm pretty much on my own then?" Grigorii smiled. "The way I like it. Probably just need a bit of Irish luck to get a win."

"You've spent quite a bit of time on your own lately," Alex replied. "At least, I assumed it was you taking out the bad guys in the woods over there. It sort of fits in with your call before you went off the map."

"I guess that's for me to know, and you to guess at," the Russian answered. "But let's just say that you're not far off the mark," he added with a grin. "What else do we need to cover? You really just wanted to know if I was up for it, is that right?"

"That's about it mate," Alex admitted, drinking the last of his coffee. "I will present the whole thing to the PM tomorrow and look for a green light. If I get it, you'll need to pack your bags for few weeks of holiday here in the UK."

Grigorii pushed back his chair and stood up. "That sounds good to me," he said. "So what can we do around here for an hour? Maybe a good pint of Guinness or something?"

"Now you're talking," the SAS man responded. "I came out here on the Heathrow Express, so no point in holding back. Let's find a boozer. Help you to sleep on the flight home."

The two men shook hands just over an hour later, Alex going as far as he could go before crossing the British border at Customs.

"Safe trip mate, and hopefully I'll be in contact tomorrow sometime. You know how it is with politics though; they might just change their minds on the whole thing once I lay it out for them."

"Just let me know, whichever way it goes," the Russian replied. "I hope I can be more useful to you on this job, Alex. I messed up a bit in Africa, allowed my men to run me more than I ran them. This time will be better, I assure you. Just me and you." Grigorii took Alex's hand in both of his. "Thanks for a second chance."

Alex stood and watched the man walk over to the customs officials, passport in hand. Alex turned, started his own journey back into the city. He glanced over his shoulder, seeing Grigorii passing through the barrier to the airside of the terminal. He didn't look back, didn't slow down.

'So he wants a chance to redeem himself,' the SAS man said to himself.

He hoped that he would be able to give him that chance. He hoped that between the two of them, they could stop the murders in Northern Ireland.

Alex headed towards his train.

21st April 2027

Whitehall, London, UK

The meeting today was held in the Ministry of Defence Building, just off Whitehall. Constructed in the middle of the twentieth century, at least half of it underground if rumours were to be believed, it had always struck Alex as an uninspiring and ugly stone block of offices, plonked accidently in the middle of so much history. It was also a short walk from the Palace of Westminster, one of the reasons for the choice of venue. Alex suspected that the second reason was to give the military men a feeling of presenting on home turf.

It was the usual band of four from the political side Alex noted, though on this occasion Mike Sanders had also insisted on 'joining the party', as he'd put it. This was either the launch or the demise of the plan to bait the killers, to try and draw them out with Alex's 'fake news' idea. In Mike's eyes, that meant that he should be there – in the end, the idea had come from a SAS member, so if it all went tits-up, it would be his boys who took the flak. That's just how these things usually played out.

"Before we proceed, do we have anything new to report from your side Colin?" Dominic asked the senior policeman. "Just before we hand the floor over to Alex and Mike."

Colin Shankly glanced quickly around the table, checking that the rest of them were ready to kick things off. He hated having to go over things twice just because one of the politicians happened to be too busy texting someone when things were meant to start. It had happened to him far too often, but not on this occasion.

"A couple of things that might be useful to us one day but right now don't bring us any further forward," he told them all. "One of the weapons that the terrorists are using has been used during all four murders to date. Another one has been at two of them at least. This is all the latest from the ballistics people," he continued. He glanced down at his notes, just checking that the facts were correct. "On top of that we have got some tyre tread impressions from the last shooting, though they don't help us much. Pretty much a standard tyre type, probably on about half the family saloon cars in the Province."

"But it is something," the PM stated, trying to put a positive spin on things. "It could help secure a conviction, couldn't it? If we find the people behind all of this?"

"It could, but first we have to find them," Shankly confirmed. "But the biggest positive so far is that we have found human hairs on the window frame that the killers used to enter the McAvoy house, and we're using them to work-up a DNA profile. We've already tested them against the family, and they don't belong to either of the adults. If we're lucky, we'll have whoever they do belong to on one of the DNA databases."

Everyone in the room was silent for a full ten seconds. "Always saving the best till last, Colin," Nicholas Thomas said, thinly veiled sarcasm in his voice. "I would have considered that that should have been the first thing to tell us. Could be a game changer."

"Enough, Nick," the PM interjected sternly. "Like the other stuff, it means nothing yet, but God, it would be great if we got a match. We need a little luck."

"It may not even be from the terrorists," the police officer said, his voice tight. Once again, Alex felt the tension between the two men, a place where there should be none. If the Northern Ireland Secretary and the Chief of the PSNI couldn't work together, then what hope was there?

"Quite," Dominic added. "Anything else Colin?" he asked. "Anything from the rest?" His eyes ran over the others, then turned to Mike. "Do you want to lead, or is this all Alex's show?"

Alex hoped that Mike would want to run with the baton, at least in the build-up. He could just imagine being on the end of the next tongue-lashing from Nicholas Thomas.

"I'm going to let Alex run with it," his boss replied. "He's done all of the work, so it seems wrong that I should steal all of the glory." He grinned, trying to lighten the mood in the room.

"So let's all play nice," Ruth Maybank added, one of the first interventions that Alex had seen her make. He looked towards her, receiving a winning smile. "You will have to get used to the politics of it all Alex. Sometimes it can even be fun."

He guessed that that would never happen, but took a breath anyway, pulling his notes closer to him, more to buy another few seconds than because he needed them. "Thanks," he said looking towards the Prime

Minister. "This shouldn't take long, and most of it you already know. Let's just say that we've spent our time putting a little meat on the bones."

For the next twenty minutes he laid out his ideas, including his meeting with Grigorii, then took another twenty minutes of questions. Mike Sanders supported as necessary, but the junior soldier was left mainly to his own resources.

'Give me a bunch of terrorists any day,' he thought to himself. 'These guys were far more dangerous.'

The meeting broke-up soon afterwards, the only people left in the room now being the two SAS men and the PM. "I'm sorry about my colleagues," Dominic said, half a grin on his face. "Like Ruth said, you do get used to it, but perhaps that's not something we should boast about. It's a cut-throat world."

"Makes SAS selection look like a doddle, doesn't it Alex?" Mike said jokingly. "It took me forever to get used to it, and I spent plenty of time in the university debating society before joining the ranks." He was more serious now, watching Alex for a reaction. "If it gets too much, just tell me mate. I can sit in on this stuff, you can do the real work."

The PM was shaking his head, his eyes troubled. "I hope that it never comes to that," he told the young soldier. "You keep the meetings grounded, bring a little realism into our rather secluded lives. I like you at the table, and I think that Ruth is also gaining respect for you. Stick with it."

Alex wasn't too sure how to answer that, everything he thought to say sounding a little empty. "I'll do my best," he finally said.

"So all of the team now have something to work on," Dominic concluded, gathering up his papers and looking at his watch. "They all know to run things by you before they release anything, so we still keep a bit of central control on the whole project. If you don't like anything that comes up, just let Mike or myself know and we'll sort it."

"Thanks sir," Alex replied. "I also hope that it never comes to that, but I have to admit I sometimes feel more than a little out of my depth here," he continued. "It's good to know that I have support if needed."

The Prime Minister shook their hands, clearly indicating that the meeting was now over. The two soldiers left the old grey building together, Mike turning right to collect his car, then suddenly spinning back around to face Alex.

"Can you be in Hereford later this week? Latest beginning of next week?" he asked, a slight frown crossing his features. "Maybe you could get Grigorii over here by then? He could join us."

"Anything in particular boss?" Alex asked, wondering what was on the cards and how he could ask the Russian to get himself back into the country again in just a few days' time. This was typical of the military; if they'd thought it through a bit more in advance, then Grigorii could have stayed over for the week. As it was he was just going to clock a lot of airmiles for nothing. "Something I need to prepare?"

Mike grinned, tapping his nose. "Just a new little toy that our boys are learning to play with," he said, a twinkle in his eye, obviously enjoying the intrigue. "I thought that perhaps you and our new Russian friend might also like to have a go with it."

With that, he span away, heading off towards where he'd parked his vehicle, leaving Alex to dwell on what was to come.

The junior man watched the colonel go, bemused. When his boss rounded the corner, he simply shrugged his shoulders and turned towards the nearest Tube station, before halting again and taking out his mobile phone. Best that he called Moscow right away, at least giving their travel people the opportunity to start the ball rolling. Then he should also give Grigorii the heads-up, a chance to get packed, perhaps even before he got the call from his own superiors.

And he really must give Andile a call.

23rd April 2027

Armagh, Northern Ireland

A different pub, again out in the countryside, just beyond the town's outer limits, but this one with a pleasant little beer garden. The weather was fine for April and the chances of being overheard outside were much less than they'd be inside, so the three men sat at a wooden table close to the carpark. The drinks were ordered, a pretty young waitress away arranging them. Business wouldn't commence until the girl had delivered and left them be, and the three tried to make small talk to fill the time.

"Did ye watch the footie last night?" Paddy asked, pulling his leather jacket back on as the sun disappeared behind some clouds. "Still nippy out, isn't it?"

"I don't watch football," Frank said. "Game for bloody prima donnas and girls," he spat dismissively on to the grass. "Give me a good game of rugby any day."

Declan was nervously tapping the table, a bundle of energy impatiently waiting to get started on the real business. He couldn't wait to tell them his plans, and how he intended to implement them. Frank gave him a funny look. "What's with you?" the older man asked. "You're doing my head in with all that tapping."

"Normally means he's got something interesting to tell us," Paddy said. "That's what I've noticed."

"As long as it's just interesting," the old boy said. "Not something feckin' stupid."

Declan forced a grin, glanced over to the bar door where the young waitress had just re-emerged. "Here's the drinks coming lads," he said. "Then we can really get started."

The girl delivered the drinks, turned and left, Paddy watching her wiggle away. "A nice bit of skirt, that one," he commented. "Great arse."

"Way too good for the likes of you," Frank quipped with a grin. "Ye wouldn't know where to start."

"Okay!" Declan shot out, getting their attention before they started talking more rubbish. "Let's get down to why we're here."

The other two men sipped at their drinks before placing them on the table. "Ready when you are skipper," Paddy replied, making a pretend salute with his right hand. "You're the boss."

Declan thought about saying something, of giving the young upstart a reminder of what they were there for, but a glance at Frank warned him that it wasn't worth it. The kid's dad still had connections from the past, could still be of use. He bit his tongue, knowing that one day his chance would come.

"The first thing I wanted to say, was that we got some good press from the Telegraph. People know why we are doing what we do, without having any clue as to who we are. That's what we wanted. They know what our cause is, but they don't know us." He picked up his pint, took a mouthful of Smithwicks. The Guinness here was dreadful.

"I've also been doing some thinking," he continued, leaning in, the others following suit. "If we want to be taken seriously, then we have to get bigger. Not much, but more than a hit every month, I'd say." He inspected the faces of his comrades, looking for understanding. "Are you with me?"

"I'm with ye," the boy responded. "I've always said we should be doing more. There's too many of those bloody Prods out there, so making it a few less would keep me happy."

Declan glanced to Frank. "And you?"

He got the barest nod in return, hardly a stunning endorsement. It was hard to read what was going on behind the old man's rheumy grey eyes; he'd never been a man of many words, more a man of actions, at least as a youngster if the rumours were to be believed.

"Are ye with me Frank?" he asked again.

The man rubbed his brow thoughtfully, still saying nothing. He lowered his hand, finally raising his eyes to Declan's. "The more of us there are, the more chance of someone saying something out of turn," he eventually declared. "It's where we messed up in the past, and I'm damned sure that's how we'll get caught now."

Declan forced a grin, coming out more as a grimace. Frank never let things go easily, everything needing to be fought for. And always 'the past' had to be revisited.

"I've thought about all of that," he countered. "We don't need to meet the new people at all, so they'll never even know who we are."

"And how will that work Declan?" It was Paddy this time, his face creased in a frown. "I mean we have to know the people, or how will they know what to do? They can't just charge around killing politicians willy-nilly, can they? If they are also a part of 'One Ireland', then they have to fit in with our planning."

"And they will," Declan replied. "Will the two of you just give me a chance to explain!"

Frank just sat and stared at him, eyes empty, no words. Paddy looked puzzled but followed the old man's example.

"I will advertise our interest to find recruits on the Dark Web," Declan began. "You've both heard of that, haven't you? It's a way to use the internet without people being able to track you, meaning that you can work more or less anonymously."

"Can't the police also access it?" the boy asked. "I thought I read that they did that sort of thing."

"They do to some degree," Declan agreed. "But even they can't monitor everything."

"But you'll still need to leave your details on it, won't you?" Paddy was showing more understanding than Declan had expected, perhaps a good thing, perhaps a bad one. At least this way it meant that he was forced to explain more than what he usually would have, maybe enough to show Frank that everything had been well thought through.

"That's the best bit," he said with smile. "All I leave as a contact is a phone number and a window of time that the phone will work. Anyone interested has to call the number in the time window, or I disappear again."

"You mean like a burner phone, or that's what they call them in the movies."

"Same thing Paddy. And the beauty of them is that you can buy them anywhere, shove in a SIM card and use it. Then chuck the thing in to the Irish Sea if you want when you're done."

Frank was still just staring, but Paddy looked impressed. Then a cloud fell over his face, a thought crossing his mind. "So let me get this right, they call you, and you agree if they can join, right? Then what? When do we get to meet them?"

"That's the beauty of it Paddy; none of us ever get to meet them. They never see us, they never know our names." He thought he saw a slight awakening in Frank's eyes, a tiny spark of something; could it be agreement? He continued. "I just outline our ideals, see if they have the same ones. Then I arrange a contact point, a time window where I can put a message on the Dark Web. They check there daily, and I can put a new burner phone number on there any day that we want. They call, I give them a job, they do the hit, and 'One Ireland' claims the victory."

"Jesus," Paddy mumbled. "It's like a bloody movie that."

Frank was looking at the boy, a question ready to be spoken. He paused, not wanting to look stupid Declan guessed later, then finally spoke. "It sounds great Declan," he started, still an edge of doubt in his voice. "But is it possible? Can you really do this with no links back to any of the three of us?"

"I can," the computer expert stated confidently.

"Frank, I think he can. I've seen it on the telly, and I've read stuff like this in the papers. I think it can be done." Paddy lifted his beer, downing a healthy slug. "It's been around for years now," he added.

"Not only that, but I can also do all of the computer work from my office, so anyone tracing it back will end up with the council offices in Craigavon, not us here in Armagh."

Frank finally allowed himself a small uncertain smile, lifted his pint. "Holy feck. I must be getting too old for this stuff. Too much technology."

"That's why you work with us young folks," Paddy told him and clinked his glass. "Let's drink to new members."

25th April 2027

Belfast, Northern Ireland

Colin Shankly was in full uniform, the black shiny peak of his cap reflecting the early morning sun around it's silver trim, the same light reflecting from the row of medals above his left breast pocket and off his gleaming polished buttons. He smoothed down his moustache and one of the make-up people reached over and tried to apply a little powder to his cheeks.

"Please, none of that," he told the girl. "Sorry, but I'd prefer to look terrible than start wearing that stuff." He had his cue cards in his left hand, tried to get a final look at them. It was almost time.

"Two minutes," one of the television people told him, holding up two fingers to ensure there was no misunderstanding.

Despite it being springtime, the weather was still chilly, the wind blowing off Belfast Lough today, the sunshine feeble. PSNI had deployed checkpoints on Knock Road two hundred metres out in each direction from the headquarters building, normal precautions when the Chief Constable was making a television appearance. It would do little for the image of law and order if the head of police was taken out in front of the country's major TV networks.

"Are we ready to go sir?" asked the public relations coordinator. She took up a place to the right of the Chief, adjusting her own hat and straightening her tie. There'd be no words from her today, but it was always best to look the part.

"One minute," came the continued countdown.

Colin had a final check on his words, deciding to ad-lib and just keep them to hand in case of emergencies. He drew a slow breath, puffed out his cheeks and exhaled. "Let's get on with this," he muttered mainly to himself. At least it wasn't live, so if needed, a second chance was always there.

A thumbs-up from the presenter who had already recorded her piece, a ten second count in, and then they were off.

"Thanks for giving us the chance to give you all an update on where we are with these cowardly murders of some of our brave politicians in recent weeks," he started, pretending to be responding to the TV anchor. "For us, even one death is a disaster, a return to the dark days that we all hoped we had left far behind us, but four is just not acceptable at any level. Our people are working day and night to apprehend the people behind all of this, and we are presently following up on many different avenues of investigation." He took a hurried glance down at the cards, looking for the next bullet point to get him going again. "Our forensic people recently came up with some details of the automobile used at one of the crime scenes, and we also have some closed-circuit TV footage of one of the terrorists dropping off information at the Belfast Telegraph offices here in the city." They had all agreed to be vague about how little information they actually had, and also not to mention the possibility of the DNA. Always best to keep something up your sleeve.

"We believe that this is a small cell, operating independently. We believe that they have limited resources, meaning that they will be dependent on others to obtain equipment to execute their crimes. This means that they may borrow vehicles or steal them, perhaps need time off work on the days of the murders, access their weapons from people who were involved from the days of The Troubles. That means that people in the street, people like yourselves, may have seen something, might have overheard something in the pub, noticed a peculiar request at work. If you have, then please report it, however minor it may seem to you at first. Once my officers include it in the bigger picture, it might just make a significant difference. We are showing secure and anonymous numbers on the ribbon at the bottom of the screen, and as I have just said, please call, however insignificant the incident may have seemed at the time."

Everything until now was pretty much the truth, facts bent slightly to suit the situation. Now he looked directly into the camera, putting on his best poker face, looking stern and emotionless, in control of things.

"As we all know, even in troubled times, someone will always find a way to take advantage of a situation, and usually not in a positive way. We are experiencing this as we speak. Criminals have noticed that the 'bad old days' may be returning, and they know that this will bring with it certain demands. Our border people have experienced an increase in weapons finds in the docks, small caches to date, but up on only a few months ago. The sources are varied, but the majority are ex-Russian military guns, coming in hidden in containers of other goods." He paused, looking at his paperwork for the close out.

"Again I ask you to keep your eyes open, but also your ears peeled. We know tourism is on the up again post COVID but be heedful of foreigners. If they don't fit the usual tourist profile, then be suspicious." He knew that this was all pretty general, a little wishy-washy even, but it had been the best that Alex and himself could agree on. "Do not try and apprehend anyone, that is the job of the PSNI. Just call the number and let us know what it is you've seen or heard and let us take it from there." He again looked straight into the lens, a stern expression on his face. "We will treat all calls seriously, so don't think that you might be wasting police time. We are here to serve you as best we can."

The red light on the television camera flicked off, filming complete. Colin knew that his people had a good chance of being inundated with hoax calls, but the plea for assistance had to be believable, needed to be swallowed by the killers.

Alex's new 'fake news' was out there.

Three hours later, on the steps of Stormont, the Northern Ireland Secretary was about to do his own bit towards the subterfuge. At his side was the Home Secretary, Ruth Maybank, sent across that morning by Dominic Wild to ensure that Nicholas Thomas toed the party line, guaranteeing that there'd be no snide remarks about the earlier address by the Chief Constable. Of course, Thomas didn't know that this was the reason – he'd been told that this was considered crucial to getting the plan off the ground, that having it presented with such high-ranking people in attendance would give it more realism. He'd agreed to it, especially when it was made clear to him that he would be doing the speaking, not Ruth.

His statement was to be broadcast live, allowing the journalists to pose a few questions after the announcement. It would contain much of what Colin Shankly had already said, just with a more political leaning, condemning other countries for attempting to interfere in UK politics. He would mention Russia, their rumoured arms dealing within the Province, a caution that outsiders should keep out of UK based affairs.

The piece only took three minutes to run through, reading from notes that had been written by Thomas but edited by the rest of the task force. It contained praise for the work of the PSNI, the only major objection from the man.

"We must project a united front," the PM had told him on the phone. "And that means supporting Colin for his press release. If you can't agree to that, then I'll simply have to ask Ruth to handle the presentation." At that, the NI Secretary had relented. He'd toe the line.

With his words done, Thomas offered the chance for the journalists present to quiz him.

"Are members of the Irish Assembly now getting additional police protection?" a lady from the Belfast Telegraph asked, a microphone held towards the politician.

"The PSNI are increasing patrols to ensure their safety, and where necessary we will put additional security on their homes."

"Have measures been put in place to replace those members who have been murdered?" this from a young man from the Coleraine Times. "As I understand, they all had duties within Stormont, and obviously those duties won't just go away."

"We are initially employing temporary stand-ins, so no-one should worry that issues in their own regions will be neglected. Individual parties will obviously be looking at permanent replacements for their people."

"Where is this information coming from about the Russian involvement?" an older bearded man from the Derry Journal asked.

The NI Secretary hesitated, thinking about the best answer.

"This has come from our intelligence gathering people both here in Northern Ireland and back on the mainland," Ruth Maybank said, leaning slightly across Thomas. "We can also deduce this partly from the goods that the seized weapons were packed with, but we also have intercepts from GCHQ that confirm certain things. These clearly indicate Russian involvement, and as Nicholas has said, this is wholly unacceptable to the UK government."

The NI Secretary scanned the reporters, the TV people indicating that he should wrap things up. "Anyone for anymore?" he said with a winning smile. He gave the hacks a full ten seconds, then closed things down. "Many thanks for your attention, and we promise to keep you all informed of any new developments."

"So far, so good," the PM said, watching the second interview in his private office in Number Ten. "The lies are out there, the lures are set. Now it just needs the fish to take them. And of course for me to do my bit for the cameras," he added jovially. "Sorry to drag your people into all of this Nikolai, but you do understand that we need to catch these bastards. I'll need to make some accusations about you on camera but you know that this is just a part of the ploy."

"And I shall be suitably offended and totally bombastic about the UK blaming anything in the world on someone else," the Russian President told him. "Which is just what the rest of the planet will expect to hear!" You could hear that he was enjoying this, playing the part of the cuckolded spouse. "I know why you are doing it Dom and I hope that one day you will return the compliment," he added.

"I hope that I never need to," the PM replied. "But I think we both know that this is little more than a hope. It seems that the COVID crisis slowed up certain things in the world, but with that gone, the usual shit is back on the table."

"If it wasn't so, why would they need us?" the Russian responded. "It's never really been any different."

Dominic sighed, wondering when his opposite number had become a philosopher. He was in front of the cameras in just under an hour, needed to run through the words that he'd agreed with Alex and the rest. "You're right," he said with a sigh. "And when the day comes for that support, you know that you'll get it."

Alex watched the PM's performance later on Sky News, pleased that he knew the truth. To a layman it would appear that the Prime Minister was about to go to war with the Soviets, so forceful was his presentation.

He hoped that the ruse would work and bring the bad guys out into the open, but also prayed that it didn't ruin what had nowadays become a good relationship between the UK and Russia. If anyone could pull off such a fragile balancing act, then he was sure that it would be Dominic Wild.

Within the hour, the Russian President had reacted, demanding from Moscow that the British presented evidence to back up their accusations. It would make great press the next day, but would it achieve it's real aim?

Alex hoped so. The next day he was meeting Grigorii again. The game was running.

For better or worse.

25th April 2027

Armagh, Northern Ireland

Declan had called an emergency meeting, the three men coming together without the pleasure of a drink, all squeezed into his car in a parking area near the centre of the city. As usual in Ireland, the rain was winning over the summer and the car windows were rapidly steaming up. He cracked his own open a little.

"Did you both see the news earlier?" he asked, twisting in his seat to meet the eyes of Frank, sat as usual in the backseat. Paddy sat next to him in the passenger's seat, a carryout coffee in his hands.

"I think everyone saw it," the old man answered. "But what's it to us?" He seemed upset about being there, maybe had had to cancel something with the wife to be there at all.

Paddy just sipped his coffee, wondering what all of the fuss was. He'd seen a little of the news, but not everything, just that the Russians seemed to pissed off with the Brits about something or another. He couldn't see that as any sort of a bad thing.

"We got a mention from the PSNI puppet, that Shankly bloke. Seems that they have something on us."

"Come on Declan," Frank replied. "Their comments were all bloody vague, something on the car, a picture of you on CCTV. It can't be anything useful, or we'd not be sitting out here now, would we?"

"But they're trying to turn folks against us." Declan hadn't liked that bit. He saw himself as a freedom fighter, someone who was trying to get all of the Irish – especially the Catholics – the Ireland he believed that they all wanted and deserved. Back to the way it had been before the English generals had started carving it up, awarding themselves Irish estates for service to the crown. "We need the folks to be with us."

"It was forever the same Declan," Frank stated, dismissing the whole thing. "They're clutching at straws, I tell ye."

Sitting on the edge of the exchange, Paddy was now becoming bored. He could have been playing pool with his mates, maybe got lucky with the new barmaid down at his local. "So is it something or is it nothing?" he asked, puzzled. "I promised to meet my mates tonight, that's all."

"It's nothing, so we can all get on," Frank said, sliding across the seat.

"Hold on a sec," Declan demanded. He tried to push his concerns to the back of his mind, to focus on the positives that had come from the news. "I think I might have found us two new members, one from just outside of Derry, the other from Belfast. What do you think?"

Frank paused. "They'll be just sleepers though, isn't that right?" he asked. "You keep them on standby until we need them. No meetings, no contact, just like you said."

Declan nodded his agreement. "That's the plan, but what about arming them? What about us?" He'd been giving it quite some thought. Their own weaponry was badly dated, and the new boys might have none at all. "There was mention on the telly of new guns being smuggled in, something to do with some Soviet connection. Maybe they can help."

"So how would ye contact them?" Frank asked. "I'm sure they don't run adverts in the local papers."

Declan thought about this for a minute, knowing that he had to reply fast, before the other two walked away. In his rush to organise the meeting he hadn't completed his usual planning, something he'd learned to do to deflect Frank's line of negative questioning.

"Same as how I contacted the two new lads," he told them. "I'll start looking tomorrow."

"You'll have to show me this Dark Web stuff Declan," Paddy said, emptying the coffee beaker. "Maybe I can find a decent woman out there too."

In his mind, Declan was shaking his head, wishing he'd never met the two of them. On the outside he forced a false smile. "We can do that Paddy," he said.

Nothing more to add, the two men slipped out of his car and were gone. Declan sat there for a full minute, letting the misted windows clear from their breathing, the rain pinging off the car roof, then drove for home.

26th April 2027

Heathrow Airport, London, UK

For the second time in just six days Alex and Grigorii met at the Arrivals area of Britain's largest airport. Heathrow's traffic volumes were slowly increasing back to pre-COVID levels, though it still lagged behind the hectic Charles de Gaulle in Paris as the busiest airport in Europe. Some would say that this was a good thing, but the commercial managers and financiers pushing Heathrow wanted their title back and the cashflow that would come with it.

Today there was no hanging around chatting; Alex had organised a fast taxi transfer to the nearby heliport, where the SAS had an AS365N3 Dauphin 2 helicopter operated by the Army Air Corps waiting for the two of them. In its royal blue civilian livery it could have been waiting for any well off businessman or sportsman, and that was just the way the Regiment liked to operate – way below the radar.

The two men wasted no time boarding and the army pilots seemed equally keen to be on their way. Alex had explained what he could to Grigorii during the taxi transfer, his voice quiet to flummox their eavesdropping taxi driver. Now in the helicopter, they could finally talk openly.

"We're actually flying up to Hereford?" the Russian asked, seemingly a little surprised. "You're letting an ex-Spetsnaz man inside of your secret lair?"

"That's what the boss decided," Alex responded, also wondering what Mike was playing at. It was either a new chapter in détente, or they were going to seriously limit access to the Russian, maybe just whip him out to Pontrilas for some sort of a demo. "I still don't even know why he's asked me out there today, never mind yourself. Just know that he found it all very funny and wanted to show me something new."

Grigorii raised his palms and hunched his shoulders, a 'who knows' gesture. Alex shrugged too, unable to add more on the subject.

"So the rest of the plan is approved," Grigorii said, a statement not a question. "I've seen the heated TV debate between my leader and yours, but as I understand it, this is all staged, all a part of the bigger plan."

Alex nodded agreement, happy with how smoothly things had progressed. "For now, everyone seems to be toeing the line. I'm sure that there'll be hiccups along the way though."

Grigorii grinned. "Aren't there always."

The helicopter didn't land in the SAS barracks as Alex had expected it to, just skirting the southern edge of Hereford and heading out towards the Brecon Beacons. Clear of the city the pilot started bleeding off power and height, descending towards a large rural area that Alex knew to be Pontrilas, a training area used by the SAS. As the aircraft came closer to the ground, a section of a Boeing 747 Jumbo fuselage came into view, along with a mock-up of a village.

"Our close-quarter battle training area," Alex pointed out to Grigorii. "Plus the old Jumbo for our counter terrorist training. Needs to be updated one day soon. No Jumbos left now."

The Russian nodded his understanding; similar things he'd already encountered in his home country.

They could also see a group of men and women close to the hulk of the plane now, all standing in a loose semi-circle with two men in black futuristic suits standing in the centre. It appeared that they were presenting something to the assembled troops, but at present it wasn't clear what.

The pilot was almost on the deck now, landing at a safe distance from the group who were now holding their hands over their ears, all watching. The wheels touched, and the pilot turned and gave Alex a thumbs-up.

"Thanks for the lift," Alex said before removing the headset and opening the rear door.

The SAS sergeant and the Russian slid out, Alex helping with a small backpack, Grigorii taking a medium sized suitcase. As soon as the two of them were clear of the rotor disk, the helicopter blades began chopping harder into the cool air and the machine began lifting off the ground. After a quick scan for obstructions, the aircraft turned away from the men, dropped its nose and rushed away, taking it's cacophony of noise along with it.

"Nice aircraft," Grigorii commented. "Our own are generally a little more 'rough and ready' nowadays."

Alex looked across towards the assembled group of soldiers, noting that Mike Sanders was heading their way. "This is the boss coming now," he told his colleague. "You met with him in Moscow last year."

Grigorii winced; Alex and himself hadn't exactly hit it off in that meeting. It had taken a long time for them to reach a point of anything resembling trust, but he hoped that they were now well on the way to it. The past was the past, and it had been Alex that had selected him for this latest task, so that had to mean something. "Are the ladies over there also with the SAS?" he asked.

"Yeah," Alex replied. "Been almost ten years now since we started recruiting the girls. Some of them make us blokes look soft! They're good."

Mike was almost with them now, advancing with a wide grin on his face. "How was the trip?" he asked as he reached them, extending his hand towards the Russian.

"Long, but fine," the man answered. "Thanks for laying on the ride here, and also for letting me see what you people do. It makes me feel more… accepted," he finished, finally finding the word that seemed to fit.

"Welcome to the team," the colonel replied.

"So what's the plan boss?" Alex asked.

"Come on over. I'll introduce you both." He smiled again, a boyish grin. "I think you're going to like this."

The two men that they'd observed in the centre of the group were from a company called Gravity Industries. Alex knew from Mike that some of his colleagues were working with them exploring military options for their Jet Suit, something that had been around for a number of years now, but only seemed to get better and better.

"And with the latest battery technology," one of them was explaining to the assembled SAS troops, "we can stay airborne for around thirty minutes on one charge."

"A few stats," the other man continued, the two of them obviously accustomed to working together. "The suit weighs in at just under thirty kilos with the batteries fitted and consists of five turbines, all spinning at about a hundred and twenty thousand rpm. The best air speed we've recorded to date is just over a hundred miles per hour, but that feels bloody fast when you're not protected by a cabin, I can tell you."

No-one wanted to dispute that, but Alex could tell that most of the troops were keen to see it, and not just hear about it. They wanted a proper demo. Some of them wanted a lot more than that.

"We started the company back in 2017," the first man continued. "COVID slowed things up a bit, but I have to say, it's now gathering pace with all sort of applications, from leisure, to rescue services, to military. This should be a great year for us."

"So, some more facts and figures," the second man cut in. He paused, his face splitting into a cheeky grin. "Okay, I jest. I think I know what all of you want, so let's go and see the thing work."

He led them around to behind the fuselage of the 747 where a third colleague was waiting, suited up in a black sci-fi like outfit, boots and helmet, a larger jet engine on his back, two small turbines on each forearm. He looked a little like some sort of Luke Skywalker, except in black.

"This is my mate Jason, and he's going to be the entertainment for the afternoon." He gave a nod to the man in the suit. "Ready when you are mate."

The man in the suit adjusted his position, crouching slightly. He seemed to press something in his hand and the five separate turbines started their wind-up, the whine starting low and rising to a high pitched scream. The two men from Gravity Industries held out their arms, moving the soldiers back a little, giving their pilot room to manoeuvre. Alex guessed that the take-off and landing were probably the least 'controlled' events, the same as he'd found when pilots had let him go 'hands-on' in helicopters and planes.

The man appeared to be checking the function of his equipment, similar to the pre-flight checks of your typical pilot, just a final inspection before committing himself to the skies. The turbines seemed to accelerate a little more, the dust below them blowing in the direction of the onlookers.

And then he was off the ground, perhaps six feet up in the air, a sort of low hover position, finding stability by adjusting the smaller turbines fitted to his arms. He held the position for a few seconds, checking that everything was as he expected – all the 'Ps & Ts' in the green as pilots would say, referring to their engine pressures and temperatures – and then another adjustment and he rose upwards once more, settling at around twenty feet.

"So as you can all see, it's a vertical take-off application, no need for any sort of forward speed in take-off," said the second Gravity man, the comedian as Alex had branded him. "Means you can basically operate out of anywhere, lift off from the back of a Land Rover for example."

The Luke Skywalker lookalike gave the men on the ground a nod, received one in return. He leant his body slightly forward, adjusted his arms and began drifting forward, moving over the top of the old Boeing aircraft. The SAS crew looked on, no words needed. The man adjusted himself once more, settled down on top of the Jumbo, a gentle touchdown.

"It obviously takes a lot of practice to land like that," the man on the ground continued. "But you can see how useful it might be. It's not too noisy, you could fly in from the terminal, approach from the tail so none of the bad guys see you, and land directly into a hostage situation."

The man in the Jet Suit lifted off once again, taking up a high hover above the fuselage. He glanced around him, then leant forward and he was off, quickly gathering speed.

"The applications are only limited by your own imagination," the man continued, obviously a line from their sales patter. "We have weekly brainstorming sessions to try and think of new market applications, and we still haven't stopped coming up with new ideas."

The pilot was about two hundred metres away now, leaning through a long righthand turn at about twenty feet. He altered his position, leant even further forward, and began speeding up. Seconds later he whizzed over their heads, speed indeterminate, but well over fifty miles an hour.

"Makes getting around in the Brecon's a little easier than the way you guys usually do it," the comedian quipped.

"You're welcome to come and try our way," one of the soldiers responded, amusing the rest of them.

"I'd probably not last two days," the man replied, also smiling.

'More like two hours' Alex thought to himself, looking at the man's physique. It had been some time since he'd visited a gym, that was for certain.

Luke Skywalker was on his way back in now, slowing to a hover above them, then gently descending to about a foot or so above the ground. He levelled himself off, got balanced, then dropped the last inches to the earth, all under perfect control.

"It looks easy – and it is – but it needs a lot of practice. I haven't seen anyone manage it on their first attempt," the Gravity man announced, a definite challenge for any Special Forces operative. "But you guys can have your turn tomorrow," he continued. "I know some of your boys tried it with us in the States, and they were pretty good, so hopefully you'll all like it."

"We get to fly it?" one of the troopers asked.

"Tomorrow morning, back in the Lines," Mike Sanders announced. "But for now, let's get all of your questions over to the Gravity Industries people, then they'll do some ground training," he said.

Behind him the turbines wound down, the Jet Suit finished with for the day.

Mike glanced across to Alex and Grigorii. "Come on then you two, fun over. I'll drive you back to camp. We can run through things. You'll be heading for Ireland tomorrow morning Grigorii, so we've got quite a lot to get through."

Half an hour later they were sat in Mike's office, Grigorii and Mike with sparkling waters, Alex with his usual cup of coffee. Mike had been right; the fun really was over, and now the colonel was all business.

"The politicians are very keen to get things moving, actually requested that you fly directly into Belfast this morning, but I managed to buy us a little time." He had a map of the Province spread out on the table that they were sat at, a decent Ordnance Survey one, quite detailed. "I hope that you enjoyed the little display we put on this morning. I see it as having great potential for our people, but also for the Special Boat Service. Imagine having a hostage situation on an oil tanker, then suddenly you have ten SF boys landing on the bridge."

"I know our people are playing with something similar," Grigorii replied. "But I think they have some problems balancing the jet outputs. You can imagine the consequences of one side being too powerful."

"Quite," Mike said, forefinger to his lower lip. "Sort of like walking with one leg longer than the other."

"We are also concerned about reliability issues right now. With a plane you can glide back down, with a chopper there's always autorotation, but with a jet pack..." The Russian let the thought hang.

"Good point. I'll raise that one tomorrow with their boffins. Not sure how they plan to get around that one." He opened a leather pad, put a pen on the page. "Right, let's get back to the here and now."

"Do we need to take notes boss?" Alex interrupted.

"I doubt it, but I might need to if you have any questions at the end. Anything I need to take up with other parties." He took a mouthful of water, then continued. "Some of this is new, most of it old hat, so I guess that Alex has briefed you on it. Just to be sure, I'll run from the start, but don't be afraid to step in if something's already clear."

Grigorii found this approach sensible but unusual. Normally he would need to sit through a full presentation from such a senior officer before questioning anything, and even then he'd need to think very carefully before he did. The wrong question could be terribly costly in Russia.

"So, where to start?" the colonel asked rhetorically. He took a deep breath, released it and began. "Your flight tomorrow is at eleven o'clock in the morning from Bristol and it's straight into Belfast International. We've organised a hire car for you there – you're okay driving on the left I assume? – and we've also booked you into the Europa Hotel in the city for the first two nights. After that, it's up to you where you stay, but this is nice and central, and nothing in Northern Ireland is more than a couple of hours drive away, so easy to get around."

Grigorii nodded, signifying both his understanding and his ability to drive in the UK. It wouldn't be his first experience of driving on the wrong side of the road.

"Please stay in the Europa for at least the first two days. I've arranged that the Police Service of Northern Ireland arrest you from there, probably the day after tomorrow."

"Arrest me?" the Russian asked, slightly shocked.

"Nothing to worry about," the SAS colonel replied, grinning. "I just want to raise your profile a bit, get you mentioned in the local papers. Of course you will be annoyed, object to your treatment and all of the rest. All part of the 'fake news' that Alex has put out there."

Grigorii nodded, now understanding the plan.

"It might then be wise to remain in the hotel for a week even, give the bad guys a chance to check out the Russian guy who was hauled in by the police. The papers will also be fed a rumour that you're an arms dealer." Mike winked at Alex now, still amused at his soldier's plan. "You can thank your friend here for these ideas. I think he's been watching too many movies myself, but no-one else came up with a better idea."

"It's a way to bring you to everyone's attention quickly," Alex told Grigorii. "We have no idea how long before they plan their next murder, so I'm hoping that they'll move on you before they do. Then we have something to chase."

"Political pressure?" Grigorii asked.

Alex nodded. "I'd prefer to give you a few days to find the lay of the land, get your bearings. You know how it is though."

To the Russian, it all seemed to be a reasonable plan, but he was pleased he was forewarned of it. Getting pulled in by the Irish police on his second day in the country would have been a little uncomfortable, even for an ex-Spetsnaz man. "I understand," he said.

"From there," Mike continued, "things are a little bit loose. Everything depends on the fish biting." He handed Grigorii a mobile phone and charger. "Anything you have now I suggest you leave with us and we'll hold it here. This is a secure phone, and the only number in the memory right now is for Alex. He is your direct back-up. He will organise whatever you need, including our support if it comes to it."

Alex nodded agreement. "Call anytime Grigorii. I have no family and my girlfriend doesn't live in this country. I'm ready and available whenever needed. I can also be in Belfast at a moment's notice, courtesy of the SAS flight that we used today. Just call. No unnecessary risks."

The Russian wondered for a moment if the Englishman was referring to their previous operation together in Africa. His 'unnecessary risks' had cost five men their lives.

"There's no hidden meaning in that," Mike said, reading his mind. "It is something that we tell all of our people before they go out on operations. Perhaps Alex will show you something afterwards if there's time. A reminder we have here in the barracks of what can happen when things go awry."

Grigorii gave a curt nod, believing the British officer's words. "Do I have a weapon? Even a knife or something?"

"Not for the flight in," Alex replied. "But I have organised a nine millimetre pistol to be in your room safe ready for your arrival. If you need more, just ask. I have direct access to the Chief Constable of the PSNI, the only person in their police force fully briefed on what we're doing. I can also give you his number."

"I'm impressed. It seems that you've thought of everything," Grigorii commented. "But I'm not sure that I should have the number of the Irish police chief in my cell phone."

"Good point," the SAS man responded. "Not really the best idea I've had today. We all know that nothing is ever perfect, and even the best laid plans can go to shit when things start to fuck-up." He looked at the colonel, received a brief nod by way of reply. "That's about it for now. I can give you the guided tour if you fancy, then we can decide whether to stay in Hereford for the night, or if we get you closer to Bristol for tomorrow's flight."

The three soldiers stood, Mike Sanders extending his hand. "Good luck."

It was now three o'clock in the afternoon, Grigorii beginning to flag a little after an early start in Moscow and the international time difference, but the tour of Stirling Lines was almost over. Alex was leading the way to his final point-of-interest for the day.

"This is the Clock Tower," he explained to Grigorii. "Soldiers who don't make it back from operations have their name put on it, even if they aren't buried here in the city. It's a symbol of remembrance for them, but also for us guys that do get back. It sort of 'keeps us real'" he explained. He paused letting the Russian read the poem on the tower, The Golden Road to Samarkand by James Elroy Flecker.

We are the Pilgrims, master; we shall go

Always a little further: it may be

Beyond that last blue mountain barred with snow

Across that angry or that glimmering sea...

"Samarkand is in Uzbekistan," the Russian said after a few seconds. "Ex-Soviet Union."

Alex nodded. "I read up a little on it when I passed the selection, wanted to know more about what I was letting myself in for," he explained. "For us that do come back, it is a memory to our comrades. It's also a reminder to us. If you don't die, you don't get your name on there." He pointed at the smallish clock tower. "We say that means that you've 'Beat the Clock.'"

Grigorii bobbed his head, understanding. "Looks like we've both managed to beat it," he replied. "So far at least."

27th April 2027

Belfast International Airport, Northern Ireland

The key to the hire car was waiting at the collection counter, just as promised, and the flight had been on time, a little early even. It was raining, a fine drizzle, but the sun was shining through, an odd combination in many places but not in Northern Ireland, even at the end of April. How else would you keep the fields so green?

Grigorii threw his bags into the boot of the hatchback, a Mercedes A series, not too big, but a car that didn't look out of place for a man on business, even if his only supposed dealings were in weapons on the black market. Starting the engine, he played around with the satnav, trying to work out how to program the Europa Hotel into it, something that turned out to be remarkably easy at the end of the day. He adjusted his seat, tweaked the mirrors, and pointed the motor towards the city, thanking God that the car was fully automatic. It made life so much easier.

Twenty-five minutes later and he was negotiating the city traffic, following the instructions from the navigation system. Traffic was busy, but it was the lunchtime rush, so it was to be expected.

Pulling up outside of the hotel, he left the car for the valet service to look after, grabbed his bags and checked in.

In his office in Craigavon, Declan was again surfing the Dark Web. Finding an arms dealer in Northern Ireland wasn't proving quite as simple as he'd explained to Frank and Paddy, and not nearly as easy as finding his two new recruits. It shouldn't really have come as a revelation to him, but it did. Being a bit of a technology geek he thought that he could do almost anything with a keyboard and a decent computer, but it was proving not to be the case.

He decided to have a break from the search, either to do some actual office work, or maybe just to have a look at the news. The papers won through, and he clicked on the Belfast Telegraph's homepage, flicking down the headlines. They were running a follow-up story about the rumoured arms deals, suggesting that this and the recent murders of politicians meant that the Province was slipping back into the bad old days, a return to the Troubles.

"Make us a single Ireland and all of this will go away," he mumbled to himself.

The article continued, mentioning that locals were always the ones who had to suffer the hardships, outsiders either just stirring things up or benefiting from them. In the past it had been American money supporting the cause it reminded people, while their taxes paid for the presence of the military and the increased policing. Weapons and explosives had been smuggled in, sold to the IRA and others at premium rates. Where would that money come from today the author asked? If it was Russian weapons, who was going to pay for them?

Declan leant back in his chair, eyes drifting to the view outside of the window, but not actually seeing it. His mind was floating over the journalist's questions.

How could he contact these supposed Russian dealers? And if he did find them, how was he going to pay for the guns?

Now that he was really thinking about it, he realised that he didn't even know how much a pistol cost. His own had been sourced by Frank from an old Republican Quartermaster that the man knew. He'd never met with the ex-IRA man himself, it had all been handled by the old man, but he suspected that it might be Paddy's father. The man had connections. He also assumed that there were more weapons available from that same source, but they would also be from the bad old days, old and unreliable. His own gun was from the seventies, so around fifty years old. Trusting your life on a fifty-year-old gun was dodgy. A broken firing pin, a stoppage at a critical moment, a jammed slide; anything like that could end up costing you your life.

He had to figure out a way to get new guns. Even better, guns and explosives. It was time that they moved up-market, organised a spectacular.

He shut down the computer. Enough for the day. It was three-thirty and he would tell the boss that he had a job back in the Armagh office, get himself off home early. Driving always helped him think.

Grigorii had unpacked his things, first checking that the pistol was available in the room safe as promised. He discovered that Mike Sanders and his team didn't make empty promises, finding a nine millimetre Browning wrapped-up in a canvas bag, two boxes of ammunition in there with it. Not his favourite weapon but one that would serve its purpose if needed. He seriously hoped that he wouldn't be needing it.

He checked around the room for a better place to hide it, but the room safe was probably the best. He changed the combination from the one that Alex had passed to him. Better that he was the only person with access.

Nothing was scheduled to happen today, so for now he had a few free hours ahead of him. He'd never been to Belfast before, so he grabbed his jacket and decided to go and explore.

It was always useful to know your surroundings.

The twenty odd minutes it took to drive back home hadn't brought Declan any closer to solving his problem of how to obtain more reliable guns, so the question remained with him as he unlocked the door to his home.

He dropped a teabag into a cup, flicked on the kettle. Picking up the television remote as he moved towards his sofa, he kicked off his shoes.

Frank and Paddy were absolutely useless to bounce ideas off, basically replicating anything that he put forward, just reformed into their own words and in their minds now their own thoughts. He often wished that he hadn't involved them in the early days, bided his time until more suitable partners had materialised but what was done, was done. It wasn't the sort of job where you could just chop-and-change at will. A loose end or a disillusioned ex-colleague could drop you right in it.

The kettle clicked off, the water boiled. He poured a cupful, the teabag rolling to the surface, it's motion reflecting his thoughts. He couldn't decide which way to turn, where to look for inspiration.

He sat down on the sofa, mug in hand, knowing what he wanted, but unable to see a route to get him there.

28th April 2027

The Europa Hotel, Belfast, Ireland

The police literally came through the door at three in the morning, smashing the lock off in the process.

Grigorii woke with a start, unsure where he was, his third different room in three nights. His initial reaction was to strike-out, try and injure the people storming his room, but then he cottoned on to what was happening; this was the staged arrest, just made to look extremely real. He guessed that the British government would be funding the room repairs.

"Get up!" he was ordered, the room light switched on and blindingly bright, revealing four men with pistols drawn, stab vests emblazoned with POLICE in bold letters front and back. "Out of bed! Now! Hurry!"

He rubbed his eyes, slowly rolled his legs out of the bed. Obviously not fast enough for the officers, one of them grabbing his shoulder, pulling him clear of the duvet. "Take it easy," he growled, annoyed that the men were getting so carried away with their job. He then remembered that his real identity was probably not known to these people. To them he was a gun runner.

He stood up, feeling a bit exposed in just his boxer shorts. "Can I get dressed?"

Three of the police officers kept their weapons pointing at his torso, the fourth extracting his handcuffs. "Quickly!" the man said. "Then you'll be coming down the station with us. You're under arrest for smuggling weapons." He reeled off Grigorii's rights, all the standard stuff.

The Russian pulled on his jeans, a T-shirt, jacket and shoes, held his hands out in front of him to accept the cuffs. He was awake now, knew better than to fight, understood that it would all be over soon enough. If he hadn't been warned of the ruse then he might well have reacted differently. It was very authentic, the officers more than a little enthusiastic. They really thought that they were on to a winner here.

Cuffed, he was led towards the lifts, a hotel staff member left to determine how to secure the room, the wood splintered all around the lock. He wondered if the safe would be opened and what the reaction would be to the pistol in there.

"Can I take my phone?" he asked, realizing that this was his only link with safety.

"I'll get it," the last man replied. "Get him downstairs and into the car. I'll be with you all in a second."

They bundled him into the first lift, pressed for the ground floor.

'Welcome to Belfast' he thought to himself.

He'd been processed, finger printed, and dumped into a cell in a police station on Lisburn Road, not too far from the hotel. The cell had a toilet and washbasin, a small metal bed with a mattress about three inches thick. He could hear the muffled sound of voices from another part of the building, but it seemed that no-one had any interest in dealing with him right now. Not sure what to do, he did the thing that most servicemen would try to do in his place; he lay down on the bed and attempted to sleep.

They hadn't removed his watch but had taken the laces from his shoes and checked that he wasn't wearing a belt, standard stuff to avoid a suicide. It was now just gone four in the morning. He suspected that he'd be held at least until daybreak, so the potential for two to three hours more sleep were on the cards.

Pulling his jacket over his upper body and head to cut out the light, he dozed off.

They woke him at seven, two policemen, one with a plate of unhealthy looking baked beans and scrambled egg, all sort of mixed together.

"Get this inside you," the man ordered.

"When can I get out of here?" he asked. "And why am I in here in the first place?"

The second man had stayed by the door, blocking the exit. "You'll find out soon enough," he said. "Looks like somebody important will be here to see you, so they must have something solid against you. Doesn't look too good."

"Somebody important?" Grigorii asked.

"Aye," the man replied. "We've been told to expect a visit from our senior management, so you've definitely upset somebody." He stood aside to let his colleague out of the cell, slammed the steel door shut. "Anyway, eat your breakfast. We'll be back for the plate in twenty minutes," he called out.

The Russian sat on the edge of the bed and ate the lukewarm food. He noticed that the cutlery was all plastic. He wasn't going to slit his wrists with this stuff, that was for certain.

It was quarter to eight when the cell door was next swung open. With the two men from the previous visit was a moustached man in police uniform, the braid on the shoulders indicating that he was from the higher echelons. He took off his hat and turned to the others. "I'll handle it from here," he said, dismissing the two of them. "Just lock the door and give me ten minutes."

Grigorii had done his homework after being briefed in Hereford and knew from his Google search that the man in the cell with him was the Chief Constable of the PSNI. He also knew that this man was briefed in to Alex's plan.

"I thought I should come down and see the man who's agreed to be the bait," the policeman said with a smile. "Sorry about the early morning wake-up, but we really need this to look authentic. As far as the men out there know you really are suspected of being a weapons dealer." The two shook hands, then took a seat at either end of the bed.

"I guessed as much," Grigorii replied, "though smashing down the hotel room door was perhaps a little extreme."

"Probably a little expensive too," Colin added.

"So what's the plan from here?"

The Chief smoothed his moustache with the thumb and forefinger of his righthand. "We'll hold you here until about midday, then release you due to lack of evidence. Between then and now, I'll get something to the press about holding a man suspected of arms dealing. A Russian man. That will get them a bit excited, so that when we eventually let you go they'll want to talk to you." He crossed his arms over his chest. "Of course, you'll complain about being rudely awakened, pushed around a bit and then fed some dreadful food. Tell them you're only here as a tourist, that you'll complain to your embassy in London, anything to get you some column inches. We want people to notice you."

Grigorii nodded, all of this roughly as Alex and Mike Sanders had outlined.

"I'm hoping to get the television people involved, then whoever is behind the murders of the politicians is more likely to see you."

"Makes sense," the Russian agreed. "And you'll release something else after my protests I guess?" he added. "Something to throw some more suspicion back on to me?"

Shankly nodded, getting to his feet. "That's about it," he said. "Do you have everything that you need? Is the revolver okay, or would you prefer a Russian model? I can get hold of almost anything with Mike Sanders assisting."

"For now, it's great, and if these people don't move on me I won't be needing it anyway."

"Would you like my personal number?" the Chief asked. "You could call me anytime."

Grigorii was already shaking his head. "I don't think that would be too wise," he said. "If I do get to meet these people, having the contact number for the head of the police over here might not be the best idea." He also stood-up, the meeting almost over. "I have Alex's number, and I think it best I pass everything through him. He can get you if I need some help."

Colin extended his hand, hearing the key in the lock behind him. "Good luck," he said softly.

"Let's hope I don't need it."

Shankly was as good as his word and at twelve o'clock two police officers once again opened his cell door, now not making any effort to box him in.

"You're free to go," one of them told him. "Looks like you've got away with it this time, but I don't think that the Chief is very happy about it."

They led him through the building, returned his personal effects, had him sign some forms. "Do you need a lift back in to town?" one of the men asked, clearly hoping that he didn't. "Or would you like me to call you a cab?" he added more positively.

"I'll walk," Grigorii answered. After eight hours couped up in the small room he was happy to stretch his legs. It would also allow him to give Alex a call, update him on things.

"Suit yourself," the man replied.

Five minutes later he was outside and free, trying to get his bearings and decode the directions that a desk sergeant had given him. It was a dull grey day that awaited him, but at least it wasn't raining. He began walking towards the built-up area ahead of him, taking out his phone as he walked and opening the screen to find Alex's number. It was a simple thing to do; it was the only number that he had on the phone.

The SAS man answered on the third ring.

"Enjoy your night in the nick?" he asked, clearly amused by the whole thing. "I heard that Colin came to visit you too."

"Yes, he did," the Russian replied. "He also said that I'd be getting contacted by the press, but so far nothing. I'm just walking back into the city," he added.

"They'll be at your hotel mid-afternoon. Colin has already informed them about your arrest, and now he'll tell them something along the lines that they've released you, but that the PSNI is not comfortable with you being out. Basically just getting them interested, then they should do the rest. You know how the media are."

Grigorii continued walking, thinking how well orchestrated the whole operation was to date. He wondered if it would go so smoothly if they tried to replicate something like this back home in Moscow. Probably not, he decided. The press were a little more controlled back there, most likely not interested in his side of the story, afraid that the state would block it anyway.

"Yes, I guess I know how your media are," he said. "Did the Chief manage to get the television people involved, or is it just the papers?"

"Both," Alex replied. "But I'm not sure just who will come to the hotel today."

"Hopefully, the TV," the Russian answered. "That's the quickest way to get this show on the road, as you people would say." He was getting further into the city now, could see a few landmarks that he recognised. "I'll get off soon. Almost back at the hotel."

"Give me a buzz later," Alex said. "Just to let me know how the press goes."

"Will do."

Alex wished that he was there in Belfast, directly supporting Grigorii, not sat in London waiting for the politicians to decide that they needed another get together, an update about nothing. He was a hands-on type of man, not a desk jockey. Sitting and waiting was not something that he enjoyed, though he'd needed to do a lot of waiting over the years. It was a large part of every soldiers life.

At least the plan was up and running, and if they could get Grigorii on to the television that evening, he knew that things could move fast. If the killers took the bait, then they could possibly wrap the whole thing up within a few days.

He stood up from the hotel room's writing desk, his laptop still switched on. He'd researched everything that he could think of, checked flight availability to Ireland from Heathrow and Luton. He so wanted to be there.

He switched off the computer, pulled on a pair of Nike trainers. It was time to go for a run and clear his head. It would stop him dwelling on what could go wrong, what else he could do from there to help Grigorii, how to make things safer than they already were. He hated putting others in harm's way. If he'd been there, he would handle it better, able to influence outcomes. Standing in a hotel room over three hundred miles away was not the place to be.

He sighed, tied his laces and let himself out of the room. A run would help.

The call came to his new room just after three, the receptionist telling him that a film crew were in the Europa's reception. Did he want to see them?

The hotel couldn't have been any more apologetic about the early morning wake-up call he'd received, giving him a new upgraded room, offering him a free evening meal in an attempt to compensate. He'd accepted, not made a fuss, as if having the police waking you up in the middle of the night was just a normal thing.

"I'll be down in a few moments," he told the girl.

Unconsciously he checked his appearance in the full length mirror by the door of the room. He had showered since leaving the police station, pulled on a pale blue shirt and a pair of Levi's. He now pulled on a black leather jacket – he guessed that this was similar to how a gun runner would tend to look in the movies, so why let the press people down?

He contemplated taking the pistol from the room safe – it had been hard to get it moved from the previous room, the hotel trying so hard to assist in the move, someone always trying to carry shoes and clothes from one room to the other. In the end he'd asked them to leave, said he didn't like other people handling his clothing.

"No need for the gun," he decided. So far no-one knew who he was, so no-one should be targeting him.

He left the room, taking the lift to the reception, spotting the camera crew immediately, a young woman with them, pointing to a spot in the corner that she thought would be good for the interview. He crossed to them, introduced himself.

"Thanks for agreeing to see us," the girl said, flicking her long black hair over one shoulder. "I'm Joyce O'Brady from the BBC's Ireland office. We heard about your run-in with the police this morning, in fact the Chief Constable has been quite vocal about things. He doesn't seem to think that they should have released you." She stopped for a second, picking up a small rucksack, the camera team already moving to the area that she'd indicated. "We'd appreciate it if you could give us your side of the story."

He nodded, following her across the reception area. People were now gathering around the place, trying to see why the BBC were there in the hotel. "I'd be happy to do so," he said, a Russian accent creeping in. "It wasn't quite the hospitality that I expected in Ireland, not what people had told me about."

"It's not normal," Joyce told him. "We're usually a very friendly bunch over here."

The camera was now set-up on a tripod, one of the crew checking lighting levels, another taking out a boom microphone. Joyce took out a small mirror from her bag, checked her appearance in it.

"Right, if you don't mind standing over there, I'll be just here, and the microphone can be between us. Should keep it out of the shot." She indicated where she meant, one of the team setting it up. "I like things to look natural, not staged if it's alright with you. Have you done this type of thing before?"

"Never," Grigorii replied. "But I think I should be fine with it. What do you want me to say?"

"Just tell it like it was," Joyce told him. "I'll do a quick intro, then I will ask you to tell me about the arrest this morning. I can then ask about your time at the police station, just how you were treated and that sort of thing."

"That sounds fine. It's not going out live is it?"

"No, no. We can repeat sections if you're not happy with them, then I'll put it all together when I get back to the studio. Should go out on the six o'clock local news if you want to watch it."

Grigorii smiled. "I should tell my mother to look out for it," he said. "But I don't think it will make it as far as Moscow."

"You never know," the lady told him with a grin. "With all of this hoo-ha between your President and our Prime Minister lately, it could develop into quite a story. Russian-Anglo relations aren't at their best right now. You might become quite famous by the time you get back home."

He allowed himself a short laugh, feigning shyness. "Let's hope not," he said. "In Russia we prefer to keep ourselves to ourselves, not to be too much in the public eye. Being anonymous is often for the best."

"But you're still sure that you want to do it?" Joyce said, wondering if he was having second thoughts.

"I'm fine with it," he replied. "I think it is only right that I have my say. I must let people know that I'm not a criminal, unlike what the police are saying."

"Good," the lady said. "Let's put that right then."

The cameraman gave her a thumbs-up, everything ready to go.

"Let's do it."

"Have a look on the Northern Irish news this evening Alex," Grigorii told his friend across the water. "It was a BBC news crew that came to the hotel, some reporter called Joyce O'Brady. She recorded a few things, but it will be cut down to about three to five minutes for broadcasting, at least that's what she expected."

Alex smiled inwardly. The Beeb was about the best he could have hoped for, and there was a good chance that it would be aired more than once, probably six o'clock, perhaps ten in the evening and again in the morning. "Perfect Grigorii," he acknowledged. "If this doesn't get you noticed, then nothing will."

"The report will also have a police statement, something to do with them being unhappy with having to release me, so we will get two bites of the cherry as they say. If our targets miss one take, they should get the next."

"You're right, and I'm sure that Colin Shankly can stir things up a bit if the coverage isn't enough, say something controversial, perhaps even rile-up the bad guys a bit."

Grigorii was sat in his hotel room, an instant coffee next to him, beside that the Browning pistol. "I guess this means that I need to be prepared for the worst," he said. "Contact could come in any form, and just how quick, well… who knows."

Alex considered this, aware that it was certainly true. He also knew from history that the Europa had been the most bombed hotel in the world back during the Troubles, having recorded over thirty bomb attacks. He decided that this wasn't the time to be telling the Russian that. "I'm having a telephone meeting with Mike Sanders tomorrow, partially to evaluate how the first part of the plan has gone, but it will also give me a chance to ask some questions. I'm not too happy with you being over there alone, and I want to come over and supply closer back-up support."

Grigorii hesitated before responding. "Would the terrorists not be on to you immediately?" he asked. "Any hint that you're a member of the SF and they'll quickly disappear to wherever they came from. The trap would be ruined."

"I know that, but I'm going mad over here mixing with bloody politicians and second-guessing on how you're managing things. I know I can't stay in the hotel, but I could operate from a safe house, or even a bed in the police HQ." Grigorii could hear the frustration in the SAS man's voice, understood how he was feeling. "If I was there in the Province, then I could be on hand if needed, perhaps bring one or two of my team to form a QRF – Quick Reaction Force," he added, not sure if the Russian Forces used the same terminology. "To get me there from here is going to take too long to be of any use."

"I understand Alex, but I think you need to let the bad guys show their hand first," Grigorii replied. "It could be tonight, tomorrow, or they may not even take the bait at all. I think that I'd hold off for now."

Alex nodded to himself, also very aware that screwing things up now by being impatient would end the whole operation. It wasn't just his own head on the line, it was Grigorii in the line of fire in Belfast, and his boss here in Hereford. A cock-up by him would be a 'SAS mistake' and that meant Mike Sanders. He couldn't do that to the colonel.

"You're right," he finally admitted. "But I'll still run the idea by him, perhaps not an immediate move, but to have a team on standby for if things hot-up." The idea already sounded more saleable. "For now I'll just have to keep massaging politicians egos, playing to their whims."

"You're learning fast," the Russian said jokingly. "We should have a bet on which one will claim the plan to have been their own if things go right. And which one blames you personally if it all goes to pieces."

Alex gave a short harsh laugh, almost a bark. "I think I can put a name to both of those people right now, and they both share the same name."

"I won't ask."

"I wouldn't tell you anyway," the soldier said. "But I will tell you if I'm right when this is all over. Whichever way it goes."

28th April 2027

Armagh, Northern Ireland

Declan was busy sticking a Tesco's Finest pasta dish into his microwave, a typical meal for a man living alone. It was either that or something from one of the local takeaways. A can of beer sat open on the worktop, a sure sign that he wouldn't be doing anything else that day that vaguely resembled work. Within five minutes the food would ping, then that and the beer would join him in front of the television for a lazy evening of nothingness.

His phone rang, the opening bars of Smoke on the Water, Deep Purple's best known song, the guitars bashing out the chords.

"Shit," he muttered after looking at the caller ID. Bloody Paddy. The last person he felt like speaking to at this moment, even more so when the microwave also pinged, meal ready. He considered just ignoring it, calling back later once he'd been fed. It was just delaying the inevitable, and anyway, maybe it was something from the boy's father, someone he really didn't wish to piss-off. He picked up.

"Have you got the telly on?" Paddy asked, his voice excited. "Switch it to the BBC news. Hurry!"

The television was on, but the wrong channel. He grabbed the controller, pressed the 'one' button, waited a second whilst the channel changed.

On the screen was a woman reporter he'd seen before, name he couldn't remember. She was saying something about a claim from the PSNI that they now had proof of Russian involvement in the recent arms finds, that the weapons had all the signs of being ex-Soviet military.

"....and in the early hours of this morning the police arrested a man here in this hotel, actually smashing down his room door before taking him down to the police station in Lisburn Road." She indicated a slim bald headed man in a black leather jacket standing close-by. "He's agreed to give his own side of the story to us, though he'd prefer us not to disclose his name right now."

The camera panned on to Grigorii, hands in pockets, nodding to the woman. "Go ahead," she told him.

"Yes," the man started, looking a little unsure of himself. "It was about three o'clock this morning when these people smashed down the door, ran into my room. I was dragged out of bed and made to dress, then they took me to some police station, locked me in a small room, left me there." His English was heavily accented, totally unlike when he spoke with Alex. "They accused me of selling guns, but this just isn't true. It was quite frightening though, nothing like I had been told about the friendly Irish people back in Moscow."

Declan was glued to the screen now, food forgotten, Paddy jabbering in his ear. "Yes, Paddy, hold up," he said. "I've got it. Let me watch it now and I'll call you back." A ribbon on the bottom of the screen informed him that the interview was being conducted in the Europa Hotel, Belfast.

"Were you abused, roughed-up or anything?" the woman was asking.

The Russian pulled aside the collar of his jacket and shirt, showed a livid red mark on his neck. He'd applied it himself with the iron in the room, but who was to know that. It looked the part. "One of them held me against a wall, told me to admit everything. I tried to explain that I had nothing to tell them, so they pushed me around a bit, threatened me. They weren't too happy when they had to let me go, didn't even offer me a ride back to the hotel." He looked at the reporter. "They are not like you and your team. Not nice people at all."

Declan was certain that the police wouldn't have pulled the man in without good reason and breaking down the door of a room in the Europa nowadays was just unheard of. This man had done something bad.

The hotel interview was closed out by the female lead, apologising for the treatment that the Russian had received, hoping that the rest of his stay in Ireland would be memorable for all of the right reasons. The man thanked her, the scene switching back to the studio where the reporter rounded things off.

Declan switched off the TV. This was like a gift from the Gods. Though he thought he could find most things online, tracking down a Russian gun runner wasn't proving too simple. Even the Dark Web seemed to have its limits.

His phone rang, Paddy again.

"What do ye think?" the man enquired. "Is this the guy we need to talk to?" He sounded excited, as though he'd just found a leprechaun's pot of gold.

"It depends on who's story you believe Paddy," Declan responded, the two sides of the tale still fresh in his mind.

"But he looks like a gangster, and he is Russian. What do you think?"

Declan considered both of these minor points, trying to make sense of the whole thing. For once he actually had more faith in the official line, the story from the police service. The man had looked the part, but of more importance was the way that the police had acted. Smashing your way into a room in a major hotel at three in the morning wasn't something that was done on a whim. Added to that was the present international tensions between the British Prime Minister and the Russian President. The PSNI would have needed to be fairly certain before ruffling any feathers. Permission for such an operation must have come all the way from the top.

"I think we need to talk to this guy," he finally admitted.

Declan rang in sick the following morning, a plan of action now clear in his head. He knew where the Russian was, but didn't know his name. He couldn't just call him up, but he was pretty sure that anyone on reception duty would now know who he was. Not every guest had their door knocked down in the middle of the night, then got accused of being a weapons dealer. And then the TV interview.

He drove towards Belfast, avoiding the rush hour. The plan was simple; a printed note explaining that the telephone number attached would be open between six and eight o'clock the following evening if the Russian wanted to do business. A stop on the way at a random superstore, a new burner phone, a new number and SIM. Peel off the sticky label that always seemed to come with the new SIM, stick it on to the note. Put the note into a blank envelope. Hand in to the hotel reception.

He entered the hotel, a baseball hat on his head, a pair of sunglasses on his face. The lobby was relatively busy, Declan looking like just another tourist drifting through.

Approaching the reception desk, he picked out the youngest looking girl, smiling at her as he reached the counter.

"I'm dropping this off for the Russian guy who was on telly yesterday evening," he explained, taking the envelope out of his inside pocket. "Joyce O'Brady promised him that we'd leave it for him. It's a link he can pass over to friends back home in Russia so that they can also see his five minutes of fame." He grinned at his joke. "Can I leave it with you to pass on?" he asked.

"No bother sir," the girl answered. "I'm sure he'll appreciate it, especially after the hassle with the police." She smiled. "Do you need to meet with him, or should I just have it delivered to his room?"

"I'm sure that if it was Joyce, he'd be happy to meet up, but as it's just me…" He shrugged. "I'm just the messenger, but thanks."

He waved, turning from the desk. The whole exchange had taken less than two minutes.

Driving back towards Armagh he wondered if he'd done the right thing. He'd certainly have been captured on the CCTV in the lobby, but the cap and sunglasses would mask his features, his clothes unassuming, something any tourist or local might wear. The girl might remember something, but quite probably not. He was just another punter asking her for help, one of a hundred or more during her shift.

The question now was would the man get the letter, and if so, would he call? If not, no loss, just no further forward. If he did, then it was clear that he wasn't the innocent that he'd tried to portray during the interview.

30th April 2027
Stirling Lines, Hereford, UK

The boss had taken the decision to have a face-to-face meeting with Alex instead of the phone call. It was something that he preferred when situations were developing, something that he'd had drilled into him as a young officer at Sandhurst. "Never assume" had been one of the favourite phrases of one of the old instructors. "If you can look them in the eyes and ask them the tough questions, do so."

He also felt it would be useful to drag Alex away from the politicians for a few days, give him a chance to mix with his peers, to wind down a bit.

There was also a third reason, but he'd hold that in reserve for now.

"So someone has contacted Grigorii?" Mike was saying, already knowing the answer but giving Alex an opportunity to add his own take on things.

"That's right boss, but we can only assume who that someone is right now." Alex was pleased to be back on camp, away from the boredom of a hotel room, the nervy meetings with politicians, in his own space. Here he was surrounded by the familiar. "We have scanned the hotel's CCTV, tied the drop-off down to one man, the receptionist confirming the ID. We've also studied the footage that we have from the Belfast Telegraph building again and the man appears to be the same one, that based on estimated height and build. It looks like they've taken the bait."

"Could the receptionist describe the man? Add anything new?"

"He kept his sunglasses and hat on, even inside the building. She thinks that he might be bald, or at least have very short hair. Doesn't help us too much, but that was about all she could add. She was coming to the end of her shift at the time, probably seen dozens of people by then, just wanting to go home."

"No prints, no handwriting?"

"He's been careful, everything printed from a computer except the phone number, and that's come straight from the SIM card producer's packaging. We are busy working out where it was sold, so that might give us a lead, but if he's careful enough to hide his identity like this, then I guess he's not going to buy the goods close to home." Alex paused, a sudden thought occurring. "But if we can find where it was bought and when, then we can see if there is any more security video available there…"

"…and perhaps the man isn't quite so careful in it," Mike added without being asked. "Who's following up on the SIM details? Is it one of Colin's people?" The colonel had the phone out of the charging cradle, ready to place a call, to chivvy-up whoever needed pushing.

"It is. I felt it would be best handled across there. The window for contact is quite tight, so I already pushed them to rush things through."

"A quick call with the organ grinder might just move his monkeys along a little faster," Mike said with a grin. "Use all of your assets Alex, and right now I'm one of them."

Alex sat silently while his boss spoke to the Chief Constable, explaining the need to hurry things through. The call was short and to the point, neither side needing many words, both their goals identical.

"Have you agreed a time with Grigorii to place the call?" Mike asked once his own call was over.

"Quarter to eight," the soldier answered. "I thought we should keep them waiting, try to get under their skin a bit. I also don't want any meetings agreed until the morning at least." He hesitated, the next words the most important to him. "We need to get some back-up over there before any meeting is agreed. I'd like to take a few men over there, be on hand in a QRF role."

Mike Sanders grinned. "I thought you'd never ask," he said. "You've never been much good at sitting on the side-lines, have you?"

Alex let out a sigh of relief. He'd truly thought that the boss would try and keep him in London, coordinating and controlling, away from the thick of the action. He was once more shocked at how well the colonel could read him. There'd been absolutely no need for him to dress-up the request as he had, he could have just laid it out in clear.

"Thanks boss," he said, a sly grin on his face now. "I'd like to take three other men from the counter-terrorism team, head across there today. We need to be on hand for when that call is made, just in case the bad guys insist on something tonight."

The colonel nodded his approval. "Anyone in particular, or shall I just ask for three volunteers?"

"They're all good boss," Alex responded. "Let them put themselves forward. It's short notice, almost the weekend and some may even have other commitments. Volunteers are fine."

"Commitments can be dropped, as you well know, but I agree with you. You can also swap people around later if this goes on for a while. Just let me know." Mike glanced at his watch. "Ten-thirty, so still plenty of time to get packed and away. I want you to do something else before you go, should only take an hour or so. Meanwhile, I'll get on to Terry Smith and get you your volunteers."

Thirty minutes later and Alex was suited-up and ready to fly, but not to Belfast. Not yet.

The turbines were running-up, the man from Gravity Industries leaning in to check that the gauges were all in the green. Alex could feel the thrust from the jets even before they were at flight speed, trying to remember all of the hints and tips he'd been given on flying the Jet Suit. The last short flight had been just a practice in the hover, each solider tethered to the ground during their attempt, safe in the knowledge that they couldn't go anywhere.

This time it was for real, and he was the second one up. The first soldier had done a lap of the parade square in record time, then taken almost as long getting himself back down to earth. It had been a great laugh to watch, but Alex wasn't laughing now – he was wondering how he would do, whether his attempt could be even worse.

Checks over, the instructor stood back, giving Alex the all-clear, permission to go.

The toggles were next to his thumbs, a further trigger at each index finger. The rest was all about moving his arms, pointing the jet thrust away from where he wanted to go, in this case up. Aiming the jets at the ground, he slightly upped the power, feeling the weight on his feet lessen at first, and then disappear. He looked down, the parade ground now about two feet below him. Now three, four, five.

He levelled out, scanned the area around him as he'd been trained to do. There was no point flying into a lamppost or powerline.

A couple more minor adjustments and he was away, gathering forward momentum, gaining more height.

It was an incredible feeling, like flying at really low-level in a small helicopter, but with no floor below you, no Perspex to deflect the wind. Before he knew it he was at the edge of the parade square, needing to stop, gain more height, or get a turn in before he collided with a building. The brief was to turn, to follow the extremity of the square. He altered the position of his left arm, felt his body change its angle. His direction across the ground also changed, and he was about thirty degrees through the turn, the building looming. He chanced a bigger arm movement, turned faster, almost too much, almost going back the way he had come.

Playing the power, experimenting with his arms, he got back on track, gathered speed again.

He completed the turning manoeuvre another five times, finally facing towards the group who still awaited their own flights. It was getting simpler with each corner, and he was feeling more confident with every second in the air. More adjustments as he neared the landing point, carefully lowering the jet outputs, trying to sink slowly to the tarmac. It seemed to be working, he was slowing nicely, he was losing height.

Less than a metre above the ground, two metres from a large 'X' that had been marked on the ground, and he was getting cocky, in the end, too cocky. He fingered a switch, took off far too much power, dropped to the ground like a stone, landing on his feet then falling forwards on to his knees. The instructor was with him in seconds, killing the jets with an emergency button, the sound of the turbines replaced by the sound of his colleagues having a good laugh.

"Your turn next," he yelled at them, a wide grin on his face. He'd survived.

"I thought that it might take your mind of the Irish situation for a short while," Mike Sanders said to him as the SAS team loaded their bags into the minibus taking them to the airport. "You've been in the thick of it for the last few days, so I thought a bit of hands-on action might do you some good. Clear the brain out before your trip."

"Thanks boss, it was just what I needed. Too long in meetings lately, and not the sort of meetings that I'm comfortable in either."

"I know Alex, but you always need to broaden your skillsets, and I thought this would be a good thing for you. I'm hoping that I can persuade you to consider taking a commission one day soon. You'd make a good officer."

"Me?" Alex replied, pointing to his own chest, shocked.

"Our unit needs good leaders Alex, and I count you as one of them. You're great as a sergeant, don't get me wrong, but I believe you'd serve the Regiment much better as an officer." He paused, before continuing. "You proved how good you were in South Africa. You were out on your own there."

Alex hesitated, still surprised by his leader's statement. It wasn't that he wouldn't want to take the step-up, but it wasn't even something that he'd ever considered. He was a non-commissioned officer, a sergeant, and he always thought of other people as captains and lieutenants. "I don't know what to say boss," he finally managed. "Thanks, I suppose."

Mike Sanders shrugged. "It's a part of my role to spot potential and try and drag it out. You have that potential," he said. "Anyway, let's not dwell on it now. Stay focused on the here and now, consider it while you're away, and let's talk again when we've got this Irish thing out of the way."

Alex looked over his shoulder to where the team were now finished loading the bags, two of them already strapped into the minibus. The third man was looking at Alex, waiting to go.

"Thanks boss, and I will," he said. "It's just a bit of a shock, not something I'd given much thought to before now."

The colonel smiled. "Give it some thought, but don't let it cloud your vision. You've got a job to do now and I think another of your supporters will be pleased if you do it as well as you did the last one in Africa."

Alex frowned, wondering who Sanders was referring to. The colonel noticed this, made a decision to say more. "The PM also asked me why you weren't an officer. He can also spot potential when it stares him in the face. See you when you get back."

Mike turned to go, leaving Alex standing there open mouthed.

"You ready for the off?" a voice asked from behind him. "The lads are ready to go, and we need to move if we want to get that flight."

Alex filed the last conversation into the back of his mind for the time being. He needed to get things moving, talk to his team. What happened afterwards was a discussion he'd have in the future.

30th April 2027

Europa Hotel, Belfast, Northern Ireland

It was seven o'clock in the evening, just forty-five minutes from the planned call with the anonymous contact. Alex and his team were due to touchdown in the next few minutes, a back-up close to hand, help within touching distance. Though not a man prone to panic, it was comforting for Grigorii to know he would soon not be alone in a foreign and quite probably hostile land.

The pistol lay on the bedside table, never far from him since the contact had been initiated. They now knew where he was, and he was well aware that kidnappings during the Troubles had been a commonplace occurrence. Better to prepare for the worst and pray for the best.

His phone beeped once, a message from Alex that the plane was down, that the team would be in the city within the next hour. They'd agreed to keep the line open – no calls between them – until after the contact had been attempted. "We may have plenty to talk about after the call," Alex had said. Grigorii knew it to be true but was also aware that the contact he was about to have may come to nothing, just some sicko reacting to the TV broadcast, someone wanting his own five minutes in the spotlight.

"But I don't believe so," he muttered to himself. He knew about the CCTV from the hotel, the match with the video from the newspaper offices. Too many coincidences for it all to be nothing.

He glanced down at the bedside clock for the twentieth time in the last thirty minutes. Seven-oh-five. Forty minutes and counting.

He crossed to the kettle, put together the makings of an instant coffee. Anything to distract him from the ultra-slow passage of time.

A police car waited for them outside of the International Airport, compliments of Colin Shankly. There was no need to go covert just yet, though they all wore civilian clothes. Right now it was all about speed, getting Alex and his team to a safe house that the PSNI kept near the centre of the city, walking distance from the Europa. Once there, they could make plans to drop below the radar, to go fully undercover.

Alex looked around the team.

Paul 'Smithy' Smith was another who had been with him in South Africa, reliable, the team joker, and also the unit's sniper. Someone like that could be invaluable in Ireland, possibly posted on a hillside close to the border, a man who could provide covert cover for Grigorii if a face-to-face meeting eventually happened. Paul was asleep in the middle of the backseat, seemingly unfazed by everything that was going on around him. It caused Alex to smile. He wished that he could relax right now.

The second volunteer had been Jeff Crosley, a scouser with a dry sense of humour and a wild mop of tussled black hair that wouldn't be tolerated in any other military unit. His skin was well tanned from both the sun and wind, causing him to be used in many of the Regiment's forays in the Middle East, often in full Arab dress. He was also a great linguist, but his main military skill was in the handling of explosives.

The last man was an unknown to Alex, a newish recruit that had only joined an active troop in the last month or two. Dave Rose owned the nickname 'Daisy' but only from his friends. At six foot three and about a hundred and thirty kilos of muscle, outsiders would think twice – at least – before addressing him that way. Despite his obvious love of the gym, the man was also an electronics genius, the main communications man in the team. He also had a first class degree in computing, was a specialist in cyber security, and it was said he'd once hacked his way into the White House.

'A fair mix of skills' Alex decided to himself. Hopefully, he wouldn't be needing any of them. Something in his gut told him that the likelihood was that he would though.

The police driver interrupted his thoughts. "We'll be there in about two minutes. I'll drop you around at the service entrance to the block, and someone there will help to get you in nice and quick."

Alex thanked the man, making sure that the rest of the crew had got the message. Daisy was shaking Smithy, bringing him back to the present.

They were ready to go.

Five minutes to kick-off, Grigorii forcing himself to stop pacing the length of the room, moving across to where his cell phone was plugged into the charger, planning to leave it attached to offset any risk of a battery malfunction. He'd been running scenarios through his head, thinking through possible conversations, deciding on excuses if he needed to delay things. He knew that he was wound-up like a spring, the same as he was before any operation, any leap into the darkness.

He checked his watch again, checked again that the number on the paper was the same as the one he'd already programmed into the phone. Check, check, and then check again. Preparation was everything, the best way to mitigate risk.

Three minutes to go.

He briefly wondered where Alex and the team were right then, whether they would be in place and ready to react. He hoped that they were, but he also prayed that he wouldn't be needing them. The soldier in him wanted action. The human being wanted to come through all of this in one piece.

In the PSNI apartment not far away, Alex and his team had dropped off their bags, claimed their beds. The place was massive, with four separate sleeping rooms, a kitchen, lounge and two bathrooms.

Now they were all crowded around the island in the centre of the kitchen, testing out the weapons that Hereford had organised to be waiting for them. Each man had a standard military pistol – the Glock 17, a replacement for the trusty old 9mm Browning – but they also had four Heckler & Koch MP5K machine pistols, a stubby little lightweight weapon, perfect for close quarters battle. There was also one Accuracy International L96A1 sniper's rifle and this had been claimed by Smithy who'd already stripped it down, checking that nothing had been damaged in transit. It was a weapon normally designated to him, so the sighting should be fine, but bangs and knocks could alter this.

Alex checked his watch, noting that the time was already quarter to eight, knowing that Grigorii would even now be playing his part. He mentally crossed his fingers, hoping that everything went to plan.

"Have the weapons ready to go lads," he ordered the others. "I don't think that anything will happen tonight, but we all know that plans are made just to be torn apart. Be ready."

They all finished lightly oiling their selected weapons, reassembling them swiftly. Smithy was the last to be ready, finally finishing the work on the rifle.

"Are we okay to get some kip?" Daisy asked. "Just in case we get rolled out in the middle of the night."

"No bother," Alex said. "Let's go two up, two down. I'll stay up for now, at least until I hear from Grigorii. You guys can decide who sits up with me, and the other two can get some head-down."

"I'll stay up with you," Smithy said moving through to the living area with his assortment of guns. "Give me a chance to have a play with the telescopic sights. Shame I can't get a few sighting shots in, but maybe in the next few days a chance will come." He gave them all a grin.

"Perfect," Alex replied, pleased to be paired with someone he knew well. "So you two can get some shut-eye now."

The two men headed to their respective rooms. Alex stayed in the kitchen, nervously waiting for the call from the Russian.

Grigorii checked his watch again, took a deep breath, and pressed the green button on his phone, the pre-programmed number beeping out it's tones for each digit, sounding like a techno tune on drugs. Somewhere in Ireland, a phone rang once, twice, then stopped, no sound coming out of the earpiece. Grigorii hesitated, wondering if he was being diverted, or possibly recorded. "Hello?" he enquired. "Is anyone there?"

The voice that answered sounded as if it was speaking through a facemask, maybe just a handkerchief. Not distorted but muffled.

"Are you actually an arms dealer or not?" the man at the other end of the line asked him. "The police say yes, but you say no, so what are you?"

Straight to the point, the Russian thought. A good sign perhaps. Impatient to be getting on with things, and he knew from experience that rushing something often led to errors.

"Who am I speaking to?" he asked, emphasising his accent. "Are you going to identify yourself, then I can do the same."

For a few seconds there was no response, the man considering the question. "I think you need to answer my question first, don't you? If you say you are the seller, I'm the buyer. You want my money, then you have to play my game."

Grigorii thought about the best way to answer this, anxious not to scare the man off. "Let's just say that I have access to certain weapons, and that I can get them into this country if the money is right." He let the message sink in, then continued. "Please note the last part of my statement; if the money is right," he repeated.

"We have money," Declan lied, still wondering where he could get the funding, hoping that Paddy's father still had the right contacts to get them help. "What type of guns do you have access to?"

"What would you like?" It was the Russian's turn to ad lib now, small lies to catch a big fish. "I have mainly Russian equipment, but my people can get their hands on other brands if needed. What are you hoping to do, and perhaps I can give you some free advice?"

The Irishman was again silent, considering his own answer. "The make isn't so important to me, but I need relatively new and highly reliable stuff. Russian is good with me, but so is American, British or German for that matter. I'd leave that to you."

"I prefer Russian," Grigorii responded, building on his character. "And can I ask what you need to do with the weapons?"

The voice in the earphone laughed, obviously amused to be asked such a question. "I'd have thought that much was obvious to you. This is Northern Ireland, and things haven't changed too much over the years. Pistols. That's what we need."

Grigorii deliberated on how to answer. He didn't want to annoy the man, needed to keep him talking. "Can we meet somewhere, discuss things face-to-face?" he asked.

"That's not going to happen," the voice shot back.

"Then how can we do business? We need to meet at some time to agree on your requirements, then I can price things up. Payment can be electronic, but the hardware will need to be delivered to somewhere, to be handed over."

Grigorii had the feeling that the man hadn't thought this part through, possibly was even surprised that the call had come at all. He could feel him considering the options, formulating a reply. "I can meet with you anywhere you like," he tried, wondering if the bait would be taken.

Another pause, more rushed thoughts. "Give me your email address," the voice told him. "This number will disappear after this call, but I will mail you another number tomorrow. There'll be no words, just a number and a time. We will talk then."

Cagey, Grigorii thought. Someone who probably hadn't done this sort of thing before, no pat answers, no practiced plan. He gave a private Russian email account that would leave no connecting URLs for the man to follow.

"I look forward to hearing from you," he finished. "Soon, I hope. My people will probably move me out of Ireland shortly, especially after I was hauled in by the authorities this week." He hoped that this would panic the man a little, keep things moving along at a decent pace.

"You should hear from me sometime tomorrow," the man told him, hanging-up immediately, no goodbyes.

Grigorii sat for a moment on the edge of the bed, thinking about how the conversation had played out, what he could possibly have done better.

It was time to call Alex.

30th April 2027

Armagh, Northern Ireland

Declan was annoyed with himself, knowing that he'd handled the call badly. He simply hadn't been prepared, not got enough background, hadn't done enough research online, all things that he was usually so good at. He still had no clue as to how much a pistol even cost, didn't know bugger all about Russian weapons, not even a manufacturers name.

"Fuck!" he scolded himself.

He looked at the time. Eight o'clock. Too late to bother with getting dressed and going somewhere to get another phone, too late to quiz Frank about where they might get hold of some money. He would need to get a new number in the morning, then email the details to the Russian from his office in Craigavon.

How could he handle the man's request to meet up? That would be exposing himself, giving away his ID.

Shit, this was all such a mess. Should they just stay small, drop the idea of pulling in more parties? They had guns that had worked so far, they had taken out the enemy. Why change things?

But Declan knew why change was needed. Continue as they were and Ireland would always be a divided country, the Brits would always control their future. And that just wasn't acceptable.

He went to his fridge, took out a small can of beer.

A thought suddenly occurred to him, something from nowhere. It was an old adage that his father had used when he was still alive. "Why keep a dog and bark yourself" he'd often said.

Thinking of his dad also made him more determined to move things forward. The old man had died when Declan was just five years of age, knocked down by a British Army Land Rover in the city. The police had claimed it was just an unfortunate accident, but years later locals had told him that it had been deliberate, that his father was involved with the local republicans, part of the IRA cell that operated in Armagh. He'd decided to believe the latter.

"And now I have a dog," he mumbled to himself, picking up his cell phone. "One more call before we get rid of this phone," he said, this time with more grit in his voice, placing the beer on the counter.

Opening his laptop, he swiftly found the number for Robby Tohill, his latest recruit in Belfast. He'd never met the man, but that didn't mean that he couldn't use him. Tohill would be his dog.

Robby Tohill took the call in his local bar, happily downing his fourth pint of the night. The place was a 'right kip' in Irish terminology, not the sort of place you'd take your girl on a night out. 'Spit and sawdust' would have been a generous description, the paint flaking off the walls, the carpets worn through in places all the way to the wooden floorboards underneath. It smelt of stale beer, unwashed bodies and farts.

"Tohill," he answered to a number that he didn't recognise, scratching carefully at a tattoo of a skull on the left side of his face. It was a new one, still slightly scabbed, unlike the multitude of others that covered his body.

"Robby, it's the man from One Ireland," the voice in the cell phone replied. "If you're up for it, I have a job for you."

Robby moved away from the bar, phone to his ear, pint in the other hand. Reaching a corner far away from anyone else, he took a seat, eyes roaming quickly around the room. "Do I get a name?" he asked.

"No, no names," the man replied. "Safer for me, safer for you too."

Robby took a slug of the ale, not happy with the answer but sort of understanding it. "What sort of a job?" he asked.

"You'll have seen on the local news that there's a Russian in town that the police say is dealing in weapons," Declan responded. "I'd like you to meet him, probably tomorrow, see if he's for real."

"You intend buying some hardware?"

"I do," the man in Armagh replied. "We're using some bloody antiques right now, so I want to get my hands on something more reliable, something new. Not just for me, but for the group as a whole. I want you to have a look at what this guy has got, see what he's about."

They spoke for five more minutes as Declan outlined his plan. Tomorrow he would know if the Russian was for real, or if this was just a trap.

And all at no risk to himself.

Two o'clock in the afternoon and Declan sat at his desk, reflecting on his plan. All of the pieces seemed to fit together seamlessly but he still had one decision to make.

On the way to the office that morning, he'd called into the nearby Tesco store, picked-up a new phone and SIM card. Using the email address that the Russian had given him he'd forwarded the new details, giving a call time of one o'clock, his lunch break, a time he knew that he would be free.

He'd followed up with a call to Robby Tohill, agreeing a time and place for the meeting.

The call with the dealer had been better, Declan much more in control of things this time, giving the Russian orders rather than being quizzed by the man. He'd told him where to be and when, and then added a further request to put the man to the test; bring a Russian pistol, something not more than a few years of age, and also a box of suitable ammunition to go with it. The more specific demand and the limited timeframe would show him whether the man could deliver or not.

He'd had a final call with Tohill, telling him to bring some sort of a bag, that he would be given a gun. He would talk to him again if the meeting was a success, tell him to go somewhere and test fire the weapon.

And now he just had to make the final decision on his list. Would he physically witness the meeting or not?

As soon as Grigorii finished the conversation with the anonymous caller, he called Alex, explaining the latest request from the killers.

"I need a pistol, and quick," he said. "Do you think Colin Shankly will have something that I can borrow?"

Alex's brain was racing, searching for an immediate solution. "I'm pretty sure he would have weapons at his disposal, but probably not something Russian," he answered after a few seconds. An idea suddenly flashed in his head, a place to get hold of an unusual weapon at extremely short notice. "I need to give Mike Sanders a call. We have an assortment of foreign weapons in Hereford. It gives us a chance to train on our enemy's kit, just in case we ever need to use it."

"But how will you get it here by six-thirty? That's just over five hours away now."

"I'm sure we can do it. A helicopter from Hereford will just need about an hour, maybe two at the outside I think. Let me make a call and then come back to you."

Alex had cut the connection, Grigorii left anxiously pacing his room. Things were out of his control again.

It had taken fifteen long minutes until Alex rang back, time which the Russian spent cleaning his Browning. Being prepared was what kept you alive but it also took his mind off the waiting.

"We've got a MP443 Grach that should keep your man happy," Alex told him. "We also have a few Makarovs but they're a little older, and that might piss him off if he's asked for new. They'll have a chopper in Hereford in the next half hour, landing in Aldergrove Airport by about four o'clock, so it works out fine."

"Do you have ammo to go with it?"

"All on the way mate. I guess you're more than familiar with the weapon?"

"Not one of my favourites," Grigorii replied. "Not as reliable as the old Makarovs even, but as you say, it will do the job for tonight. How will you get it to me?"

"I'll deliver it myself. Do me a favour and check out what the trade entrance for the hotel is like. I can meet you there. Let's say five o'clock, give the pilots a bit of breathing space."

"See you at five."

The choice of the meeting place had been Declan's, somewhere that he knew would be busy on the weekend, plenty of Joe Public in attendance, harder for the authorities to set-up a sting operation. It was also close to the Europa, so no excuses for the Russian showing-up late.

The bar was named Robinsons and it was just across the road from the hotel, a pub that everyone in the whole of Belfast was familiar with, famous throughout Ireland for as long as he could remember. It was an old style establishment with colourfully tiled floors, long wooden bar, and loads of ales to choose from. Not that there'd be much drinking tonight.

It was five past six when he watched Tohill walk through the front door. They both knew that the Russian was already in there, knowing him from his TV appearance, something that they could use to their advantage. They knew him, but he didn't know them. He'd instructed his new man to let the Russian wait a little while, to stand-off and make sure that he was alone, not communicating with others. Tohill took a chair at the bar, watching his target as the man tried to clock all of the faces in the room, trying to decide who he was meant to be meeting. He'd taken a corner table away from the main crowd, a place where he could show the contents of his holdall without others seeing them, a sensible approach given what he should be carrying.

Declan watched Tohill making his assessment, saw him eventually get up and go and join the dealer. He'd taken the decision to be present only about an hour before, come straight from the office. As neither Tohill nor the Russian knew who he was, he considered it a safe choice. He wanted to see things for himself.

He watched as the Russian scanned the bar before holding his bag open for Tohill, showing him the contents. Words were exchanged, the foreigner clearly not happy to handover the weapon without payment. It was a gamble that Declan had decided to take; he wanted the weapon to be test fired, wanted to try it out before exchanging cash. If it didn't happen, if the man refused to part with his hardware, then at least this meeting had proved that the man had guns available, that he was really what the PSNI believed him to be.

Tohill necked the last of his pint, stood to go. The Russian also got up from his seat, said something to the Irishman and handed over the holdall.

They'd got their weapon and made their point.

Sat close to the pub doorway, Alex finished up the last of his shandy, got up and left the bar. He wanted to be out ahead of the man with the gun, then to follow him. To Alex, it looked like he wasn't the brains behind the operation, but he might just lead him to their base.

"I'm coming out now," he said, pressing the transmit button on a tiny radio. The click from Smithy pressing the same on his set told him that the message was received. His crew were positioned a few doors along from Robinsons, one to the left, one to the right, Smithy observing from across the road in the Europa.

Alex crossed the road, took out a street map, pretending to be searching for something on it, to all the world just a confused tourist.

"That's the man exiting now," he informed the others. "Get a picture in case we lose him." He knew that Smithy had a Canon camera with a reasonable zoom on it and hoped that Colin Shankly would be able to assist in finding the target if he gave them the slip. It was a gamble, but one that he had to take.

"He's coming your way Daisy," he heard Smithy warn the big man. "Jeff, if you start moving now, get yourself in somewhere behind him."

Alex watched the scouser leave the doorway he'd been stood in, passing the pub and closing on the target. He kept half an eye on the pub door, waiting for Grigorii to leave, wanting to talk to him and see what had been said but knowing that he couldn't. If the bad guys had surveillance on him, then that would blow the whole operation.

"He's getting in a taxi," Daisy's voice came over the earpiece. "Shit, there's just the one! We're gonna lose him."

"Did you get any pics?" Alex asked, praying for the right answer.

"No problem boss," Smithy responded. "All done."

"Okay," Alex said, trying to sound casual about it all. There wasn't much that they could do about it, so no point getting excited. "Stand down. Go back to the safe house. I'll be there soon."

The taxi went past, a tattooed face in the rear passenger's side window. He looked quickly to see if another one was anywhere to be seen, but just like Daisy came up negative. Just then Grigorii came through the pub's door, heading straight across to the Europa. A small crowd of office workers went in to Robinsons, a couple of men and a woman also leaving. Any one of them could be a part of the pick-up, but in all likelihood, none of them were.

One man came out alone, watching as the Russian walked through the hotel entrance. Alex wondered if he was showing too much interest, or perhaps just thinking about where to get his next drink. He considered whether to go across and start a conversation with him, just ask directions or something, when the man abruptly turned and marched away.

'Just another bloke with nowhere in particular to go,' he decided. He took out his phone and called Grigorii. It was time for a debrief.

3rd May 2027

Armagh, Northern Ireland

Declan was left with a decision to make; to contact the Russian once more, or to run while he was ahead. He now had a free pistol, and more to the point, a handgun that worked well. Tohill had stolen a car, driven up into the Mountains of Mourne, found a deserted spot close to the highest peak – Slieve Donard at just under three thousand feet – and completed a test firing. By all accounts the Grach had performed well, with no stoppages and easy to handle.

So, to run or to trade? He needed to decide. Fast.

If he ran, he'd won a gun, a substantial achievement by any means, and he was still totally anonymous to both the dealer and to the authorities. He had armed his Belfast asset free-of-charge. Meanwhile, he and his local team still had antiques, and he had no idea what the man in Derry had in his arsenal, if anything.

The other problem with running was who could he then use in the future to get more weapons from? He was certain that his actions would become known about, then he would not only need to find another dealer, but he would also need to find one that was willing to work with him. They said that there was no honour between thieves but to get blacklisted by the Russians might get around, and then who would do business with him?

There was also the fairly major problem of the Russians possibly looking for compensation. He'd be the target then.

And of course, there was still one further problem. Funding. He hadn't spoken to Paddy and Frank yet about the gun business, hadn't sounded out whether or not there were connections that could assist with money. That needed to be done, and soon.

He sat at his desk pondering his options.

Lunch first, and then a decision. He got up from his computer, grabbed his jacket. He could walk to Tesco and get a sandwich, picking up a new phone in the process. The walk would clear his mind.

It was two days since the meeting in Robinsons and Grigorii was again getting frustrated with sitting in his room, waiting for something to happen. At least Alex was busy, chasing-up the photos they'd got from the meet, chasing the SIM card details down through the PSNI people, checking CCTV footage from the place of purchase. So far, no concrete results, but it had to be better than sitting in a hotel with no idea when – or if – the bad guys would ever get in touch.

Grigorii had added his own details to the description of the man he'd met with, the major identifying mark being the skull tattoo on his face, clearly quite recent. Evidence of other tats on his hands and neck would also be of use, something that would be on police files if he'd ever been involved in a crime, if he had a criminal record. And he'd looked the type who would have one, that much was certain.

He picked-up his cell phone, glanced again at the screen. Nothing.

He flicked the mouse for his laptop, the screen leaping into life, hoping for some new mail. Again nothing.

He thought of calling Alex, just for a chat, but knew this wouldn't help his colleague at all. Killing time was something that soldiers had to become good at, almost as good as they should be at killing people. It never got any easier though.

Alex was in the PSNI headquarters for a private meeting with Colin Shankly. They'd had their first bit of luck; the images that Smithy had taken outside of Robinsons had been matched with one Robby Tohill, a known bad boy in West Belfast, a record including two counts of GBH, an arrest for drug dealing, and a strong suspicion that he'd been linked to the Provisional IRA back in the day. The next decision that they had to take was what to do about him.

"If we haul him in, we show our hand," Alex was saying, the discussion already ten minutes old, the subject going around the same circle for the second time. "Then Grigorii might as well get the next flight back home."

"But we might get the weapon back, take another one off the streets," the policeman pushed back at him. "And maybe he can give us names and addresses of the other key players. That would be the end of it."

Alex frowned, looking again at the police file on the man. "Do you see him as a major player, someone that could organise the hits we've seen to date?"

Shankly sighed, running his fingers through his hair. "I know what you mean," he said, now smoothing his moustache, a sure sign that he was a little bit nervous. "But right now he's out there somewhere with a gun and ammo, and there's no saying that he isn't planning to use it."

The soldier nodded his agreement. It was a decision way above his paygrade, but if they got this call wrong, then they would certainly lose any chance of catching the thugs that were assassinating the local politicians. "I understand," he replied slowly. "And anyone dying is one too many, but if we lose this thread, this possible link to something bigger..." He tailed off. "In the end, I guess it's your call," he finished, feeling beaten.

Colin shook his head, disagreeing. "You have the backing of the PM, Alex, so either we agree on something between us, or I hand the responsibility over to him." He stretched his legs out in front of him, crossing one ankle over the other. "It's a big call, and we can't get it wrong."

Alex was silent for a few seconds, tossing ideas around his head. "How about we put Tohill under surveillance, ready to pull him in if anything starts to look bad. I can use two of my team if this helps, otherwise you can run it as a police operation. In the meantime we give the big fish a chance to contact Grigorii again."

Shankly nodded, a fair compromise reached. "If you could use your people initially, then we'll pick it up from this evening. You can mobilise a lot faster than I can."

Alex nodded.

"By the way, we got details of where the SIM card and probably also the phone were bought, some superstore in Lisburn. We have a time of purchase and we've managed to get all of the store's CCTV for the section that deals with mobile phones and accessories. I have people working through it now, should have something back within the next hour I think."

"That's great news," Alex exclaimed. "Perhaps I should stick around to see what they come up with."

The Chief Constable got to his feet. "Let's go along now and see how they're doing. Maybe they have something already."

They walked along a busy corridor, plain clothes and uniformed police officers moving in both directions, tied-up in their work but greeting the Chief as they passed. Up some stairs to the next floor, then Colin held a door open.

"Let's see what you lot have got," he announced loudly, addressing everyone in the room.

A young woman in jeans and a blue jumper attempted to put down a ham sandwich, trying to quickly swallow the part in her mouth, looking more than a little embarrassed at being caught out by the boss. She wiped her mouth with the back of her hand, coughed, placing the half-eaten meal down on her desk.

"We're just done sir," she finally managed to get out.

"Perfect timing then Kim," Shankly said with a grin. "Don't let me stop you eating though."

The lady started tapping letters into her keyboard, sliding the mouse around the pad, clicking on icons. "This is the section of video five minutes either side of the purchase time," she said, giving a final click on the left mouse button.

The camera was black and white, mounted on the wall behind the till, the image acceptable but not sharp, typical for in-store video. You could see the back of the sales girl's head, no-one at the counter. The girl put her hand inside her blouse, adjusting her bra.

"You get to see all sorts on these things," the police woman said with a smile.

Someone appeared on the far side of the room, looking at a display there, it's contents unclear.

"I played with the zoom earlier. The guy is looking at SIM cards."

The man turned, coming towards the till, a couple of things in his hands. He wore a baseball cap, sunglasses, his jacket fastened up to the neck.

"He's got a mobile phone in one hand, the SIM card in the other," the girl updated them.

Reaching the checkout, he took out a wallet, counted some money from it.

"And he paid in cash," Alex noted. A credit or debit card would have been better, a possible address to chase down.

The man in the picture suddenly looked up at the camera, hurriedly turning away, pulling the peak of the hat down a little lower on his face.

"That's when he realised that the store had CCTV," the girl said, stating the obvious.

"Can you stop that there?" Alex asked. "Wind back to when he looks at the camera, freeze it there." He was watching carefully now, something in the image familiar. Then he had it, even with the disguise. "He was also in Robinsons the other night. I clocked him when Grigorii was leaving. He stood and watched him cross the road to the hotel."

"Shit!" It was the Chief Constable who uttered the oath. "We were so close to him."

"But no closer now than we were before with that hat and the glasses," Alex added.

"Is there enough there to run facial recognition software?" Colin asked.

"We can try it sir," the girl replied. "But we'd need to have it on a database somewhere to make a comparison."

"Give it a try."

Alex was thinking hard and fast, looking for another avenue to search. "Does the store have any other CCTV? Does it cover the parking areas? Maybe we can pick him up on the way to his car, get a plate number?"

"We'll get on to that," Shankly said. "Kim, can you get me the latest address on record for a Robby Tohill please? Print it off and give it to Alex here. It's time we got a break, and this might just be it."

Daisy, Jeff and Smithy had been despatched in two vehicles to take up residence in the street where Tohill lived. It wasn't the best set-up, but it was just for a few hours until the PSNI could put together a full observation team and find a nearby building that they could work out of.

Alex called Grigorii, filling him in on the latest developments.

"And no contact to date?" he asked at the end, hoping to be told that he was wrong but knowing that he wouldn't be.

"Nothing."

Patience was a virtue they said, but at that moment Alex would probably have disagreed. "These guys are starting to piss me off," he said into the phone. "We need to somehow change things and get the upper hand."

"Tell me about it," the Russian agreed. "I'm the one couped-up in this bloody hotel. At least you're out there doing the chasing."

Though Alex didn't say anything, he knew exactly what Grigorii meant. It was a complete role reversal from just days earlier.

5th May 2027

Armagh, Northern Ireland

"In the old days, I'd have been out there with you, you know," Sean Murphy told Declan as they sat alone in a private section of a downtown pub. "I was never much good at sitting on the side-lines, at least not until my hips gave up the ghost. Then I had no real choice."

Declan nodded, trying to show his understanding, still nervous around the old man. The meeting had been set-up by Frank and Paddy, Frank an old friend of Sean, Paddy his only son. It had been agreed that only the two men now present would participate; the less who knew the truth, the better for them all.

"I was a good friend of your father, you know," the older man continued, not giving Declan any chance to interrupt until he'd said his piece. "You may have heard the rumours, but your dad and me were a part of the local IRA active service unit back then, the ASU as the Brits would label us. I was one of their youngest commanders, younger than both Frank and your dad." As he said this he looked all around the room for anyone that could possibly hear the admission, old habits dying hard. "The squaddies hated us, couldn't pin anything definite on us, but they were fairly sure that we were behind their problems. I'm sure that's why your da' was taken out the way he was," he added.

He took a sip of his Guinness, Declan wondering if it was time for him to talk yet. These were all old stories, things he'd already heard. He was about to speak when the old man jumped back in again.

"Frank has told me about your situation, so you don't need to go into details. You need cash for weapons, and I think that I can help." His old eyes narrowed, the wind-weathered face of a farmer looking at the younger man, trying to read what was behind his eyes. "Back in the day, I was also the quartermaster for the IRA here, organising weapon supplies all along the border from Warrenpoint to Derry. I would usually get them shipped in, sometimes on bigger ships in to Warrenpoint, Greenore and the like, sometimes in to smaller harbours on fishing boats, south of the border at Carlingford, occasionally into Kilkeel. Sometimes they'd be organised via Dublin, and I'd just have to arrange transport to get them over the border." He now had a faraway look in his eyes, his memories of those distant days still clear. "I still have a lot of them in caches up and down the border, but Frank tells me that you don't want my crappy old guns."

Now he finally paused, waiting for the younger man to explain his thinking. Declan swallowed nervously, wiped his lips with the sleeve of his jacket.

"The guns we're using now must be over fifty years old, Sean," he began. "If we get a blockage, a misfire with the old ammunition, a firing pin fracturing, then we're up shit creek without a paddle, as they say." He stopped, wondering if more was needed. He needn't have worried though; Sean was ready again to resume his tale.

"I understand son," the old man said. "We were the same in the old days, until we started getting funding from the Yanks. You know how they are – 'I have Irish ancestry' is their favourite saying. 'I want to help the cause,'" he mimicked the American accent. "Most of them have never been near Ireland, and their Irish links are so bloody dated that their pet dog probably has more Irish blood in its veins!" He grinned at that one. "But I have to admit, we did like their money." He lifted his glass, indicating for Declan to do the same. "Slainte!"

"Slainte!" Declan returned, wondering if this meant that the discussion was over. He hoped not, as he still had no idea if he could count on the old man for funds or not.

"We also stored explosives, especially the plastic stuff, Semtex they called it. Probably the most stable stuff we ever got our hands on," Sean continued. "Probably still got a tonne of the stuff stowed away around here in the woods, all in its original wrappings. Better than when we used to make our own bombs with fertiliser and the likes. Never knew if it would work until it did, and even then, it sometimes went off before we were ready for it. Bloody dodgy days, they were." He looked at Declan over his glass. "Did you know that Frank was the ace on bomb making back then? I suppose not. The man never talks too much."

The conversation might have been illuminating but it wasn't going anywhere fast. Declan glanced surreptitiously at his watch, desperately wanting to move on. "So you still have explosive, and you still have guns," he ventured. "Do you still have any money though Sean?" He felt uncomfortable being so direct, but for now he'd heard enough of the man reminiscing.

The old boy gave him a sly grin. "I thought that you'd never ask," he replied, humour in his voice. He tapped his fingers on the wooden table, thinking a bit before he went on. "You see, if you want to be a leader, then you have to lead, and up to now you were letting me do that." He stopped the tapping. "And in answer to your last question, yes, we still have funds, even had a little more money coming in since the COVID thing passed over and America got rid of the Trump fella."

Declan suddenly realised that all of this had just been a test, a challenge to see if he would dare to talk over the old guard. He decided that it was time to continue in the same vein, to lead. "Then it's the million dollar question, Sean," he said. "How much are you willing to spend on us?"

The old man considered this, swirling the last of his beer, clearly enjoying the negotiation. "Perhaps if you'd be good enough to go up and buy another couple of drinks, I could have a wee minute to consider that question."

Declan knew now that the decision had been taken long before the meeting. This wasn't a true negotiation, it was simply a test to see if old Sean thought he was up to the job. It looked as if he'd passed.

It was too late in the evening to be going back to the office, so he went to a nearby restaurant where he knew one of the girls, asked her if he could use their business computer to send out an email. It wasn't as secure as his usual methods, but it would do for now. He needed to get things moving again with the Russian dealer.

He ordered a double espresso coffee while he tapped away on the keyboard, partly to pay for 'borrowing' their system for a couple of minutes, partly to sober him up a little after his drinks with old Sean. After routing his message through a number of hubs, he was ready to send.

It was a quick and simple message, no words wasted.

The gun was fine. Let's talk again at 0800 tomorrow morning.

He added the number for his latest disposable handset, pressed send.

It may have been short and sweet, but now was the time to move things forward. He'd had a productive few days all in all. He had a supplier for his guns, he had a banker with money to burn, and the same person also had a supply of plastic explosive. And he also had a man on his team who could handle the stuff, who had made bombs before.

An idea was forming in his mind. A big idea, something that back in the day Sean would have described as a 'spectacular'. Something that would really put his little group One Ireland on the map.

With no contact from the terrorists for a few days now, political will behind the operation was waning. Talk was that the stake-out at Robinsons had perhaps been compromised, either that or the surveillance on Robby Tohill, this causing their targets to go in to deep cover. There was rumour that the whole operation could be shelved, Alex arguing that they needed to give things a little more time, 'others' suggesting that the SAS must have messed up somewhere along the line and that they should now stop wasting public money. With so few people copied in to the operation, Alex was fairly sure where the rumours were coming from, but with no progress to report he was running out of options and arguments.

They'd been so bloody unlucky with so many parts of the operation. The CCTV had been inconclusive, no matching from the facial recognition computers; the car at the superstore had been too far away to get details of the number plates, the video only in black and white, so car colour indeterminate. Tohill had so far led them nowhere, basically just staying at home or going to his local for the past few days and nights, no meetings, nothing suspicious. If the operation was shut down, then he'd be dragged in, but Alex had little hope that the man would lead them anywhere fast. To Alex, he was just a bagman, someone to run the errands.

Things had looked bad, on the point of collapse, so when Grigorii had received the email he'd forwarded it immediately to Alex, following it up with a call. "It's still on," he'd told the SAS man. "Look on your computer." It was a great relief for Alex, keeping the operation alive.

Grigorii called the number at bang on eight o'clock in the morning as directed, still trying to decide on why there had been so many days of silence. The same voice answered on the second ring, again muffled, as though speaking through a mask.

"I'm ready to order," it told him, directly to the point.

It was a version of what Grigorii had hoped to hear, something he had practiced for. "Same as I got you before?" he asked.

"Just the same model, but new this time. And ten of them."

The Russian decided to test the man. "So that's nine plus the one your man took with him?" he asked. How would the man react?

"I said ten, and I meant ten," the voice ordered, a touch of anger apparent. "And all of them brand new. The one we have was to test the water, let's call it a loss-leader." A snigger followed the final remark.

Grigorii knew that the buyer was trying to play hardball, decided to play a little of his own, at the same time being careful not to get the call cut-off. "It'll take a few days to get an order like that together. Is that okay with you?"

"As fast as you can," the voice told him. "How much?"

Grigorii knew that the market value for a 9 millimetre pistol was around six to seven hundred pounds per weapon, but on the black market? "Twelve hundred per gun," he responded, trying to make it sound final. It was a guess and a gamble, not giving in too easily on the price, knowing that what he was offering couldn't be sourced just anywhere.

"Ten grand for the lot," the man countered.

Grigorii paused, pretending to consider the offer. "Done," he finally agreed. "How do we exchange the goods?"

The man still seemed uncertain about this part of the operation, hesitating before answering. "First you need to give me the exact date that the goods will be available to me here in Ireland. Then we will fix a handover." Grigorii could almost hear the man's brain ticking, trying to gain the upper hand once more. "And let's be clear on payment. Half upfront, the rest once I have the guns in my hands, not before."

If this had been a real business arrangement Grigorii would never have taken such a risk, but this was no deal, just a fishing trip with the pistols as bait. "I can live with that," he replied after a short pause.

"I will be in contact with you again tomorrow, I hope. I will need all of your details by then. Any final discounts, delivery dates, the rest. Be ready."

The line went dead.

Alex set the wheels in motion through Mike Sanders, getting the hardware to Belfast as soon as sounded reasonable. They'd decided that a week for delivery sounded fair; guns would usually be shipped in, so this would take some time. Giving a delivery in two or three days would indicate that the stock was either available in country, or that they were being flown in, an unlikely scenario with airport security. Better to move them in a container or hidden in a cargo of ten thousand tonnes of wheat. That would be the cover story.

"By the way Alex", Mike said after agreeing the details. "The hair sample that the PSNI picked up at the McAvoy house. It's come back the same as the facial stuff, nothing on our DNA databases, no match."

'Another blank' Alex thought, careful not to voice his disappointment. "Something will break soon boss," he responded, trying to sound upbeat. "They've just been lucky so far."

Mike sighed. "You know politicians. They want results like yesterday, while they can take weeks on end debating who should get the funding for a new office desk." He still sounded under pressure, more subdued than usual. "We need a break," he finally added, the implications seeming clear to Alex. "Keep at it," he finished, a forced positivity in his voice. "You usually have a way of making things happen."

"I'll give it my best."

Declan had called a team meeting, the Armagh one at least.

"We never got to discuss and agree a new target last time," he told the two men after explaining where things stood with the sourcing of new weapons. He'd been thinking quite a lot about his recent conversation with Sean Murphy, and not just on the funding issues. He looked at Frank, wondering if he still had it in him. The man was key to what he had in mind.

"Another politician?" Paddy whispered, his eyes alive with excitement.

Declan nodded, taking his time. This was going to be a big one, a game changer, a real variation on the way they did things. A 'spectacular' as they'd have said in the past. He'd decided to meet in a playpark this time, no-one around but the three of them, no other ears to overhear the conversation. This plan could risk no leaks.

"I think that it's time for a big one," he replied, noting that even Frank was taking notice. "I think we should take out Nicholas Thomas, the Northern Ireland Secretary."

6th May 2027

Westminster, London, UK

Preparations for the Dominic's visit to Stormont were highly secretive, at present the press pack still totally in the dark. It had been decided that it would be good for morale, a confidence boost for the whole Province and a sure sign that the terrorist murders of politicians had come to an end, that the PSNI was again in control of things. No killings had occurred for over two weeks now and the news about weapons deals also seemed to be dead. The police had even issued statements that they'd intercepted three shipments in the same period, all giving a positive spin to things.

But within the corridors of power the few who knew about the trip were still highly nervous. Three days was a very short time to prepare everything, but a long time for something to leak out. And as they were all well aware despite their positive front, the bad guys were still out there, and still trying to get their hands on guns.

"I'm still not happy about the visit," Ruth Maybank told the other three people assembled at the table. She wore a bright red jacket over a crisp white blouse, standing out in stark contrast to the others in their charcoal suits. "The risk is still too high."

Colin Shankly nodded agreement. Security would be his overall responsibility, no matter who else the UK police, military and others organised to form the defensive wall around Dominic Wild. They still had Tohill under observation but were really just chasing the shadows that made up the rest of the terrorist team. They definitely knew of at least one more person out there, but despite all of their sources for intelligence gathering they had no real idea of the size of the group.

"I believe that we're overthinking it," the NI Secretary chipped in. "I live over there, drive to work every day, and things really do seem more relaxed right now."

"You live over there part time, you go to work with an armed police driver and have a second police car escorting you, so of course you feel okay. And you have twenty-four hour security on your house," Ruth reminded him. Colin Shankly was pleased that he hadn't needed to tell them this. It would only have started another argument.

"The PM will have the same," Thomas said petulantly. He was really of the opinion that if it was good enough for him, then it was also good enough for anyone else. "In fact, he'd be flying in, his chopper landing on the lawns of Stormont, so he's actually even safer."

"I'm coming, and that's it," Dominic interrupted. "I am also the PM of Northern Ireland, and that makes it my duty to show the people that things are okay. That I have confidence in how things are running across there."

The Chief Constable had flown in that morning, this his first brief on the planned trip.

"Will you be in and out on the same day?" he asked. "Makes security much easier, as Nicholas has just said. Helicopter in, helicopter out."

The PM frowned, his lips forming into a tight line. "I'd like to have a night there," he told them. "I think it would look much more reassuring for the people. Have some sort of semi-official dinner with local dignitaries, politicians, wives, then out again in the morning," he added.

It was Colin's turn to frown. This was turning into a security nightmare. He started thinking about manpower, cancelling all police leave, where was safest place to host such an event.

"A great idea," the NI Sec agreed. "Great for morale."

Dominic Wild turned towards the Chief Constable, temporarily excluding the rest of them. "Could we make it work Colin? Can we handle it without undue risk?"

'Damned if you do and damned if you don't' the policeman thought, trying to shape a politically correct response. "In Northern Ireland there will never be no risk, but if we can keep the visit under wraps until the last minute, I can ramp up your security and keep the threat low," he told them. His protection was the statement about keeping of the visit 'under wraps'. He knew that the politicians would say that it could be done, but in truth, he knew that such a thing was verging on the impossible.

"Then it will happen," Dominic announced.

Other preparations were also underway, but not in the warm corridors of Westminster.

Declan and Frank had joined Paddy and his father for a drive from Armagh towards Monaghan and the north/south border. The landscape was made up of rolling hills, a lush green under the early summer skies, a peaceful looking land that hid many dark secrets. The roads were narrow and empty, houses infrequent and mainly white painted farm buildings and pale yellow bungalows.

As they came closer to Middletown and the border itself, Paddy took a right turn, following the Coolkill Road, this even narrower than the one they'd just left.

"Not many people coming out this way, as you might well remember Frank," Sean said, staring at the sights and conjuring up memories of days gone by. "We used to do this trip together occasionally. The only people you'd see back then were farmers and bloody squaddies on patrol."

A little further on, he signalled that his son should take a rutted farm track, Declan getting out to open the gate. About five hundred metres further on they could see a small, wooded area.

"Just up by there, son," he indicated.

A minute later and they were all out of the car, Sean limping on his failing hip joints. He stood at the front of the vehicle, scanning the ground around him, trying to find landmarks. Finally he pointed to a large oak, walked slowly towards it.

"Should be about five paces behind that tree," he told them.

The other three men followed, Declan and Paddy both carrying shovels from the boot of the car. Five metres beyond the tree, Sean stopped, looking once more for markers.

"It's been about seven years since I was out here, the trees are all much bigger now but I think this is the spot," he told them. "Shouldn't be too deep, a foot or two maybe."

Declan and Paddy moved forward to start digging, the two older men watching, Sean lighting up a cigarette.

"You say there's Semtex here too?" Paddy asked. "What if we put a shovel through it?"

"It'll be fine lad," Frank told him. "Most forgiving stuff I ever worked with," he added.

"Let's hope that you're right," Sean said blowing out a cloud of smoke. "Or we'll all be back in Armagh before we even know it."

Alex had decided to take a bit of a chance and call a meeting including Grigorii, the Russian being collected from the hotel by a taxi that actually wasn't one. He was whisked away to the same police station that he'd once been locked-up in not long before, taken in through a side entrance and then directly to a small interview room.

The room contained the four SAS team members and Colin Shankly. The Chief took control of the meeting, briefing them swiftly on the Prime Minister's intended visit.

"Just what we all need," Smithy offered with a grin once he'd finished. "A bit more pressure."

Alex said nothing, a thoughtful look on his face, eyes focused on the far corner of the room. "Not being rude, but can your people handle the security requirements right now?" he asked Colin, then added. "We're ready to help, but you know the place much better than we do."

"I've got it in hand," the policeman replied. "I'm not too happy with it, but if he really can just fly in unannounced and then out again the next day, I think it will be almost impossible for someone to organise something in so short a time." He grimaced, then went on, "But I somehow doubt that something that big will remain a secret for too long. You all know how people talk."

Alex considered this, trying to decide whether or not his own team could really offer anything to assist the police. "Smithy here is a sniper if that helps?" he finally suggested.

"I have snipers too, and I think it will be better for coordination and control to have one party running it all," Colin responded. "Simpler for everyone."

"Okay," the soldier agreed. "It's not really why I called us all together, but thanks for putting us in the picture. Better than learning from the press after the event." He leant back in the chair, clasped his hands behind his head. "As we all know, the DNA, the CCTV and the car sighting at the superstore have all brought us no further forward. We have their messenger – Tohill – under observation, but he's not taking us anywhere." He leant forward, crossing his arms in front of him on the table. "Sometime in the next day or two we will receive the ten Grach pistols for the trade.

145

And sometime in the next three days or so we should hopefully know where and how the trade will be completed."

"Are you disabling the pistols, removing the firing pins or something like that?" the policeman asked, a hopeful expression on his face.

"I don't think that's a good idea," Grigorii butted in. "Tohill might look like an idiot, but he seemed to know his guns."

"And Grigorii will be the one in the firing line if we cross them," Alex added.

Colin Shankly nodded, understanding but clearly not happy about putting a pile of weapons out on the street. "Understood."

"If all goes to plan, they'll never get their hands on them anyway," Alex said, trying to placate the man. He could see both sides of the argument, but his main concern was putting a man on the ground with a poor cover story. To be caught out would be almost certain death. "What I was trying to get from today was an idea of where these people will probably insist on meeting for the exchange."

The others nodded agreement, knowing that to be one step ahead of the terrorists was crucial.

"That's obviously very hard to say," Shankly started. "Things went very quiet during the coronavirus crisis, so we can only fall back on history and what I would probably do in their shoes."

"That's the best we can hope for."

"Well Alex," the Chief began. "Historically the terrorist likes to have the border at his back, a place to run to in an emergency. Even in the seventies and eighties – the height of the Troubles – the border was pretty porous. Now we have less patrols – just us and the Guardai, and no military presence – so it is even worse now than it was then. That's where things happened most of the time back in the day."

Grigorii nodded his agreement on this. "That makes sense."

"The other problem that we have is it is a long border, and though our links with the Guardai are not too bad nowadays, assistance will probably be limited or too late." Colin stood, walked over to a wall totally covered in a map of the whole of Ireland, north and south. "The main border crossings are manned since the breakdown of the Brexit talks, which means that they are probably not realistic crossing points." He swept a hand over the map, halting and tapping on Newry, Armagh, Enniskillen, Strabane and

Londonderry. "These points also have major cities close by, and that means a higher police presence, so not where I would want to be hanging out if I was a bad guy."

"All makes perfect sense, but doesn't help us much," Alex said. "There are so many gaps between these places that they still have plenty of choices on where to do a runner."

"Totally true," Colin replied. "But keep in mind that in an emergency they have to get to the border from the agreed handover point, and then they have to get from the crossing point to somewhere of safety. You'll notice that the roads become more sparce out here," he waved his hand over some of the countryside between the cities, "and many of them are basically tracks, not great for a high speed escape."

The others were now on their feet too, studying the highly detailed Ordnance Survey map.

"So, the second thing I said I'd do, was to say what I would do in their shoes." Colin stayed at the map, using his index finger to draw out a circle close to Newry. "This is the main crossing point between north and south, the main road between Belfast and Dublin. And in my eyes, should you want to disappear, the best place to do it would be into the biggest city." He tapped Dublin.

"But surely that's also the most secure of all of the crossing points?" Daisy asked. "And I thought we'd agreed that they would be avoided?"

"One hundred percent right big fella," the Chief agreed. "We wouldn't cross there, but that is the road that you would want to be on as soon as you could be." He pointed to a place close to Newry called Forkill. "See all of the tracks around here? See the mountain, the forest, perfect places for the handover. And here's the border," he pointed to the line on the map, shifted his finger again. "And here's the motorway, all the way down to Dublin."

"We need to steal a car, but one that won't be missed for a few days," Declan told the team.

They were moving into stage two of the plan, and Declan had taken a week off work, spending part of each day in the Stormont Park area of Belfast, spying out the lay of the land around the Parliament Buildings, the roads in and out, and the routines of the ministers. His main interest had been in one man in particular.

"Then we need to get one from the airport, a ferry terminal, something like that," Frank replied. Declan had noticed that the man had found a new lease of life since the trip to the arms dump, a fresh spring in his step.

"I think the airport," he agreed. "Long-term parking, preferably after watching a family leaving for a holiday."

Frank agreed. "Do you want Paddy and myself to sort that one out?" he asked. "You seem to have enough on your plate right now."

"If you've finished the other task, that would be great. I'll keep up the surveillance."

"Do you not think you could use that Tohill character for that?" Frank asked. "Would save you a lot of driving."

Declan had considered this too, but his prize was too big to risk using someone that he didn't know so well. If his plan worked, they would have a major scalp to their name. If it went wrong, then they'd either all end up dead, or rotting in a prison somewhere on the mainland. It just wasn't worth the risk. "No, this one's for us."

9th May 2027

Stormont, Belfast, Northern Ireland

Dominic and Ruth boarded the twin-engined Super Puma helicopter at the Barclays London Heliport in Battersea at eight-thirty. It was the closest helicopter base to Westminster, but it was also close to the home of the PM. He'd always stayed close to his home and first ever constituency, even during his working days as a doctor, when he'd repaired people at the nearby St Thomas' Hospital. He was a bit of a home boy at heart, never straying too far from his roots.

The flight would take around two hours, giving both of them a good opportunity to catch-up on some of their reading from the bottomless pit of correspondence that crossed their desks, just another part of their jobs. It was reading with no interruptions, so they both hoped to get an efficient return for their efforts.

As the helicopter left the ground, gaining height rapidly, they both took a moment to gaze out over the city. Dominic remembered how deserted it had become during the COVID crisis and loved to see it buzzing once more, lanes of traffic cramming the M25, boats and barges packing the Thames. Life was almost normal once again.

Ruth wondered about the day ahead. She had a very high regard for the PM; he'd brought her in, given her the opportunity to become what she now was. In politics she was as loyal a follower as one could find, someone who truly believed in Dominic Wild and his aspirations for the nation.

Clear of the city the helicopter steered to the northwest, and she took out the first file that she needed to study. It was going to be a long day, and she was sure that both she and the PM would have to face a few challenges along the way, and also a sore face from the fixed smile that they'd both be adopting until bedtime. And then of course there'd be a whole raft of 'peacekeeping duties' as the two of them called them. Yes, Nicholas Thomas would be out to score points over Colin Shankly all over again.

She sighed, eyes going from the scenery outside to the business on her lap. If anything was going to stop Dom from taking it to a third term, it was the political in-fighting, not the people's vote.

Nicholas Thomas had ordered the pick-up from his bachelor pad in downtown Belfast for nine o'clock. He hated starting early almost as much as he hated finishing late, unless of course the late finish included some evening function with people he actually enjoyed being with. His day in the office was usually a short one, and with the PM not arriving before ten, he'd seen no reason at all to change it.

It was a two-bed flat near the centre of the city, giving him great access to all of the amenities. His wife had refused to leave their Hertfordshire home – 'Belfast is far too dangerous for the kids' – and he hadn't fought too hard to get her there. It meant he was a single man during the week, and able to escape from work every Friday afternoon to return to the UK. (Further shortening an already short week).

The doorman called over the intercom to announce the arrival of his car and police escort. He glanced at his watch, deciding that they could hang on another few minutes while he finished his coffee and cleaned his teeth. Time was on his side.

He glanced out of the living room window with views over the River Lagan and sipped his coffee.

"No rush," he reminded himself. "Time enough."

Declan had watched Nicholas Thomas plus his one car escort as they had made their way along the Upper Newtownards Road every morning for the last four days, never quite the same time, but always driving the same route from the city. Even with no security training per se, he knew that this was careless and wondered if the police were at fault, or if the Northern Ireland Secretary himself simply demanded this. Whichever was the case, it made his job easier than it should have been, something he would not be complaining about.

He was sat on a bench just along from the turnoff for the Parliament Buildings, Frank down the road a little towards the city to give him an early warning, Paddy up the hill on the same Newtownards Road, just in case someone decided to change the route for some odd reason that morning.

He'd parked the stolen Honda just opposite the junction for Stormont, directly where the target car would need to drive by to get the NI Secretary to work. The vehicle would have to pass within three metres of the Honda.

He glanced at his watch, wondering what time the man would decide to show his face today. He didn't know the man at all but knew that if they'd ever met one another, he would likely have hated him.

The ride across the Irish Sea was a bumpy one, making reading difficult to a point that first Ruth and then the PM simply gave up on it.

"Sorry about the turbulence," the co-pilot said over the intercom system, turning in his seat to address them. His harness made this difficult, the metal seat even more so, but he just felt that it was a little rude to address the PM without at least attempting to face him. "The good thing is we are making great time. The tailwind is about thirty miles an hour. Should get you there early."

Dominic smiled at the man, though his stomach wasn't happy at all. "Just keep them informed of our arrival time. People will panic if we suddenly pop around the corner and nothing is prepared," he said with a grin, knowing that everyone would be on standby even now.

"We're in constant contact," the young man replied, turning forward again.

The police driver put on a brave face, angry at having been kept waiting for fifteen minutes for the NI Sec. It wasn't the first time that it had happened, and on one occasion the man had even had him drop-off some random woman before allowing him to take the route to the office. The man was just a pompous fool as far as he was concerned. He felt sorry for his wife and kids back in England, but more than that, he just wished that he'd go back there himself and join them. There simply had to be better candidates for the job.

"Why have we stopped?" Thomas asked from the backseat, looking up and laying down his newspaper. "Is there some sort of problem?"

"Just the usual traffic sir," the policeman answered. "We could turn on the lights and siren if you like, but you told us before that this isn't really necessary."

"I have the Prime Minister coming today," the politician complained.

"Shall I put the lights on sir? Get the escort to run in front, clear the traffic a wee bit?" the driver asked.

Nicholas Thomas hated the way the Irish used 'wee bit' to describe anything from two minutes to two hours. It provided no clarification at all. He looked at his watch, realising that the helicopter wouldn't be due for probably another hour, at least forty minutes. He picked up the paper again, turned to the crossword.

"Just keep going as you are," he ordered. "No need to attract unneeded attention."

'Some people are just never happy,' the driver thought. "As you say sir," he said aloud. 'Wanker!' he didn't say, but it was so clear in his mind that he thought the man might have somehow heard it anyway.

Declan took out his cell phone, making certain that it was the right one. It wouldn't do to use the wrong one, especially today. Of the other two, one was not going to be used until he was ready to talk to the Russian again, something he was delaying until this was all over. And the other one…

"Still nothing Frank? No sign of the man?"

"Just normal traffic Declan," the old man replied. "Keep calm young fella. He'll get here when he gets here. You know how it is."

Frank was the main part in today's mission Declan reminded himself before responding. No point in upsetting him. The man looked the same as always but it was as if his mind had gone back twenty years, a freshness in his words and actions since they'd dug up the arms and explosives on the Coolkill Road.

Declan grinned to himself. It had been a great place to hide the weapons he decided to himself. "Cool kill," he said aloud. It had a nice ring to it.

The traffic was moving again now and Nicholas knew that they would be at the long pale grey building that was Stormont within ten, latest fifteen minutes. He watched out of the window as people struggled up the hill, some probably on their way to work, some with dogs heading for the park. It was a blustery day, looked as if rain may come later, a typical Irish summer.

"Do we have any news on the PM's helicopter?" he asked his driver.

"I had an update in the earpiece about five minutes ago sir," the man replied. "Should be with us a little bit early, probably twenty to thirty minutes out. Depends now on air traffic control, not the weather."

Nicholas looked again at his watch, then looked ahead at the traffic. All being well he'd be there at least ten minutes before the PM, possibly up to twenty. Still time for a final cup of coffee, then get them all ready for the cameras that he'd had organised. Another chance to lead the news.

Declan's phone buzzed, the one that connected him to either Paddy or Frank.

"Yes?"

"The car's just passing now," Frank whispered into the microphone. It was as if he thought the occupants of the car might hear him.

"I'm ready," Declan informed the man, hanging up and putting the cell into his right jacket pocket. Carefully he extracted another handset from his left pocket, what he would call 'phone three.' He pressed the button on the side, ensuring that the screen lit up, that the thing was on and ready. There was just one number programmed into the phone, and he selected it, starting to walk slowly away from the junction and towards Frank.

Looking away to his left, Nicholas Thomas could see the Irish Assembly buildings, knowing that by now everyone would be there ready to receive the PM, many with butterflies in their stomachs, praying that their small part in today's proceedings would pass without incident.

He could see the junction up ahead, the long drive through Stormont Park all the way to the massive building.

Another glance at his watch, not really aware of doing it, not seeing the time, not admitting to himself that he was also a little nervous. TV cameras had that effect on people, even if you placed yourself under their scrutiny fairly often.

The car lined up to turn at the junction, the driver happy that today's pain was almost over.

That's when it happened.

Declan stopped walking, moving to the edge of the footpath to let others pass by, looking back up the hill to the junction and the position of the official's car, then pressed the green button to call the one number on phone number three.

"We've been told to change course and land in the International Airport, Prime Minister!" The pilot interrupted Dominic's thoughts, the PM's eyes on the approaching coastline, then the large green spaces beyond it that made up most of Ireland. He switched his gaze towards the two crewmen, neither of them looking his way, one leaning over the central console, adjusting switches and dials, the other focussing on unheard incoming radio traffic.

"Why is that?" was all he could think to say.

It took a couple of seconds before the captain answered. "Sorry, I'm still receiving information, but it seems that there has been an explosion very close to the Parliament Buildings and the local police want to route us away from the scene." He stopped again, another message coming in.

Dominic considered the situation for a second, very aware that the security people wouldn't want him anywhere near the incident. He understood this, but he'd never been a runner, and anyway, it could be anything, not necessarily a threat.

"Tell them we're coming in anyway," he decided. Now was the time to stand strong.

The pilot relayed the message, appeared to have a debate with someone on the ground. "I have Colin Shankly on the ground. I can switch him through to you." The co-pilot thumbed a button on the intercom box, and the Chief came through to the headsets in the back of the chopper.

"Hi Colin, Dominic here," the PM said. "What's going on?"

Colin's voice sounded slightly distorted, the sound of sirens also clouding it's clarity. "The NI Sec's car's just been taken out, a car bomb on the Newtownards Road. We are still securing the scene, trying to get into the vehicle, but it's a bloody mess. I don't think you should be here," he added.

'Nicholas Thomas' thought the PM, glancing at Ruth Maybank. He wanted to go on, but should his 'wish' also put others at risk?

"We should be there," the lady told him firmly. "Those bastards can't see us running." Her voice was determined, steely. It reminded him of Margaret Thatcher.

"We're coming in Colin," he said, decision made for him. "We won't get in the way, but we need to show strength here, not weakness. We are a team."

The Chief Constable said nothing for a full thirty seconds. "I appreciate your support sir," he finally conceded. And to be honest, he did, but he also considered all of the extra problems that having the Prime Minister on the spot in the middle of a terrorist event would mean to him and his men.

"How long until we're down?" Dominic asked the pilot.

"Ten minutes, not more."

"Am I still in contact with the Chief?"

"Sir."

Dominic quickly ran some words through his mind, trying to see if they sounded acceptable to himself at least. "Colin, I'll be with you in a few minutes. Don't wait for me, just go about what you need to do. God knows you'll have enough on your hands without me." He hesitated, trying to remember names, failing. "Get the PR Officer to be ready for me. We need to prepare something for the press, and quickly."

"I'll get that sorted immediately PM and thank you. I think I need all the help I can get right now."

Dominic was about to sign off when a final thought struck him. "Can you also get Alex to be there as soon as possible. He can organise my close protection for the next few hours, free-up your people."

Ahead, through the windscreen of the helicopter, buildings were appearing, large cranes in the harbour, motorways. From close to the city centre was a plume of smoke, reaching skywards. Belfast had claimed another victim.

The team were in the middle of a brainstorming exercise, trying to envisage every possible scenario that could play out during the handover of the weapons, changing every possible variable such as surroundings, enemy numbers, armaments, and even their own injuries. It was something that they always did, but no planning could ever fully cover what actually ran out on the ground. Their ability to adapt to situations while under fire was one of the main strengths of all special forces operatives and playing these 'games' helped them do this. It also highlighted weaknesses, allowed them to correct them before the shit really did hit the fan.

Alex's phone buzzed on the sideboard behind him and he turned and scooped it up. 'Grigorii', he expected. The man was going mindless with boredom alone in the hotel.

"Alex, it's Colin here," the policeman swiftly announced, not wasting his words. "There's been an explosion here at Stormont. It looks like Nicholas Thomas is dead, a car bomb. The PM is insisting on continuing with his visit. He wants you here for close protection. Now."

Some small part of his brain froze, partially in shock, but he was already in motion, indicating to his team to get their things together, to prepare to move. "Can you arrange transport?" he asked, also avoiding unnecessary words, cutting to the chase. The man would have enough on his plate right now, didn't need Alex asking how it had happened, who was involved, or anything else like that. The important thing now was to get there.

"It'll be at your place in ten minutes. Anything else I can do?"

"Keep safe Colin. We'll be there ASAP."

Alex cut the call, swiftly briefed his team who had already bagged their weapons, ready to move.

If this bombing had been carried out by the group 'One Ireland', then his team's task had just become much more difficult. Not getting a result was simply not permitted. All bets were now off. It was time to perform.

His phone buzzed, the car waiting outside. "Let's go," he ordered.

9th May 2027

In Front Of The Parliament Buildings, Stormont, Northern Ireland

It was a hastily arranged press conference, the wreckage of the car still smouldering below where they stood, the police trying to recover it despite this. The traffic was backed-up all the way to the city centre, the press corps only available because they'd already been present and expecting happier announcements, but no doubt imagining what sort of headlines they could make out of the present circumstances. Death and destruction sold more papers than visiting dignitaries, even if they were the Prime Minister.

Dominic Wild stepped up to the dais, Ruth Maybank taking her position slightly behind his right shoulder, solidarity at its best. They'd decided to leave Colin Shankly out of it, allowing the man to deal with the horror that had already happened, one of his own people also killed in the blast.

"Citizens of Northern Ireland," Dominic began formally, glancing down at some hastily assembled words on some handwritten cue cards in his hand. "I came here today to celebrate with you all, to see what both you and your representatives had achieved in the past months since we succeeded in our long battle with the virus." He again lowered his gaze, looking for the next words of his speech. "Instead, I have arrived to find that one of your brave Irish police officers has been murdered, and with him the man tasked to help lead this country into better times, the Northern Ireland Secretary, Nicholas Thomas." He paused, partly to organise his thoughts, partly for dramatic effect. He lifted his head, looked directly into the bank of cameras. "Some people try to take this fine country back in time, to return to the days when murder was common here, when life was cheap. They don't care that the people they have just killed also have families, children, loved ones.

"This is not the first murder here in recent times, but when nothing happened for the last few weeks, I thought that we had things back under control. Today proved that I was wrong. The cowards are still out there." Behind him, Ruth wiped a tear from under her eye, probably the result of the breeze, but it looked very dramatic either way.

"Today I will make you a promise, the same one that I used to make to my patients back in the days when I was a doctor." He looked over the crowd that had gathered, mainly made up of the government staff, but also from several locals that had been in the park grounds at the time of the blast. "I promise that I will do everything in my power to fix things. I will cure this place, the same as I cured sick people during the COVID times. I will be there for you all."

He suddenly felt very tired, the early start, the bumpy flight, the shock of losing someone that he had known well. He again stared into the lenses of the press corps. "We are coming to get you, wherever and whoever you are," he said, his words crisp and clear, forceful and clipped. "Do not rest easy, because we are right behind you."

The crowd of strangers that had gathered clapped and cheered, the press calling out their usual questions, most asking how the PM would keep his promise. It was what people wanted to hear, but was it a bridge too far, a promise too large to honour?

Alex stood on the edge of the gathering, not watching the Prime Minister but watching the crowd for things that didn't fit, for threats. His men were positioned all around the gathering doing the same thing, hands in pockets that concealed their weapons.

The task of taking down One Ireland had again been ramped up, just made a whole lot tougher.

They'd left as soon as the echoes from the explosion had died away, not even waiting to see the results. They knew that the police would spring into action as soon as they discovered what had actually happened, knew that roadblocks would appear on all of the main routes in and out of the city.

Their second car was further up the hill, already pointed towards Newtownards, away from the city where the traffic was quickly becoming a tangled mess. They'd taken a right for Comber, heading along the edge of Strangford Lough, avoiding the major roads and motorways, a long hike home through Newry but a hike that kept them out of the way of trouble. The car radio kept them up-to-date with developments, at least those that the police were willing to make public. Even half an hour later they were uncertain if they'd achieved their goal, whether or not the minister had died in the explosion.

They howled like schoolboys winning a football game when the Prime Minister spoke to the press.

"We feckin' did it!" Paddy yelled.

Even Frank smiled, his newfound youth splitting his face. "It's just like the old days lads," he told them. "Except we haven't got the bloody British Army chasing our arses!"

As they neared the outskirts of Newry, Declan decided that this was definitely a day for a beer. Maybe two. A celebration.

11th May 2027

Belfast, Northern Ireland

With the Prime Minister again out of the Province, Alex and the team stood down from their close protection duties and refocussed their efforts on finding and destroying the terrorist cell that called itself 'One Ireland'.

It had been days now since Grigorii had heard from the terrorists and fixed pricing and delivery, long days where he'd needed to stay in the Europa, close to his phone and laptop, not risking missing a message or call. 'Cabin Fever' was an understatement of some magnitude; to use another American term, he himself thought that he was going 'stir crazy'. He longed to get outdoors, had started dreaming about his time spent in the forests back in Russia living out of a backpack.

"It's got to come soon," Alex told him over the phone, trying to remain positive. "Just keep your head down and watch a movie or two."

"I've watched more movies than I thought even existed," the Russian complained. "I think that if I watch another one, I'll kick out the damned television screen." He sighed, knowing that Alex was right. They'd come so far, the Grach pistols were waiting to go, all he needed now was the call from the buyers and a place to do the swap, guns for money. "I'll be all right," he conceded. "I'll spend an hour in the gym, beast some of this pent up energy out of me."

"That's better," the SAS man said. He'd been in the same position himself on numerous occasions and in various parts of the planet. Waiting for something to happen, counting the hours. And then when it did happen it generally lasted for only a few minutes anyway, during which time you were so bloody hyped-up and scared that you barely remembered them. "Something's got to break soon," he added.

"Let's hope," Grigorii replied. "I'm more than ready to go."

They'd all been invited around to Sean Murphy's place a couple of days after they'd returned victorious from Stormont, somewhere Declan had seen from the outside, but never from within. 'Who said violence didn't pay?' he thought to himself as he admired the house.

The 'place' was a long white bungalow on the outskirts of Armagh, set in around three acres of lush lawn. At the side of the house was a ride-on mower, the only way to maintain a garden so big. Inside the house was like a Tardis, five bedrooms and two receptions, most of the sleeping rooms en-suite.

"You've got a fine place here," he told the old man.

Sean's wife had been dead for five years now, finally succumbing to a two year battle with cancer. It meant that there were just the four of them, just a bunch of men with a common interest, getting the Brits out of their country.

"Back in the day, we always celebrated a successful job with a bottle of this stuff," Sean told them, pulling out a bottle of Black Bush. "You remember that don't you Frank?" he asked his old comrade in arms.

"Aye," the other old warrior replied. "And some crackin' good parties we had back then," he added.

The four men raised their glasses, faces now serious, Declan especially reflecting on what he'd just done. "Slainte!" Sean toasted them.

"To One Ireland," Declan said, adding his own salute.

They knocked back the strong spirit, feeling it burn all the way down to their stomachs. It felt good, fortifying them against any personal doubts that might try and creep into their minds following the event. It was a normal feeling, Declan had read. During the pressure of an operation the adrenalin ran high, but once the deed was done it left the system, leaving a vacuum where questions could breed.

Sean was pouring another round, moving from man to man. "You boys did a fine job today," he'd told them. He stopped at his son Paddy, a tear in his eye. "I'm proud of you boy," he said. "You're making a difference, hopefully achieving something that me and my merry band never managed." He raised his glass again. "To Paddy, my boy."

They drank down the whiskey, the boy's face red, partially with embarrassment and partly with pride. The spirit just made it a little bit brighter.

Paddy finally felt like he was somebody, that he really did make a difference. It made him want to do something even bigger, something that would really put One Ireland on the map.

Still nursing a bit of a hangover the next morning, Declan knew that it was time to move forward once again. Sean had agreed to fund the arms purchase, would organise to have the money available in cash today. Cash was his suggested method of payment, no links to bank accounts, no paper trail. Actually handing over the money was the problem area, but he'd had some ideas on how to get around that one too. The first payment would be simple; five thousand pounds bagged-up and dropped at the hotel, no meeting, no danger.

The second payment would be the one where the weapons actually changed hands, and that was proving more difficult. That money couldn't be handed over without proof that the goods were really existing, in their hands, and that needed a person. The problem was, who would that person be?

Part of Declan said that it had to be him. He was the most meticulous of the team, and he was also the leader. Paddy was capable of doing something stupid, even if his father believed that he'd finally grown-up. And Frank was too old – even in his new rejuvenated state – to be dashing around the countryside collecting guns.

Another part of his brain said that he should personally avoid dealing directly with the Russian. It put him in the firing line, and even disguised it would give away too many distinguishing features. His height, weight, voice, even his complexion would all be out there in the open. And what if the man tried to cross him, didn't bring the weapons they'd requested, tried to get more cash from the deal? How did he handle that? He'd seen the man in the flesh and he'd looked like he could handle himself. Declan was no slouch, but in a straight fist-fight he guessed that the Russian would hold all of the cards.

It was something that he needed to decide on and soon.

He would call the man that afternoon he decided, fix the meet, make the drop-off of the down payment.

He poured an instant coffee, adding an extra spoonful of granules to his mug, not bothering with milk. It was time to sit down and make a plan, and to do that he needed to get his head clear, his brain fully functional. Black Bush Whiskey certainly didn't assist in that capacity he decided with a wry smile.

It was the same voice, distorted as usual, but at least the call had finally materialized.

"I'll receive the guns tomorrow," Grigorii told the anonymous voice on the line. "But I need to receive the down payment from your side before things go any further."

"You'll have it by tomorrow."

"Where do you want to meet to hand it over?" the Russian asked. "I can get a car if necessary."

"It won't be necessary to meet for this," Declan replied. "I'll contact you and tell you where to pick it up, today or tomorrow." He decided to keep things vague. No point in alerting the man that the drop would be in the Europa itself. No point giving him two opportunities to see who he was.

"Okay," Grigorii responded. "I'll be right here in the hotel, waiting for your call." He waited for the caller to offer him something more, tried to keep the conversation going when nothing came. "What about the actual handover of the pistols and ammo?"

"You'll need a car for that," the man told him. "It will be outside of the city, so I suggest you get something with a good satnav. I guess you don't know your way around here too well?"

"I manage okay, but I'll take your advice. A car with satnav," he repeated the suggestion. "Will it be far from the city, or just outside maybe?" He was probing, hoping for any sort of a hint that might make things easier for Alex to set-up some back-up for him.

"It might be, and it might not," was all that the man offered.

Grigorii was getting nowhere here, tried thinking of something else to keep the man talking, hoping that he would say something that he didn't plan to. "Was that your crowd that got the minister the other day? That bomb down by their parliament?" It was worth a try. Perhaps it would open the caller up a little, maybe he'd become boastful.

"It was," was the sum total of the answer. Then silence again.

"It was a well-planned hit," the Russian offered. He was clutching at straws now, running out of things to say. "I doubt if I could have done any better myself."

The man at the other end of the phone said nothing, ignoring the comment. For a second Grigorii thought that he'd hung-up, the silence lasting far too long. He was about to speak himself when the man finally continued. "You'll see your money later, and I'll call again, maybe tomorrow. Today is Wednesday, the weapons swap will be Friday. Be ready."

And then he hung-up.

Declan could still feel the Russian's probing questions, could sense him digging around for extra information. He replayed the conversation in his mind, happy that he hadn't given anything away, that he had also dominated the exchange. He was calling the shots now, the Russian dancing to his tune.

He couldn't blame the man for trying to discover what the plan was. He was a man alone, Declan was a part of a team, a group of men who were clearly not worried about taking lives. Why should they not just kill the Russian, take both the guns and the money? If he was in the other man's shoes, that's what he'd be considering. It would be 'oh so easy' to double-cross him, to take him out, but it really wasn't something that Declan considered. If things went well, he would need more weapons, more bullets. He'd need the man again.

Declan also believed it wouldn't be in his interest to do anything bad towards the Russian. The man had demonstrated that he had the back-up to get the arms in a relatively short time. That meant a well organised line-up behind him, possibly with links to the Russian mafia or other powerful factions, not people that you wanted to upset.

No, Declan thought to himself. Playing it straight was the best way for all parties.

Alex called a meeting of his team, inviting Colin Shankly to also take part. They had little new, except that the handover would be the coming Friday, and that it looked as if it would not be happening in the city itself.

"It'll be the border area, just has to be," the policeman said. "I just wish I could be a little more specific."

"The man's playing it very close to his chest, and who would blame him," Alex responded. "That means that we need to be as mobile as possible. I'll talk to Mike Sanders and get us some Heli support, maybe we move out of the city today or tomorrow and stay out at Aldergrove. The aircraft could operate from there, and we'd be clear of city traffic, avoid delays."

"I can give you a police chopper if it's easier," Shankly offered.

"The SAS ones are in civvy colours, so we can be a little more subtle with them," Smithy butted in. "But maybe we could use one of your covert cop cars. You know, the ones with the lights hidden under the grill, then we can go high-speed if needed, but blend in if not."

"Perhaps two cars Colin," Alex added. "Just as a back-up."

"I'll sort that out," the Chief said, noting it down. "I can also have men on standby, just in case you need them for anything." He smoothed his moustache. "You know how these things go; always some sort of a surprise."

"Agreed," Alex said. "I think that's about it for now Colin. I'll get on to Hereford, and you can sort out your people. I'll keep you briefed."

He was about to get up when another thought struck him. It was a thought that he would keep to himself for now, but it was something that could be a game changer on the day. Something that hadn't been used yet in anger.

"I have a small boat on Carlingford Lough," the old man was telling him on the phone. "Again funded by those lovely Americans back in the day." The man loved drama, painting a picture, drawing out a moment. "You can have the use of it if it might help with any of your plans."

Declan considered this, thinking again about how to safely complete the arms handover, whether the boat could fit into any part of his planning. "Thanks Sean, that would be great, but I don't have any experience on the water. Never used a boat."

"I'm always willing to help Declan," the older man replied. "No walking for me on the boat, so no disability. I'd be as good as the next man. Just keep it in mind."

It was a possibility, Declan thought. Something different, unexpected. A safety net.

"Let me think about it Sean," he responded. "It could be a really great idea."

"Just call if I can help," the older man replied. "With anything."

13th May 2027

Joint Helicopter Command, Aldergrove, Northern Ireland

The Dauphin 2 helicopter floated noisily just above the runway of Belfast International Airport, hover-taxiing towards Lough Neagh and the southside of the complex, a place where the RAF had set-up a base in the early years of the twentieth century. In the early two thousands it had changed its title to the Joint Helicopter Command, encompassing helicopter operations from all three of the UK's military services, and providing close air support for the PSNI. Manning was presently down to minimum figures, with talk once again turning towards a total closedown of the place. Defence cuts never seemed to go out of fashion, at least not during peaceful times.

Alex watched the helicopter from the comfort of a fairly rudimentary office, a warm cup of coffee cupped in his hands to fight off the poor heating system. He wondered whether any maintenance had been done on the boiler in the last few years. He somehow doubted it.

His team slouched around on camp-beds, the other offices now commandeered for their use, outside of the city and ready to react to whatever Friday brought their way. Daisy got up and strolled over to Alex's window, just in time to see the Dauphin put down about fifty yards away.

"Let's see if we got everything we asked for, hey?" he said. Both knew that this was rare, and that more than often you received a few 'surprises'. Sometimes the 'surprises' were better than the initial request, so neither were counting their chickens just yet.

"You guys coming out?" Alex called, knowing that they were, just seemingly giving them the power of choice. Orders were usually not required in a special forces environment, not even during times of high stress. Everyone knew what he or she had to do and just did it.

They sauntered out towards the helicopter, the blades winding down to a stop, the aircrew going through their own shutdown checks. The team stood just outside the edge of the rotor disk and waited for the pilot to look up and invite them in.

The co-pilots door popped open, a thumbs-up coming from the pilot as his crewman climbed down from the cabin.

"Welcome to Ireland," Smithy offered. "First time here?" he joked.

The flyer pulled open the rear door, showing them that the cabin was laden with equipment, most probably all for the team. "Help yourselves boys," the man said. "Anywhere we can grab a brew?"

Alex pointed towards the building that they had just left, a little below the standard usually frequented by the fly-boys he guessed. "All of the makings are in there, first room on the right as you go in. Find some space for your camp beds too; this will be your home for the next couple of days, but I suppose Mike Sanders has filled you in on that. No posh hotels this week."

He received a nod and a grin in return, and the two airmen grabbed their personal bags and headed into the hut. Alex and the rest of them moved up to the aircraft, ready to offload their gear.

Behind them, the pilot called out from the door to the offices. "By the way Alex," he yelled. "Mike also gave you what you asked for. He told me to tell you that it cost about two-hundred-thousand quid, so to try not to break it." He grinned, before adding. "He also said that this will be the first real operation that it's been deployed on, so don't get it a bad name." He turned and went off in search of the coffee.

"So we got the Jet Suit," Smithy commented. "When can we have a play?"

The SAS men had turned one of the offices into a sort of armoury-come-quartermaster store, their equipment laid out all around it on collapsible tables and benches. One table contained the Jet Suit and spare batteries, the most pricey part of their arsenal, but at present the only part that had no known use. It was a back-up, something that Alex had decided could be a joker in the pack, especially if the finale played out in the countryside. It was a possible method to move fast and relatively silently, to outsmart the enemy, to put down a man somewhere that they could never expect.

They had the four Heckler & Koch machine guns, the four pistols and the snipers rifle, and now they had additional ammo to match all of the weapons. Mike Sanders had also sent over some grenades and flash-bangs, small explosive devices that basically deafened and blinded their targets for a few minutes when used.

Two ghillie suits lay on another table, and enough camouflage clothing to keep them all going for a month.

Alex surveyed it all, wondering what he would need, what would be surplus to requirement. He heard the two aircrew talking in the next room, a TV with what sounded like Coronation Street playing in the background. He also had a helicopter at his disposal, he reminded himself. Father Christmas in the form of Mike Sanders had been kind.

His phone trilled in the next office, and he dashed through to it. Colin Shankly's name was on the screen. He pressed to receive the call, phone already at his ear.

"Tohill's on the move," the policeman told him quickly. "I can get him tailed, or we can leave this to you. Your call."

Time was of the essence and Alex had only four men. If things went wrong, fingers would point his way, towards the Regiment. "We'll put two men on him, just give me directions. If your people can follow him until we get into position." He indicated that Daisy and Jeff should prepare to move, get their basics together. "I'll give them the car, so we'll need a second one as I mentioned. Can you spare that?"

Both men knew this wasn't a time for niceties, both being highly economical with their words. Greetings and pats on the back could come later if all went well.

"I'll sort that out," Colin responded. "Just keep me in the picture." He hung up.

Alex turned his attention to the team, filling in the gaps that had opened up during the short exchange.

"It's go. Now we need a little bit of Irish luck," he told them.

They were all outside at the car now, Jeff in the driving seat, Daisy riding shotgun. Both had a 9 millimetre pistol in the door pockets of the car, and under the passenger seat were two MP5s, plus a load of spare ammunition, partially boxed, some already loaded in magazines. They were getting reports from Shankly's people putting Tohill on the road heading north from the city, up towards Portrush and Coleraine, somewhere in that direction.

"Keep in touch," Alex instructed the men, knowing that they would anyway. His phone rang again, Grigorii's name on the screen this time. "Grigorii, can I get back to you?" Alex asked, anxious to get his team out on the job.

"Alex, this is important," the Russian interrupted. "Someone has just left five thousand pounds with the reception, the down payment. I just picked it up." He sounded a little breathless, as if he'd been running. "I'm trying to get a hold of the CCTV now."

"Just a sec," Alex told him, quickly informing the two men in the car of the latest development. "Get on your way," he added. "And good luck." He put the phone back to his ear. "It's all happening Grigorii," he said to the Russian. "Let me fill the gaps for you from my side."

With the money dropped-off, Declan decided it was time to start his diversionary tactics, and that meant releasing Tohill and his man called Doherty from Derry. He didn't believe that either of the men had been compromised, but if they had then so be it; the very least it would do was tie-up police assets, but his plan for the two of them was bigger than that – they would soon be getting their first real operation for One Ireland under their belts.

Following the death of Nicholas Thomas the police had raised their protective screen for the local politicians. It was a little like locking the door after the horse had bolted Declan thought, but it was to be expected. It also ruled out taking down another political figure for a little while at least.

The north coast was once again beginning to fill with tourists, attractions such as the Giants Causeway a magnet for people exploring the country's natural wonders, the affordable golf courses popular with the British middle class, combining the sporting occasion with an excuse to have a knees-up. These people were easy targets, either out on the course with a bag of clubs, or half drunk in a bar during the evening.

These were the people that were the focus for Tohill and Doherty. It would be easy, and it would draw attention far away from where Declan and his core team planned to be the next day.

As he drove back south from Belfast he reflected on how much time all the planning and organising was now taking up. It was almost a fulltime job.

They had eyes on the man now, his green Fiesta pulled into the carpark of a small Portrush hotel. Tohill made no move to get out, making a call on his cell phone, looking around the parking area as though to find someone. Another man got out of an old Fiat parked down on the main road, his own phone stuck to his right ear. He waved when Tohill exited his own motor.

"It looks like there's two of them at least," Jeff said, stating the obvious. "But what are the two of them up to?"

"The million dollar question mate," the other man answered. "There's a carpark over there by the quayside. Maybe a better place for us to park and keep an eye on them."

They'd passed by the hotel now, a rough looking place but with good sea views, it's white paint stained to a light grey, windows in need of replacement. Jeff found a spot in the parking area that Daisy had indicated, and they reversed in to allow them to watch the two men above them. They were talking, leaning on the Fiesta, appearing to be feeling one another out, as if this was a first meeting.

"I'll take a stroll across, call in to the guesthouse," Jeff decided. "Might hear something during the pass."

He tucked his revolver in to the inside pocket of his jacket, ensuring that it was well out of sight, and got out of the car. He leant back in the doorway, putting a small earpiece in, Daisy doing the same. They completed a quick radio check, then he turned, heading across the road towards the hotel.

The two men by the Fiesta stopped their discussion as he got closer to them, a fairly sure sign that they hadn't just been exchanging pleasantries. He pretended to ignore them both, wondering how he could get a decent picture of the new man. It would be good to know who he was, what they were dealing with. Tohill was a known quantity, but the recent addition to the competition was not. Colin Shankly may be able to help with that, but first they'd need to get a photo.

Past the car and almost at the hotel entrance, he chanced a conversation with his oppo. "Can you grab a photo or two on your phone when I come back down?" he asked. "I'll go close, that should draw their attention."

The sound of the transmit button being depressed squelched in his earpiece.

Entering the hotel, he asked the receptionist about the price of a room for the night. He wasn't intending to stay, but he had to make it believable in case the two men checked up on him should they go inside. It was a simple cover, but it was always important to have one. So many operations fell to pieces because people lacked attention to detail. Small things really did make a big difference.

He keyed his radio to let Daisy know that he was on his way out. The two targets were still at the car but looked as if they were ready to move. He passed close, hoping that the picture was good.

Behind him, the two Irishmen had separated, one returning to the Fiat, Tohill moving to the hatch of the Fiesta. Both retrieved overnight bags and moved towards the hotel entrance.

It looked as if they were going to be there for the night.

"So we have half of the money for the pistols, but still no meeting point for the handover," Alex summed things up after giving Grigorii the latest rundown on where things were with the rest of the team. "I don't like it," he added.

"Me neither," the Russian replied. "They hold all of the cards. We're left to react to whatever they throw at us, and we both know that's where things can go wrong. A rushed choice, and then the game's up."

The two men were silent for a moment, both searching for a glimpse of some detail that they might have missed.

"We have what we have," Alex finally sighed. "I guess we should both get some sleep. Tomorrow could be a long day." He was standing outside of the offices, Smithy and the two pilots already unconscious.

"It could be," Grigorii agreed. "But hopefully it's also where all of this ends."

14th May 2027

Armagh, Northern Ireland

Today was the day, and to say that Declan was nervous would have been an understatement. He was awake with the very first hint of daylight, unable to get any sleep from that point on, finally giving-up and making himself a cafetiere of coffee, drinking it black in front of Sky News. After fifteen minutes he flicked off the telly, unable to concentrate on the repeated headlines from the previous night.

He considered calling Robbie Tohill up in Portrush, realising that this wouldn't be such a great idea at just before five in the morning. Let the man sleep. He'd have his own worries in the none too distant future.

He took a shower, dressed, put together another pot of coffee, running his plans once more through his head.

Tohill and Doherty would storm on to one of the greens at the Ballyreagh Golf Course at around eleven o'clock, take some pot-shots at a bunch of foreign tourists, hopefully British. The Derry man knew the area best, had selected a place near to the road, somewhere that they could park and watch, wait for a bunch with English accents and then attack. They needed to injure at least one, preferably more, then run for it. A short drive would get them on the main road towards Limavady, and then onwards to Derry itself. Countless country roads offered alternative routes, and once in Derry City they'd be lost to the authorities, with the border also close to hand if needed.

It seemed to be a simple plan, but he knew that those were the ones with the most chance of success.

The best case scenario was that the police would race resources up to the area, tie up men, cars and helicopters, chasing two phantoms of men who should be well hidden by the time they had themselves even halfway organised.

Worst case was that the two of them would be caught, and if that happened the police would still have their assets working hard in the wrong area. And as neither of the men had ever met him, had no contact information to reach him, in fact had no clue at all as to who he was, then that would also an acceptable outcome for him.

Meanwhile he'd be doing some business with a certain Russian at the other end of the Province.

Sipping slowly on the second pot of coffee, Declan believed he'd made a fool proof plan.

Grigorii wished that it was already seven o'clock, at least then he could go for some breakfast. Sitting in his room waiting for something to happen was just killing him. Sleep was now out of the question.

His phone buzzed. He glanced at the clock on the TV and noted that it was still only six in the morning. That meant it had to be Alex. He was fairly sure that the SAS man had also been sleeping on a bed of nails that night.

"You okay this morning," the Englishman asked, the sound of an airline winding up its jets somewhere in the background.

"Good morning to you too," the Russian said with a smile. "Yeah, I'm fine," he conceded.

"Couldn't sleep mate, and guessed you'd probably be the same."

"Any news from up at the coast?" Grigorii asked.

"Nothing," Alex replied. "Still no wiser as to what those two are up to. Could be nothing at all."

"Did the police get anything on the second man?"

"Sorry, I forgot to tell you. The info only came through during the night." The soldier adjusted his phone, switching hands. "Some bloke called Liam Doherty from Londonderry. Bit of a crook, a few minor convictions on record, definitely a bit of a leaning towards the Republican crowd, but nothing worse than Tohill. Could be something, could be nothing."

"We seem to be getting a lot of nothing," Grigorii answered wryly. "Sort of close, but no cigar as your people would say."

Alex exhaled noisily. "I have a feeling all of that is going to change today."

It was seven o'clock when Alex's phone next rang, the soldier wolfing down a couple of slices of toast with yet another cup of coffee.

"Alex Green," he answered formally, the display showing no caller ID.

"Morning Alex, Dominic Wild here," the PM replied. "Just thought I'd wish you and the team all the best for today. We need this thing to end, to close the chapter. It would also help with closure for the Thomas family, help with closure for us all in fact."

Alex felt a momentary burst of anger. Why was the PM putting unneeded pressure on him? There was enough in the balance without Dominic adding to it all. He took a deep breath, carefully considering his words before speaking. "We'll all do our best Prime Minister," he said, leaving it at that.

It was the PM's turn to reflect on things, suddenly aware that he had said things that were best left unsaid. "Sorry Alex, I should have thought things through before this call. My bad," he ended.

"I guess we're all under pressure right now, sir," Alex responded, already calming down.

"Some more than others," the PM replied. "And some definitely with a different stress to others. You're at the sharp end, I'm sat here in number ten."

"I think I know where I'd prefer to be," Alex answered. "And it's not where you are. Horses for courses as they say."

He heard Dominic sigh, wondered what other dreadful business was passing over his desk right now, how he'd actually found the time to give some squaddie a phone call at this hour of the morning. Once again he marvelled at his country's leader, the man's seemingly endless infinity for work. "Keep safe son."

Alex heard that the line was still open, felt that he was expected to answer, his anger now all gone.

"The team is ready and we will give it our best shot, sir."

"I know you will Alex."

The line went dead.

He'd chosen his spot, using his own common sense added to the advice from old Sean, someone he used a lot as a point of reference nowadays. 'Why reinvent the wheel?' his father had always asked him. The old man had done it in the past and had lived to tell the tale, so what worked then had a good chance of also working now. Sean was a Godsend, even if his son was a bit of a liability.

"First off, try to think of how your enemies would look at something," Sean had advised him once. "Then look for a way to combat their thinking. And finally, look for things that they would never think of."

He'd tried to pull all of those things into the final plan, coming up with a list of things he needed to consider.

1. The place shouldn't be too close to home, but also not so far away that he couldn't get back there easily.
2. It should be away from towns and cities, away from places where the Russian could have back-up, support, whether from colleagues or the authorities.
3. It should have clear views around it, the final approach only possible on foot.
4. It should have an alternative way out.

He knew that meeting all of these criteria wouldn't be easy, but compromise was possible on certain points if necessary. He also believed that he was dealing with a man operating alone right now, having seen nothing so far to the contrary.

And up in the north would be the diversion to draw the authorities away from where the real action was happening.

He believed that he was as ready as he could be.

It was time to fix the meet.

14th May 2027

Europa Hotel, Belfast, Northern Ireland

Grigorii's phone jerked him back to wakefulness, hardly believing that he'd actually managed to doze off again. He grabbed at it, fumbling a little with the buttons, finally selecting the right one, noting that it was ten o'clock already.

"Hello," he barked, trying to hide his recent awakening.

"Morning," the distorted voice came back at him. "Have you a pen and paper? We need to fix the exchange. Now."

He scrabbled around to collect a pad and pencil off the bedside cabinet, wishing that he hadn't fallen asleep. Too many days hanging around doing little or nothing had numbed his brain, and this definitely wasn't the time for going at things half-cocked. He shook his head, then confirmed to the caller that he was ready.

"There's a place up on Carlingford Lough called Greencastle, up near the entrance of the lough, and close by to the lighthouse there. Less than a mile from the place is an old castle – actually it's called Greencastle Royal Castle, it might even feature on your car's GPS." The man paused, looking to his watch. "I'll give you two hours to be there, and before you say anything, I know that that's tight but that's your problem. Come alone, park in the village and walk over to the castle. That's where we will meet."

"Two hours," Grigorii protested. He hadn't looked at a map but knew where the lough was, knew that he needed to get out of the city, drive to Newry, then find a place that he'd never heard of until just now. It was a big ask by itself but added to that he needed to give Alex time to position himself and his team. "Is that even possible?" he tried, hoping for a change of heart, an additional hour.

"It has to be, because if you're not there by twelve o'clock then the deal is off, and you then become a target," the man threatened him. "Did you get the address? Last chance."

Grigorii reread the instructions back to the caller, confirmed that he was on his way.

The line went dead.

The rest of the team watched as Declan disconnected the call, watched him sigh a heavy breath of relief. It was finally on.

"Ready to go?" he asked the others, meeting their eyes, attempting to sound confident. Nods of agreement came back his way.

They all climbed into Sean's car, a white SUV that gave them plenty of space and like everything else the man owned, far superior to what the others could afford. Paddy drove, his father in the passenger seat, Declan and Frank in the rear.

Declan used the transit time to call Tohill, knowing that their part in the plan was also scheduled to spring into action.

PSNI wouldn't know what hit them.

Grigorii opened the hatch on the Mercedes, carefully putting the duffel bag of new pistols into it. They were all boxed, so no danger of metal-on-metal clangs alerting someone of something unusual in the cargo but being careful was just something of a conditioned reflex for him. It had kept him alive – so far.

He sat down in the car when the valet had got out, adjusted his seat and checked that his phone had connected to the sound system. He typed 'Greencastle' into the navigation system, checked on the system's map that the place it had identified was really on Carlingford Lough. In the past he'd had some bad experiences with satnav, knew of out-of-date programs taking people to places they had no wish to go to. It showed the right place, gave him a transit time of one hour fifty. He'd have to move fast.

Following the directions from the lady who was the GPS, he pressed another button and requested Alex's number.

With his right hand, he made a final check that his own pistol was ready in the door pocket, then waited for the connection to be made.

Both he and Alex would be very much up against the clock today, the thought reminding him of his tour of Hereford and the clocktower there. He hoped that the whole team would beat the clock once again. He'd learnt from others who'd failed that it was never something that you could count on.

"We'll be leaving the hotel in the next ten minutes, getting ourselves up towards the target area and seeing what we see," Robbie Tohill explained quickly. "All okay, all on time."

"Maximum disruption is what we need," Declan told the man. "Then get the feck out of the place, keep the coppers guessing. No overdoing it, and no getting caught, either of you."

Tohill shook his head, pissed off that the man even thought that he needed to say such things. "We know the score," he replied.

"Good," came the response. "Let me know when you've done it and you're on your way. Try and make it to Derry before midday."

"We'll be there."

Daisy had checked into a guesthouse close to the water, roughly a three minute walk from where the two Irishmen were staying. He and Jeff had hot-bedded all night, one of them constantly on watch from their car, ensuring that the targets stayed inside. During the two-to-four shift – when people were at their lowest ebb – he'd planted a tracking device on the Fiesta, hoping that it was the car that they would most likely use. They only had one tracker with them, so they needed a little luck now, but with the Ford being the newer vehicle of the two they hoped that they'd got it right.

His phone rang, Alex once more.

"Grigorii has a time and place now," Alex said, giving a fast update. "How are things at your end?"

"No sign yet, but we're both in the motor and ready to roll."

"We'll deploy in the next ten minutes, I'm just deciding how best to play it. I want to be there as early as possible, so it looks like the helicopter will be the plan. You may not be able to get me for a short while but I'll send a text once things are confirmed." He paused. "Good luck and stay safe," he finished.

They stopped not far outside of Newry on the Warrenpoint Road, Sean and Frank heading down to the water's edge to where a small white-and-wood cabin cruiser with the name 'Belfast Child' was anchored. Declan reckoned that it was around four metres in length, and certainly big enough to sleep a couple of people. It was really beginning to look like terrorism paid. He hoped that it would be his own turn soon.

The two old men busied themselves with the boat, preparing to leave the mooring and start their cruise down the lough towards the sea.

"Some feckin' boat," Declan stated.

"Great for fishing when I was a kid," Paddy agreed.

Declan sighed. How the other half lived, he thought. "Let's go," he ordered. "We still have to get through the centre of Warrenpoint, and I want to be the first there."

Paddy manoeuvred the car out of the parking area, following the road along the lough. It was shortly after eleven, and that meant they should be at least forty minutes ahead of the Russian. The plan was falling nicely into place.

"Don't spare the horses," he told Paddy, getting himself comfortable in the seat, closing his eyes and focussing on what was to come.

Smithy and the pilots stood around their leader in the makeshift office, all finishing lukewarm coffee, all prebriefed and now just being issued tasks by Alex. Every man knew what was happening but now with the latest information from Grigorii, they also needed to know their specific parts in the overall operation.

"We need cover and support for Grigorii, and we need it there ASAP, hopefully before the terrorists can get someone down there." Alex pointed out Greencastle on the OS map, detailed at one inch to a mile. "The castle itself is where the handover is planned to take place, and he's been told to walk there from what is barely a village, here," he used a pencil to circle the place. "It means that he walks in for the last few hundred yards or so totally exposed and in the open."

"So you want us to put you two down somewhere here?" the lead pilot asked, pointing at the map.

"Not possible," Alex swiftly responded. "These people might already be there, so we have to be careful, play it safe. My plan is to put Smithy down somewhere here. There's a lighthouse close by, so perhaps you can buzz that a couple of times, make people on the ground think we have something to do with the navigation channels, something like that."

"Only Smithy?" the pilot asked. Smithy was less surprised than the pilots. Alex wanted a couple of options, not placing all of his eggs in one basket and leaving no room for error.

"Yes, only Smithy," Alex confirmed. "He'll have his sniper rifle with him and will find a place where he can see as much of the castle as possible, routes in and out, etcetera. You'll have to suss it out on the ground mate, but we can talk once you get there."

"And your plans?" the soldier asked.

"I'll drive up, bring along all of the ammo and weapons we have left here." He looked at his watch. "I'm going to have to get on the road soonest, but I can also arrive a little after the bad guys and Grigorii. It sort of sandwiches them between the two of us, you on that side," he indicated the approximate helicopter drop-off, "and me here." Another tap on the map.

"What about Daisy and Jeff?"

"They stay on their task, but they may also need Heli-support at some stage. We'll all be in touch with one another, so we can change things around as they develop."

The three men nodded, clearly understanding that this was a very fluid situation. Flexibility would be the key.

"So let's move," said Alex, slapping his hands together. "Get your gear together and let's rock and roll!"

Alex was the first away, Smithy assisting in loading his car and even he was a little surprised with some of its contents.

It looked like it could be a highly interesting day.

14th May 2027

Portrush, Northern Ireland

"The two of them are leaving the hotel now," Jeff said softly, waking up Daisy from a restless snooze in the back of the car. Jeff wondered how a man so large could find any sort of rest in such a small space. It must be an artform, he decided to himself.

They watched as the two Irishmen walked across to their separate cars, each dropping their overnight bags on the back seats, climbing into their respective vehicles. The smaller Fiat was first to roll out of its slot, stopping at the exit to wait for the Ford to catch up. Soon the two pulled out of the carpark, turning on to the one way system and heading out of town.

The SAS men followed, keeping at least one car between them and their quarry but never letting them get more than a couple of hundred metres separation. It wasn't too hard; at almost eleven in the morning the traffic had calmed, most people at their places of work, school runs over long before.

After a few minutes travel the two target cars took a right turn, following a road that ran parallel to the coastline, the sea below looking calm and blue in the summer sunshine. They passed a junction leading up to the clubhouse of the Ballyreagh Golf Club, then the lead car slowed slightly, seeming to look for a parking place, then continuing on once more before pulling over to the kerb where there was enough space for the two vehicles to stop.

"We need a place to stop," Jeff said, eyes scanning the filled parking spots ahead of them. "I'll drop you off so you can trail them."

Daisy got out quickly, stuffing his Glock into the back of his jeans, eyes on the two men who had also left their cars about fifty metres ahead.

"I'll be with you as soon as I can," Jeff said, drawing away as an impatient driver behind him honked his horn.

Tohill and Doherty were now crossing the road towards the nearest fairway where four golfers were deciding who was the next to play their shot. The course wasn't busy, the men taking their time, having a bit of a joke at one another's expense. Their voices carried with the onshore breeze, drifting towards the road, just about audible to Daisy. It sounded very much like a bunch of cockneys, larking around, enjoying some occasion or another without their wives in tow. One of them lay down on the grass, pretending to use his club as a snooker cue, getting a belly laugh from the others.

Daisy smiled to himself but puzzled over why the two suspected terrorists were watching the tourists, both of them making steady progress towards the golfers. Something just wasn't right...

Suddenly, the man called Doherty reached behind his back, his hand emerging with the unmistakable shape of a weapon. The SAS man shifted his attention towards Tohill, saw that he was also removing a gun from its hiding place inside his jacket.

"Shit!" Daisy exclaimed, his own revolver already in his hand, sprinting towards the two targets, already aware that he was possibly too late.

CRACK. A report smashed out, much louder than the voices of the cockney jokers, the wind and the traffic, turning the golf course from a sports venue into a killing ground.

The joker on the ground was now curled-up in a ball, in obvious pain and screaming obscenities, blood visible on the side of his chest, the joke long over. The other three golfers froze where they stood, trying to make some sense of what they were seeing, at first unable to react to it, not really knowing how to.

Another loud metallic report as another round was fired, the Englishman closest to Tohill staggering slightly and then falling, collapsing in a heap on the ground. Not moving.

Daisy was still about thirty-five metres away but knew that he had to engage the terrorists before there was no-one left for him to defend. He was too far off but needed to do something. He dropped into a half crouch, arms locked in front of him, weapon in both hands for stability, squeezed the trigger. The round missed the target but attracted the attention of Doherty, who turned and returned fire. Behind him Tohill took another shot at the golfers, one of them now turning to run, at last out of the trance that he'd been caught-up in. The Belfast man tracked him briefly, fired again, two shots this time, the golfer thrown to the ground with a squeal, blood streaming from a wound to his right arm.

Daisy fired again, feeling a change in the air pressure as a bullet zipped by close to his left ear. 'Can't miss this one' he told himself, double tapping this time, two rounds in quick succession. The man from Derry went down, one of the rounds hitting him in the right shoulder. He still attempted to return fire with his left hand, but the accuracy was gone.

Tohill glanced around, only then realising that he was also under attack. He briefly considered joining Doherty in the gunfight with the stranger but on seeing the Derry man go down decided that it was time to get out of the place and ran for his car, all the way firing unaimed shots towards his attacker.

Daisy returned fire towards both targets, paused to change magazines, looking around quickly to see where Jeff was with the car. Two guns would have been much better than one, but at present he was alone and receiving rounds from both of the gunmen. He turned his focus to the closest one, the man already wounded, and put another two bullets his way, the man collapsing on to his back, no longer moving. He shifted his aim back towards the running man, discovering that he'd already reached his car, fumbling with the door but too far off for any sort of accurate shot. He pumped off a couple of rounds in that direction, anyway, hoping for divine intervention.

"Where the fuck is Jeff," he swore to himself. The bastard was going to get away, and there was nothing he could do about it. He stood-up, started running for the road.

He watched as the green Fiesta screeched out of the parking space, clipping the wing mirror of another parked vehicle, racing up the road, engine over-revving. He turned away, realising it was lost and walked back across to the fallen terrorist, poked him with his foot. The man was dead, nothing he could do for him. He'd got what he deserved.

Moving over towards the fallen tourists, he withdrew his phone and dialled 999. At least two of them would need medical assistance, blood flowing from bullet wounds. One appeared to be fine, just in shock, the other one, well... What a mess. He just hoped that the ambulances would be quick.

"Where the fuck are you Jeff," he muttered moving again towards the road just as Jeff appeared from around the corner, slamming to a stop, pushing the passenger door open for him.

"Sorry mate, there was just nowhere to park," he said, embarrassment evident in his voice. "I heard the shooting, turned and got back as quickly as I could!" He knew it sounded lame, but that was really how it had panned out.

"Get turned around," Daisy instructed him impatiently, jumping into the car. "The Fiesta went off that way in a hurry. We need to get after him. Fast mate!"

"Call Alex," the senior SAS man demanded, forcing himself back into special forces mode, putting the cock-up behind him and operating like a soldier once more. He pulled away, rushing in the direction indicated. "Tell him what's going down. Ask for air support. It's probably the only way we'll catch the bastard."

"On to it," the big man replied, calmer now, phone already out. This wasn't going at all to plan. They needed back-up. And fast.

The drive south had been undertaken at breakneck speed but being in a covert police car allowed him to get away with this minor transgression. The turnoffs for Newry and Bessbrook were next up when Alex's phone trilled into life through the car sound system, dragging his attention from the road to the handset. 'Daisy'. He pressed the pick-up button on the steering wheel, immediately aware of the road and engine noise that was coming from the callers end.

"How are things with you two?" he asked before the man had a chance to speak.

Jeff came on the line, their phone obviously in handsfree mode. "We've had a few problems," he said simply. "But I think I'd better let Daisy explain the situation in more detail. He was there."

The SAS soldier quickly recounted the shootout at the golf course, at least as much of it as they were aware of. Final casualty counts would come later, but he was certain that at least the gunman from Derry was out of the game, possibly one of the tourists. The other certainty was that Tohill was still armed and on the run.

"We got lucky in a way," the man continued. "We only had one tracker with us and we stuck it on his car, so we know which way he's going, at least while he stays with the vehicle."

Alex was thinking fast about how best to react, now fairly sure that this was just a diversion from the main task, something to distract people and resources away from the weapon exchange. He turned off the motorway towards Newry, trying to organise timings in his head.

"Keep on the tail of the target car," he told them. "Our Heli will be dropping Smithy off in the next few minutes, then I'll divert him up to your location. Both of these cop cars have secure comms and I'll get us an open channel to use for communicating with the pilots. They can assist you in taking out Tohill, and I'll push on to support Grigorii."

"Roger that boss," Daisy replied. "Just to give them a heads-up, we're just turning on to the Dunhill Road from Coleraine and heading in the direction of Limavady and Derry. He's heading west, possibly to get across the border into Donegal."

It made sense, running to a place where they couldn't follow. Just like the old days, and just like Colin Shankly had expected.

"Keep with them and keep in touch. I may need to turn off the ringer soon but will keep the phone on silent vibrate at least." He tried to think of anything else that might be of help, drawing a blank. "Keep safe lads," he finished.

The Dauphin routed along the coast before cutting in towards the lough, intentionally overflying the castle at Greencastle, all three men on board watching carefully for any signs of life. Luckily, they saw none, meaning that the SAS looked to be the first on the ground but they still flew two laps of the nearby Haulbowline Lighthouse anyway, a vague attempt to throw off any suspicious onlookers. It also allowed Smithy the chance to have a swift look around and get some idea of where to set-up his observation post.

"I think if you drop me here," he told the pilot as they came close to the water's edge, a wide sandy beach looking more than safe enough to put the helicopter down on. "It must be just over half a mile to the castle, and I noticed a small group of trees about halfway there. I should be able to approach behind the cover they'll provide, take up a position in them and see what things look like once in place."

"Roger. Your choice," the co-pilot replied.

The pilot was already at just over a hundred feet, so he just slowed the chopper and lost the rest of the altitude as they came over the sand. There was a small tornado of loose grit – not doing the engines any good at all, the pilot noted – but the area was tidal, so most of the ground was hard packed. Smithy had the door open before they touched the deck, his rifle in one hand, a pack with the MP5 and some rations in the other. He leaped out, sprinted out of the disk, turning to give the pilot a thumbs-up before charging the rest of the way up the beach. He wanted to be visible for as short a time as possible.

The helicopter was already back in the air and gaining height. A few people at a nearby caravan park turned to see it thunder overhead, wondering what the blue civilian aircraft was up to. As it disappeared towards the Mountains of Mourne, so did their concerns, quickly forgetting it had ever been there.

Smithy carried on at a fast pace until he had his tree target positioned between himself and the meeting point, then steadied his progress to a brisk walk. It was still about an hour before the planned exchange, and he would be in position within ten minutes. His first objective was achieved.

Alex's phone came alive again, this time Grigorii.

"I've just left Warrenpoint, so about eight to ten miles out. The roads are a bit tight down here, but I should be in position about ten minutes early," the Russian explained. "Where are you now?"

"Probably ten minutes behind you," Alex answered. "Just arriving in Warrenpoint, so if the traffic's good, I'll be there on time, perhaps even a little early."

"Any other news?"

Alex explained about the shooting close to Portrush, the death toll now confirmed as just the gunman, although one of the golfers was still critical. "Jeff and Daisy are still tailing Tohill, but he's now taken to the backroads. Not the best conditions for following someone just using a tracking device. I've tasked the Heli to get up there in support, so hopefully they can cut him off before he gets to the border."

"So it's just the two of us?" Grigorii asked, concern apparent in his voice.

"No," Alex came back quickly. "Smithy's already out on the ground, in some sort of a copse about three to four hundred metres from the castle. Easy shot for a man like him. He'll have you covered."

"I'm sure he will," Grigorii answered, sounding a little more confident now. "I'll call once I get there, let you know the lay of the land."

"Roger that. Just be careful."

The Dauphin helicopter charged westwards across the Province, trying to get to Londonderry before the fugitive did, somehow hoping to help coordinate the two SAS men and the local police in cutting off his escape to the south. With a top speed of almost two hundred miles per hour and only a slight headwind, the navigation system predicted slightly less than half an hour's transit time. It looked like it would be touch and go.

The pilot was concentrating on squeezing out all of the power he could from the machine, the co-pilot dialling in the frequency of the troops on the ground.

"Where are you boys now?" he asked when ready. "And what's your latest position on the target?"

"He's come off the main road just before Limavady," Daisy responded. "I can only guess that he's avoiding it as a major town, having a police station and therefore a possible place for roadblocks, but it's just a guess."

"Makes sense," the airman answered. "Are you close to him?"

"Just over a mile behind by our reckoning, but you know these trackers can have delays, so it could be a little bit more than that. Where are you? When can we expect you here?"

"We're twenty minutes out."

"Shit! If he hadn't come of the main drag that would probably have been too late, so thank God that he's playing cautious."

There was a silence for a few seconds, then the pilot came on air. "I'm pointing the plane directly to Londonderry as the closest point. Should be there within twenty and can then come out your way in a sort of ground/air pincer movement. How does that sound?"

It was the best chance they all had.

Paddy stopped the car at the outer border of the tiny settlement of Greencastle, the place consisting of just a couple of houses and farms, a lot of rundown farm outbuildings full of rusting machinery, and a nearby ferry terminal that linked Greenore in County Louth to the North. A short walk away was the square grey stonework of the 13th century castle, their goal. It was all a bit of a let-down considering what they were there to do, or at least Paddy thought so.

For Declan it looked just as he'd hoped – an unmistakable landmark in a pretty much deserted wasteland. The perfect place to exchange some cash for some guns. And set directly on the water, with its own pier, it also offered them an emergency route out if that's what they needed. It covered all of his bases.

He got out of the car, stretched, and looked around again for anything that looked out of place. He saw nothing, felt comfortable.

"Come on then Paddy," he said as the boy climbed out of his side of the car. "Let's go and man the ramparts."

The boy gave him an odd look, put his pistol in his jacket pocket and pressed the lock button on the key fob. "Whatever you say Declan," he said frowning. "It'll be good when this is all over. Too much like work to me, not really fighting for the cause, not why I joined."

"Think of it this way," his leader said. "No guns, no fighting. We need to do this."

They walked together towards the castle.

14th May 2027

Greencastle Royal Castle, County Down, Northern Ireland

It was ten minutes before midday as Grigorii pulled up along from the ferry pier in Greencastle. He'd already spotted the old fort just a five minute walk away, pondered over how many battles the place must have seen during its lifetime, but focused more on things that didn't fit in to the rural setting of the hamlet. The obvious recent addition in his mind was a clean white SUV, a Nissan if he was correct, though he didn't want to go over and examine it; if he was right, the presence of the vehicle meant that he wasn't the first man there. Others were likely watching his actions even now.

He carefully took his pistol from the door pocket, slipped it awkwardly into the back of his pants, then called Alex, giving him the latest update. "I wouldn't come all the way into the village – if you can really call it that, it's so bloody small. As soon as you enter the place, you'll be visible from the castle. It's a damned good choice of location on their part."

He took a swig of water from a bottle, followed that with an exaggerated look at his watch for the benefit of any observers, and listened to Alex on the car speaker.

"Thanks for the warning," the SAS man answered. "I'll stop just before the place, try and park-up out of sight of the castle. Are there any other vehicles, or just the Nissan?"

"I've driven the length of the place, and that seems to be the only car that feels out of place to me. There are a couple of older vehicles on driveways and outside of farm buildings, but I can't imagine these guys wanting to meet on their own doorstep. I think that the SUV has got to be their vehicle."

"Okay," Alex answered, mulling over his options. "I think you'd better put your hand in the fire and go and see them. I'll be there in a couple of minutes now and will try and make my way on foot to be as close to the castle as I can, probably to the SUV. That's their escape route, so they have to come back to it. If I'm there and you follow, we have them between two guns and should hopefully be able to overpower them."

"That depends on how many of 'them' there are of course," the Russian added wryly. "Okay, it's time, I'm going in. I'll keep the phone connected and hope that no-one picks up on it."

"Good luck."

Alex stopped the car on the far side of the hamlet they called Greencastle, a group of farm buildings between himself and the old castle. The road ran alongside the edge of the lough, Grigorii's Mercedes visible about two hundred metres away. The white SUV was still invisible to him and he considered driving closer.

'No' he thought. Going closer to the castle meant betraying his presence, possibly spooking the targets. This was the stopping point. From here it was on foot.

He looked over the water to Southern Ireland, the port of Greenore working a vessel on the far bank, large cranes swinging around, clouds of dust coming from the ship's cargo. Smaller vessels – fishing and pleasure craft he thought – were dotted around the lough, some in motion, some at anchor, totally unaware of what was going down so close to where they were all enjoying their day.

He picked up his pistol, checked that there was a round in the chamber, the magazine was full, and that the safety was on. He inserted an earpiece into his left ear, monitoring Grigorii as he climbed out of his car.

"Alex, an update," Jeff's voice came over the police radio channel they'd been designated.

He sat back in his seat again, delaying his exit from the car. "Go ahead Jeff."

"We have eyes on the Fiesta, and our Heli-support is now with us. We're about three miles from the border and just outside of Derry. We're going to try and stop Tohill soon, working on a roadblock with the locals," the man told him. "By the way, we couldn't reach you on the phone."

"I have Grigorii on the phone, just in a listening mode. He's heading for the castle and I need to get into a supporting position now. For a while I'll be out of contact, but as soon as things happen here I'll clear the line. Probably no more than ten minutes."

"Okay, understood. We'll be fine. I mean it's just one man, two of us, the local police and the chopper. Your focus must be on Grigorii."

Alex turned off the police radio and got out of the car, looking to find a route that would get him close to the Russian's car without becoming visible to the people in the castle.

Robbie Tohill sensed that something was badly amiss. The car behind him had been there for some time now, following him along some narrow country roads that would normally only be used by locals, turning into other lanes exactly when he did. He could also hear helicopter activity somewhere close by, low level he guessed, never getting a sighting of the machine, but very aware that it was out there.

He felt hunted. Nervous. His natural instinct was to run for the border, get into Donegal and the safety of the South, away from the jurisdiction of the Northern Irish police. He knew that he was close now. It was time to run for it.

He slowed slightly for a righthand bend, looking in the rear-view mirror and no longer seeing the suspect tail, the road behind him now clear. Perhaps he'd been imagining things. It was normal to be suspicious, tense even, after an operation. It could all have been nothing.

He straightened-up after the corner, decided to hit the gas and rush for the safety of the South.

That's when the flashing lights appeared around half a mile ahead of him.

With the roadblock coming up fast, Jeff and Daisy had backed off, not wanting to scare Tohill into finding a turnoff somewhere before he got to the police. The helicopter crew were coordinating things between the local coppers and the SAS men, letting the soldiers know that they were only about a minute behind once the Fiesta was brought to a stop.

"The target is slowing, he's seen the roadblock," the aircrew suddenly reported. "The police turned on their lights a bit too early in my view, but that's what we have."

Daisy studied the GPS map in the vehicle, looking for junctions that could ruin the trap, allow the car to escape. He saw none, told Jeff to slow down a little more, wait to see Tohill's reaction to the situation.

"The car's turning," the helicopter reported. "He's going to be coming back your way shortly."

The SAS man again looked at the map, again checking that there were no roads between them and the target. Again nothing. "Block the road Jeff."

Robbie was now certain that he was trapped, that something was going down. A roadblock, a tail car, a helicopter – it couldn't all be just coincidences.

He turned the vehicle, making the decision to run from the police. But first he had to warn the anonymous man that led One Ireland. Maybe he could help, maybe it would stop him and his team also getting lifted.

He had to try.

They watched as the stranger walked slowly towards the castle, a bag over his shoulder, no doubt the pistols. Nothing else moved in the small hamlet, as if everyone had gone home for lunch, no-one working, a midday siesta. The man was alone, as directed. It looked like the exchange would go to plan.

Declan's phoned buzzed, and he frowned as he saw the caller ID. Tohill. 'Not now' he thought but took the call anyway. You just never knew.

"We've been set-up!" the man screamed in his ear. "I've got a police roadblock up ahead, and I think I've been followed for the last few miles." Declan could hear the blind panic in the man's voice, knew that things must be bad. "There's also a helicopter buzzing around somewhere close by. It's all a pile of shit!"

"Calm down," Declan said softly, knowing that it wouldn't help matters but feeling that he had to say something. "What will you do now?"

He could hear a car engine revving, gear changes, then Robbie was back on. "I've turned away from the roadblock. I'll try and outrun them, head back to Belfast and disappear for a while," he replied. Saying it made him calm down a little. He had a plan.

"Great thinking," Declan responded. "We'll be in touch. Good luck."

He cut off the call, a little panicked himself now, but knowing that he needed to focus on the problem at hand. If the authorities had been on to Tohill, were they also on to him?

"We need to get out of here," he told to Paddy, making a decision. "The police are chasing down Tohill, so they might be out for us too."

Grigorii was trying to keep his breathing normal, his heartrate down, all the time watching the turrets and windows, doors and entranceways, looking for movement that signified people being present.

Suddenly two men appeared ahead of him, both with guns drawn, balaclavas pulled down over their faces.

"Turn around!" the leader ordered loudly. "Get back to the road! We can do the business back at the car."

The Russian raised his arms, not wanting to panic the pair, one of whom seemed a little highly strung, pointing his weapon deliberately towards Grigorii's head, coming closer all the time. He turned, walked back the way he'd just come, hoping Alex was hearing the gist of the exchange. He heard one of the men close behind him now, felt the barrel of a weapon pushed into the area of his right kidney.

"Calm down please," he said softly, hoping to smooth things. "I have the guns, and I hope that you have the money. We're here to do a deal."

"Shut-up!" the man behind him ordered.

"We'll do the business back at the car," the other told him. "We need to be quick, get the job done."

The Fiesta slowed when it spotted the car parked across the lane ahead, almost totally blocking the road. There was no way out, nowhere to run.

The noise from the helicopter was getting louder, the sound now vibrating through the vehicle, and then suddenly, it's shape appeared in the rear-view mirror, only fifty yards back and barely ten feet from the ground.

"Holy shit," Tohill mumbled to himself. "The bastards have fuckin' trapped me."

He had a decision to make, and it had to be a fast one. To surrender, or to run?

He chose the latter, pressing the accelerator pedal to the metal and pointing the car at the slight gap to the left side of the vehicle ahead. It was a chance, and he would take every opportunity that was given to him. He wasn't going to jail again.

Alex was moving carefully towards Grigorii's vehicle, using the cover of farm buildings whilst at the same time trying not to attract the attention of the locals. It was a difficult compromise but he was doing his best.

He stopped in the cover of a what looked like an old bailing machine when Grigorii's phone came to life in his earpiece. He listened to the exchange, not quite catching all of the conversation, but getting most of it.

The plan had changed, and he wondered if it was down to what was happening somewhere close to Londonderry.

Declan dropped back slightly from the Russian, called Frank on the boat, asked to be handed over to Sean.

"We need to change things around a little over here," he told him, relaying the news from Derry. "Can you be close to hand just in case this is some kind of a set-up? I'm not saying it is, but better safe than sorry," he added.

"We'll be alongside in ten minutes max."

"Perfect," Declan responded. "I think we can be done by then, one way or the other." He cut off the connection, focus again on Paddy and the Russian.

"Get clear of the car!" Jeff shouted the order, the two SAS men leaping over a drystone wall that lined a farmer's field. "You take the tyres, I'll go for the driver," he added, taking to one knee and resting his Glock on the wall, both hands clasping the pistol-grip.

Daisy followed suit, the car moving at a pace now, still forty metres away but eating-up the distance between them quickly.

"Engaging target," Daisy said, and began shooting, his aim on the driver's side front tyre. It was a big ask to get a hit, the car now moving at speed. To his left he heard Jeff's weapon also firing, saw a part of the windscreen go opaque. At least one of them was getting hits, but the screen was a much larger target than the tyre.

The car was almost on them now, trying to fit through the narrow gap between their own car and the wall.

"Get down!" Jeff shouted, dropping below the lip of the stones.

They were just in time. The sound of the car crashing into their own was followed by the sound of the engine revving out of control as the righthand side of the car went airborne, performing a giant sideways roll. The left hand wing then hit the wall, amplifying the motion, throwing the whole vehicle into the air and over their heads as they hugged the earth. It hit the ground about five metres away, slid a little and then came to a halt, engine still revving, front wheels spinning wildly.

Jeff got cautiously to his feet, Daisy following, weapons raised and pointed at the vehicle's interior.

"I'll cover, you check the target," Jeff told the big man. He held his pistol in front of him in a two-handed grip, still a little shaken from the closeness of the car passing just over their heads.

Daisy moved forward slowly, also in shock, gun at the ready. There was no movement from the car, the driver's seat on the far side as he approached. He bent down, trying to see the inside of the vehicle, assessing the situation.

"I think he's dead," he called back, eyes still on the occupant.

Robbie Tohill had been thrown halfway out of the shattered windscreen, obviously not wearing his seatbelt. His head was covered in blood, cuts from the shattered glass, but the main cause of death had been a bullet to the front of the face, a large part of the back of the skull that was now facing Daisy totally missing.

"Looks like you won the shooting contest," the junior SAS man stated, the dry military humour helping to keep him calm. "He's definitely a goner."

Alex knew that he had to get forward, closer to Grigorii's car, to try to get his eyes on the white SUV that he'd been told about. The problem was, if he was seen coming forward, he may just panic the people with the Russian, igniting the whole situation and possibly costing the man his life. It was a risk that he couldn't accept at present. Right now the deal was happening, and perhaps this was as the terrorists had always planned it. If the weapons did change hands, they could follow the car and arrange police assistance to get them back. This wasn't a time for panic.

He moved forward from the bailer to an ancient tractor, tyres flat and rotten, rust eating away at the steel. He looked ahead for the next piece of cover, wondering if Smithy had visual on the three men. To check meant switching Grigorii off, calling the sniper on his cell phone. He weighed up the odds, all the while looking for the next piece of cover.

Again it came down to 'what if they left the scene with the pistols.' And again the answer was that it wasn't an insurmountable problem. The answer was again the same; follow, roadblock, capture.

He took out his cell, disconnected from the Russian, called Smithy.

'Everything has a degree of risk' he reasoned with himself. He decided that this was an acceptable one. This certainly wasn't Grigorii's first rodeo; he could handle himself.

Paddy unlocked the SUV, opening the rear hatch, half an eye and his pistol still on the arms dealer. Declan stood back, gun by his side, his eye on the water, searching for the Belfast Child. He thought that he could see her, not more than two hundred metres from the nearby jetty.

"Put them in the back there," he instructed the dealer.

Grigorii hesitated, doing what he believed would be the right kind of reaction to such a request. "I haven't seen the colour of the money yet. Why should I give you the guns?"

Declan sniggered. "You should do so because we have two guns aimed straight at you, but I guess it's a fair question." He took a large brown envelope from his inside jacket pocket, opened the flap and showed the wad of fifty pound notes within it. "The money," he said.

"Can I count it?" Grigorii asked, playing for a little more time, hoping that the SAS men would intervene sometime soon. He placed the pistols in the back of the SUV.

"No," Declan replied. "If we're to do business, then we have to show some trust for one another."

Grigorii shrugged, pretending not to care. "If you cross me, it will be the last business that we ever do," he said. "And I assume that a growing organisation like yours will be needing more assets in the future?"

Declan grunted dismissively. "There are others," he answered, trying to be just as nonchalant. To his own ear it didn't come over as very confident, but it was out, and now he couldn't alter it. "Stand back from the car. I want to see the merchandise."

The Russian took two steps back, moving a little to one side and permitting the Irishman better access. 'Where the fuck was Alex' he thought. "Can you tell this bastard to back-off a bit?" he asked as the second man prodded him in the back again with his pistol. He was starting to get pissed off with the man.

"He's just doing his job," Declan said. He was actually quite pleased that the Russian was losing it a little. The man was far too smug.

Smithy took the call on the second ring, first confirming to himself that it was Alex. He had shifted his position away from the trees, now following a ditch to get a better view of the three men standing at the rear of the white car.

"Do you have visual on the target?" Alex asked, skipping preliminaries.

"I do, but not a great shot really. It's just bad luck but the way that they've parked means that the back of the vehicle is away from me, and that's where the three of them are right now. Do you see them?"

"Negative," Alex said. "Do things look okay?"

"I'd say that they are in the middle of the exchange. Nothing untoward that I can see though."

"I have no cover between myself and Grigorii's car. I'm worried that they might freak out if I start closing on them." Alex glanced out from behind the tractor, saw a rusted trailer ahead, ducked down and moved behind it. "Can you get a shot in if it's needed?"

"Once they go to get in the car, I can possibly hit the driver's side door at least. That would stop the car at any rate. It might also give you time to get up to the car, assist if needed."

Alex nodded to himself. He'd worked with Smithy in Africa, knew just how reliable the man was. "Let's stick with that plan for now. Keep on the phone."

"No problem boss, I've got an earpiece in. My eyes are on the optics and the rifle's ready to rock and roll."

Declan counted the boxes, chose one at random and opened it. Inside was a brand new Grach handgun, still in the maker's wrapping. You could smell the newness of it. He allowed himself a grin. Boxes of ammo filled the base of the bag.

"I won't open them all," he said. "But it looks like we have a deal."

He threw the envelope on the ground close to the Russian, causing him to bend and collect it.

"Pick it up and then back-up to your car," he ordered. "Once you get halfway, we're going to mount up and leave here. Do not follow us. Wait thirty minutes, then you can get back to Belfast."

"Jesus, you guys are really amateur," Grigorii replied, getting another poke in the back from his new found friend. "You should back-off mate," he said turning on the man.

"Just do as my boss says, otherwise I'll drill you the same way I've done with the bloody politicians," Paddy snapped, anger in the words. He was fed-up with being treated as some sort of dickhead, especially after what they'd achieved only days before. His father's praise still rang in his ears, and he knew that he didn't warrant the treatment that he was getting.

Grigorii gave him a wry smile, turning back to the boss man. "You should really teach your people manners."

Declan was also getting annoyed now. Things had actually gone so smoothly, but now the Russian seemed to be deliberately picking a fight. He sucked in his pride, controlled the red mist. "Just back-off and follow my instructions, then we can laugh at all of this in the morning. We'll have our guns, you'll have your cash." He hoped that this would end it, closed the hatch and started to move towards the passengers door. "Maybe there's a next time, but not if you piss me off anymore."

The Russian was pacing backwards away from the SUV, eyes on Paddy who had moved slightly to his own side of the vehicle. Where was Alex? "Maybe I won't agree to more business if you insist on bringing total lunatics along with you."

Something in Paddy snapped – Declan had always worried about his sanity – and he shouted an oath and brought his pistol up into the aim. He loosed off a shot, the Russian diving to the ground, rolling away. Another bullet followed the first, then he fired off the rest of the magazine, all the while backing towards the driver's door.

The Russian curled into a ball, blood pouring from a shoulder wound, then lay perfectly still.

"That'll feckin' teach ya who's feckin' boss!" Paddy yelled, pulling open the driver's door.

Alex heard the shots, broke cover, running towards the sound. Smithy's voice came through the earpiece, urgent but controlled. "Keep back boss," he warned. "I'm going to engage a target. I have one visual."

The SAS sergeant kept advancing, seeing Grigorii on the deck, not moving. He still couldn't see the SUV, certain that it couldn't be far, moving steadily forward, slightly crouched, his Glock leading the way. He heard the crack of the sniper rifle just as he finally reached a position from where he could see the white car, saw the screen shatter, heard a second shot ring out.

"I'm moving in Smithy," he yelled. "Grigorii's down!"

The passenger door of the SUV swung wide open, another figure running from it towards the water. It was only then that Alex noticed the boat swinging in to the jetty, the fleeing man heading straight for it.

"Shit!" Alex swore. He needed the helicopter, knew that it was somewhere up by Londonderry, not available for probably an hour. "Can you see the boat Smithy?" he asked, already knowing the answer. If the sniper couldn't get a line on the passenger's side of the SUV, then the vessel would definitely be in dead ground. And Alex still had about a hundred and fifty metres to go before he was anywhere near the car.

"No boss."

"Don't fire, I'm moving forward," he ordered. "Come in to the SUV and let's see what we can do."

He ran quickly forward, seeing the fleeing terrorist leap on to the still moving boat, watching as the skipper pointed the craft away from the quay, gunning the engines. He reached the Russian, the boat already about a hundred metres offshore, well out of pistol range. They had got away. His focus now needed to be on the man in the car and his fallen Russian colleague. Perhaps Smithy could do something when he arrived with the rifle.

He knelt down beside Grigorii, pleased to see that he was still breathing unaided. His left shoulder was soaked in blood, as was his left calf. Apart from that, he appeared to have gotten off lightly – Alex had counted thirteen rounds fired in his direction.

He looked back towards the lough, watching the small ship running for the opposite shore. Southern Ireland.

Taking out his cell phone, he disconnected Smithy and called for an ambulance. As he spoke, the Russian stirred, saying something unintelligible in his native tongue. He'd survive.

14th May 2027

Greencastle, County Down. Northern Ireland

Minutes later and Smithy was also at the Russian's side, a little out of breath from the run through the fields. He had his small backpack and the Accuracy International sniper rifle with him and before doing anything else had checked that his earlier target was truly out of the game. It was something that Alex chastised himself for not doing – his focus had been a hundred percent on the Russian, trusting his colleagues shooting to neutralise the threat. If his trust had been misplaced, then he'd probably been dead by now.

He looked again at the fleeing boat, making a decision.

"I've already called an ambulance Smithy but please do what you can to help Grigorii," he told the other man. "Do you think you could hit anyone on that boat out there?" he asked, almost as an afterthought.

The sniper looked out to the vessel, made a swift judgement. "Easy, but look behind it Alex," he replied. "Any mistake and we could end up shooting innocent people in the port over there. The bullet would travel much further than to the boat."

Alex looked. It was a fact, and the port was where the boat appeared to be headed, a straight run to Eire. The risk of collateral damage was too great, no matter how good a shot Smithy was. His options were running out, the decision that he had to make almost forced upon him. There was no other way.

"Look after Grigorii. I have to get my car."

The mood on the Belfast Child was sombre, Sean steering the craft and looking bleakly to his front, speechless. Though it couldn't be confirmed, it looked like his only son was dead, and all for a few guns. He felt like crying for the boy, though another part of him wanted to turn the vessel around and fight back. From the description that Declan had provided on how things had panned out, Paddy had been shot by a sniper. Returning to the scene would only mean more opportunities for the same gunman to kill more of them. Revenge would need to wait.

Declan stared out over the stern, now certain that he'd been set-up. It was a sobering thought; until now he had believed that he was controlling events, setting the stage. Now it seemed that someone else was, effectively dismantling his small band of freedom fighters.

He looked at Frank, once again acting like an old man, the vigour that he'd shown in the last days all gone. The game looked to be over, and all that they could do now was run away to the South, lick their wounds.

With no warning, he suddenly let out a loud roar, his frustrations pouring out towards the bastards that stood on the far shore. He'd be back. They would pay.

Frank and Sean looked at him as if he was mad. Sean considered pushing him overboard into the lough. He was the cause of Paddy's death, the man who'd made the plan. His mind drifted back to the old days of the Troubles, memories of other schemes that had gone wrong, operations that he had planned and led. Those thoughts saved Declan's life.

Smithy had taken two wound dressings from his pack, applied pressure to the hole in Grigorii's shoulder. The leg injury was just a gash, a flesh wound from a bullet that had almost missed. The Russian had been fairly lucky but had lost a lot of blood from the shoulder, enough to cause his body to partially shut down. Stopping that blood would save his life, but the SAS soldier still wished that he had the facility to administer a saline drip, something he didn't have with him. Fluids in for fluids out was what the docs always told him.

Somewhere not too far off he could hear the moan of a siren, the ambulance he hoped.

He glanced at the boat, still able to make out the escaping terrorists. Fifteen minutes from now they would all be in Southern Ireland, safe from the British authorities and able to regroup, plan, and kill again. The thought made him sick, caused him to look at his rifle, consider the shot, risks and all.

Alex's car came around the corner, racing towards where he was working on the Russian, braking too hard. His comrade jumped out, leaving the engine running, in a big hurry to do something.

"Let it go Alex," Smithy said. "At least we're all alive to fight another day." He pointed to Grigorii. "Even he'll be fine."

Alex was at the boot of the car, still all go, still preparing something. "Give me a hand mate," he said. "The ambulance will be here in a minute or two and like you said, Grigorii's going to be okay. We have one more chance to get those bastards out there." He pointed towards the boat, then continued removing items from the back of the car.

Smithy moved to the vehicle, suddenly realising what his leader was planning to do. "You can't be serious Alex," he said. "Nobody's ever tried this."

Alex grinned, not a pretty sight, more of a grimace really. "Somebody has to one day, and there's no time like the present, as they say." He took the main jet from the boot, shrugged it onto his back. "Give me a hand to strap this on," he ordered.

Smithy shook his head but moved behind his friend and helped to adjust the fittings. They moved on to the smaller double turbines for the left arm and finally to the two for the right. More straps, more adjustments, and then the hand grips were at the optimum position for the SAS sergeant.

"There's a fresh battery pack in the boot Smithy," Alex said, shrugging his body in to the Jet Suit, trying to get it as comfortable as possible. "I'd like to have a fully charged one to try this out. It'll give me about thirty minutes, way more than I should need."

"You're fucking mad," the sniper said softly, half a grin now on his face.

"I know mate," Alex replied. "But you know that I hate losing."

"'Who Dares Wins'", Smithy replied. "Talk about living up to our motto."

Declan knew that he had to be the first to speak, to break the silent stand-off between Sean and himself. One of them had to be the big man, to have the balls to apologise. What had happened back onshore was something that neither of them could have foreseen; he'd even gone over all of the planning with the older man, allowing him to add his own experience to the final strategy. They both owned the final plan, even if he was the leader.

He turned away from the view of the shore, walked forward to the control console.

"I'm sorry about Paddy, Sean." He looked the older man in the eye, trying to gauge what was happening in his head. "It shouldn't have happened, I should have suspected something sooner, as soon as Robbie Tohill told me about the problems that he was having. Sorry," he repeated.

The old man understood how hard it must have been for Declan to say those few words, to take ownership for the failure of the operation. He tried to speak himself, tripped over his words, tears close.

"I'm so sorry," Declan said again and the old man grabbed him, hugging him close.

"It happens to all of us lad," Sean whispered in the younger man's ear. "It doesn't make it easier, but it's a fine line that we walk, and sometimes it can go horribly wrong." He felt a tear roll down his cheek, unable to keep it in check any longer. "We'll get even," he finally forced out.

"We'll get even," Declan agreed. "I'll see to that."

The two of them turned to face forward, Greenore ahead, an invitation for them to escape and regroup.

Alex was discovering the tactical disadvantages of the Jet Suit before he'd even got off the ground, the most obvious one being that he had no hands free to hold a weapon, not even one as simple as a pistol. It was a problem, but one he just had to live with. The plan would be to land on the boat, then engage with the Heckler & Koch machine pistol that he'd slung around his neck. He'd have to be fast, to shoot before getting shot. It wasn't great, but it was the only solution he could think of.

His jacket pockets also contained his pistol in the righthand waist-side pocket, and two hand grenades in the left. More was simply not possible, the straps and equipment of the Jet Suit getting in the way.

He was nervous; he'd only had the one true flight around the parade ground in Hereford, and added to this, no-one had ever tried out the equipment in a real battlefield scenario. To make matters worse, he was going to do it over water, no safety net.

Smithy stood back a little, everything he could do to help already done. It was all about Alex now, whichever way things went.

Alex took a deep breath, pushed the button, and the turbines spooled up, running to flight speed. He looked out over the lough, aware that the small boat was already about halfway across. It was now or never.

Nodding to Smithy, he started applying power, going light and then lifting off the ground. He moved his arm positions, adjusting the hover, testing the equipment and getting a feel for it once again.

It was time.

He altered his stance, leaning slightly forward, running down towards the beach. A little more height, more speed, and then he was out over the water, his nerves on edge, confidence in what he'd decided to try now waning. What if he crashed into the lough? Could he swim with all of this kit on, or could he get it off? Questions he just hadn't considered until now flooded his mind.

With no helmet, no ear defenders or a headset, it felt as if he was doing about a thousand miles an hour, pelting his way out towards the middle of Carlingford Lough. The parade ground test flight had been relatively slow, buildings restricting faster progress. Now there was nothing between him and Southern Ireland, just a small boat in the middle of a very big pond, a boat he somehow had to land on.

It was a daunting and scary thought.

All eyes were now on the shore of Eire, less than ten minutes sailing away. That was freedom, that was safety. Behind them was now only danger and dead men.

Sean adjusted the wheel, making allowances for the turning tide, the swell and the current. He planned to turn away from the main port as they got closer, to run along the coast to the smaller harbour in the village of Carlingford itself. From there they could find a car, head further south to Dublin, lay-up for a few days, get the failed mission out of their minds. It suddenly struck him that he probably wouldn't be able to return to his home – once the authorities identified his son, then the next port of call would be there. He would need to change his name, to change his life, and that wouldn't be too easy at his age.

"Frank," he said to his old friend. "If you pop into the cabin you'll find a bottle of Bush. I think we could all do with a shot right now."

The old man got up, looking exhausted, and moved forward into the sleeping area and galley at the front of the vessel. His eyes looked lifeless, like a dead fish, his spirit crushed. Sean couldn't see him doing any more of this sort of thing.

"We need to go underground for a while," he said to Declan once Frank was out of earshot. "They'll soon identify Paddy, then they'll search out the rest of us. There's no going back."

Declan nodded his agreement, also feeling beaten. "I also thought that Sean. But we have money, so we can find somewhere to hole-up and build back from there. How much do you have left from the old funds?"

"Enough lad, but I'd suggest that we shift it to another account really soon. That's something else that they'll be searching for, checking our banks, finding out what we have." He adjusted the wheel again, starting the turn to head towards Carlingford. "Shit. We have so much to do. It's start again time."

"And we'll do it," Declan answered. "We'll do it for Paddy."

Alex was closing quickly on his quarry, sat at about twenty feet above the water, the far side of the lough rushing towards him. He could see the people in the vessel, all looking forwards towards the shore, their place of salvation. He was thankful for the relative silence of the battery powered flying suit, confident that the boat's engine was generating more noise, masking his approach.

He had no clear strategy, everything had been done on the hoof, and now he tried to organise his thoughts, to come up with a real plan of attack. The turbines on his forearms meant that he couldn't direct a weapon, so the MP5 and pistol were out of the question. The only way to use his guns was to get down on the deck, switch off the suit and go into action. That all took time, and he was relatively certain that the men on the boat also had weapons, that they would also try and engage him when he landed on board.

The problem was, he could think of no other option.

He was now less than fifty metres from the target and going far too fast to land. Changing the angle of the turbines, he slowed the speed, coming up almost silently behind the small vessel. The crew were still all looking forward, the Louth coastline almost there. It could work; he could land, drop the excess baggage, and engage the enemy. He counted three men all grouped together, so one well utilised MP5 machinegun was all that it would need.

He slowed further, now running at almost the same speed as the boat, floating above the water at just over ten feet, almost like a helicopter approaching an aircraft carrier just before landing. He wished that he had a gun in his hand, some way to do the business now, not to land at all.

He could see two men by the steering column, both looking towards the shore. A third man – older he thought – sat alone to the side, a glass in his hand, not really seeming to be a part of the team.

Suddenly, the old man looked to his left, straight at Alex. The shock on his face was clear, even from where Alex hovered, his gasped words alerting the other two. The vessel immediately slewed to the right, leaving Alex out over clear water again, and the younger of the two men at the console came to the stern of the vessel, pistol in hand. Alex moved off quickly, the dynamics of the situation now very different, the element of surprise lost.

For a moment, he wondered how long he'd already been airborne, how much battery time he had left to play with. He was fairly sure that he'd been up less than ten minutes but had no way to check. All he could do was focus on the here and now.

"What the feck is that?" Frank exclaimed, not believing what his eyes were telling him. A man was floating in the air, not five metres from the back of the boat, following them.

Sean and Declan turned to see what the commotion was all about, the former throwing the boat into a tight turn, temporarily ridding them of their pursuer. Declan pulled out his gun, staggered a little at the speed of the turn, then made his way to the stern of the boat, watching the flying man. He waited as the small vessel stabilised, running a little while on the new course, then raised his gun, pointing it towards where the threat now was.

"I'll shoot the bastard down!" he told the others, firing off three fast shots, all hopelessly wide of the mark, his stance loose and unsupported, the boat also rocking slightly in the light swell.

"Move back here," Sean instructed. "You need to lean on the cabin structure, give your gun arm some support." The old man moved towards him, the wheel left unmanned. "Frank, give me your gun and take over the helm for me."

Their target was now about thirty metres off the starboard bow, running at the same speed as the vessel, but out of effective pistol range.

They waited for their opportunity, a momentary stand-off developing.

Alex moved along with the track of the vessel, keeping a good distance from it while he tried to think of a new plan. It wasn't easy. If he had a weapon in his hand, he'd feel much better about charging forward at high speed, firing at the targets. That would at least keep their heads down, stop them focussing on killing him. As it was, the only thing he could think of was piling in at top speed, trying to smash into the two men who would all the while be firing back at him.

The odds of that plan working were incredibly poor. Suicidal. He had to do better than that. And he had to do it soon. He must have been airborne at least fifteen minutes now, and the battery life was only about thirty. Time was his enemy too.

It was an odd stalemate situation, but it had to end quickly.

An idea flashed through his brain, not one that he relished, but the only one that came to mind.

"Steer towards that harbour wall over there Frank." Sean said pointing forwards. "That's Carlingford, and that's where we'll be getting off."

"Aye Sean, I'll do that," the old man replied. "But I'll need you to do the final bit. I'm no sort of a sailor."

Declan never let his eyes stray from the flying man, wondering what he would do next. It seemed as if he was using his arms to allow the flight to actually happen, and that meant that he couldn't use them for anything else. That meant he had no gun, nothing to attack them with.

So what could he do? Tail them all the way to Eire? And then?

If that was all he could do, then it looked as if they would get away, he surmised. In ten minutes they would be ashore, running for Dublin and safety.

He was going to have to take a big gamble, and he was going to have to do it now. Time was running out, both on the battery life for the Jet Suit and also on the time it would take for the small boat to reach the shelter of Southern Ireland. Once there, he had no jurisdiction. He could pursue the men, he could take them down, but would he receive any official support for doing so? It was something that he didn't want to take a chance on.

He moved the jets on his arms, experimenting with what he could get away with. It was impossible to raise them to a height where he could clasp the Heckler & Koch, and even if he did that, it would mean releasing the hand grip, and that would mean totally losing control of his flight. He would have the weapon, but probably just crash into the lough, the enemy escaping. It was a no go.

The same would apply to using his pistol, though he found that he could raise a hand to the lower pocket height, probably even get the gun out of the pocket. The problem was once again the hand grip – having a weapon in his hand but having no control of the flight.

He moved his fingers over the controls. For basic flying, he needed to use his thumb and index finger, not more. That still left him three free fingers.

He had an idea.

They were only two hundred metres from the old harbour entrance, another fifty after that and they'd be ashore. Sure they'd need to find a ride to Dublin, but money talked, and they had enough of it.

"We're going to be fine," Sean said softly. "This boyo is stuck out there. He can follow us, but that's about it."

"If he comes close, we pop him," Declan agreed.

They watched the man manoeuvring around a little, still holding his place off their bow. It seemed like a game of chess, the man trying to overcome a stalemate situation, to find some way to make it checkmate. They couldn't shoot him, and he couldn't shoot them.

Suddenly the man turned, pointing straight towards them, his speed increasing and closing the gap fast.

He held a hand grenade in each hand, squeezed hard against the hand grip by his middle finger, his two outer fingers curled around the base, keeping it safe there. He was pleased that Smithy had insisted on removing the pins onshore, holding the firing mechanism in place with a strong elastic band, much easier to remove with almost no hands. His middle finger now stopped that same mechanism from slamming over and starting the countdown to the grenades exploding, something that would likely spell the end for the SAS soldier.

Alex saw the muzzle flashes as the two men tried to engage him, had no idea where the rounds were going, focussed totally on getting over the vessel as quickly as humanly possible. This was a once in a lifetime chance, it would need a lot of luck, but it was the only solution he'd been able to dream up given the present circumstances. It was now or never.

The boat was almost there, his height was only about ten foot above the water, and it was time to do it.

He released both grenades, watched them fall away, and then the boat was behind him.

Declan had fired off his whole magazine, Sean was still shooting. The man came so quickly, the rocking motion of the boat not helping their cause, neither man hitting his target. Shooting a man in his bed was so much easier than shooting at a moving mass from an unstable platform.

Something solid hit the deck of the Belfast Child and the man was gone, gaining height as he swept over the port bow. They turned, Sean firing off a couple more rounds before his pistol gave a metallic click as the magazine emptied, the slide locked back. Neither looked to see what had hit the deck of the boat, both still following the flying man.

"What the feck is that?" Frank asked from his place at the wheel. He stared at the small explosive device now rolling towards him, the other caught up in a coiled rope.

The two turned to see what the old man was talking about, just in time to catch the full force of the exploding grenade.

Alex watched as the boat caught alight, the flames small at first but getting bigger quickly. He guessed that he'd got lucky, that the diesel tank had caught, or that fuel or oil must have been stored somewhere on deck. Either way, the result was better than he'd dared to hope for.

One man had jumped over the side, the other two he assumed dead, either from the explosions or the flames.

It was time to get back to the North while he still could.

Smithy watched all of the action through the scope of his rifle, seeing the boat burning just when it seemed that it would get away. He gave a silent cheer for his comrade, then turned back to watch the medics loading Grigorii into the waiting ambulance.

"He got them," he yelled back towards the Russian. The man managed a weak thumbs-up, already on a drip and strapped in.

'He'll be fine' Smithy thought to himself.

He walked over to the water's edge, watching the speck that was Alex coming back towards him.

It seemed like he was going to make it, but nothing ever went totally to plan, and this was going to be no exception.

First, the main turbine failed, winding down and stopping. He tried to stay airborne with the two on each forearm, slowing right down and trying to somehow make it to the shore, but then the battery totally failed, and he was falling into the cold dark waters of Carlingford Lough.

That's when panic really set in.

Alex was a strong swimmer, but the weight of the Jet Suit, a machine gun, a pistol and all of his clothing dragged him under. At first he fought against it, tried to swim to the surface, but he was just wasting his energy. He instructed himself to stay calm, not to fight with the water itself, to focus on getting the redundant equipment removed from his body.

The arm turbines came first, the straps easiest to remove. He hit the bottom of the lough, guessed that he was around ten metres underwater, feet deep in sticky mud, his lungs already screaming for oxygen. With his arms now free, he focussed on the main jet, undoing straps and clips, freeing it from the sling of the MP5 machine pistol, ditching all of it into the murky water.

He struck out for the surface, desperate for air, cold, looking upwards to where he could see an opaque light.

Out of nowhere, a hand grabbed him, hauling him upwards, then bursting through the surface of the water, gasping in air.

"You are fucking mad," Smithy yelled at him, helping to keep him afloat.

Alex fought to slow his breathing, trying to get his heartrate under control, treading water as he did so. "Let's get out of here," he finally replied. "I've had enough fun for one day."

When they finally reached the shallows and waded out of the cold water of the lough, Smithy began laughing to himself.

"What's so funny?" Alex asked, wondering what a sight the two of them must look right now.

"I was just thinking about how you're going to explain all of this to the boss," Smithy answered, still laughing. "Quite an expensive day out you could say."

Alex frowned, then also grinned at the thought. "Yeah," he agreed. "I just left two hundred grand of taxpayers cash on the bottom of an Irish lake." He stopped, looking back to where they'd just come from. "Might take a bit of explaining."

"Especially if it's in Southern Irish waters," Smithy added. "An international incident."

16th May 2027

Stirling Lines, Hereford, UK

Alex reflected quietly on the last few days, at the hellish speed that things had moved at.

Smithy had driven them back to Aldergrove, Alex making calls to all the necessary parties as they drove. First he'd spoken to the aircrew, the helicopter on its way back to base, with it Daisy and Jeff, their car no longer safe to drive after the collision out by Londonderry. They'd all be meeting up in about an hour or two, compare notes and hopefully get out of the Province soon.

His second call had been to the boss, Mike Sanders. He talked him through how the operation had panned out, no details, just the salient points – they'd got most of the terrorists, they'd lost no-one from the team, though Grigorii had been injured. He had no update on the Russian's condition. That would be his next call.

He made the decision not to tell the boss quite how the chase had ended yet. Losing the Jet Suit would be better explained face-to-face, possibly over a beer. It would come out anyway, just not on the phone so soon after his splash in the lake.

He noticed Smithy glancing across at him as he ended the call.

"Not ready to give him the bad news yet?" he'd asked with a cheeky grin.

His next call had been to Colin Shankly, and it had been worth it, learning that the man's opposite number on the other side of the border had been in touch. Following the explosion in Carlingford harbour, the local police had picked up a dazed and drenched old man going by the name of Frank Horan who'd climbed out of the lough. He was being transported as they spoke for a handover in Newry, the nearest border crossing point. They hoped that the man would lead them to any other players in the One Ireland group, assuming that there were any more.

As he ended that call, his phone rang once more, Mike Sanders again.

"I want all of you on the Dauphin as soon as you can," he ordered Alex. "Be best if you're all back here, then we can do a proper debrief. We'll let Colin sort out all of the details at that end."

"That's fine by me boss," Alex answered. "I think I just need to sleep for a week right now."

Back in Aldergrove, they'd packed their personal possessions in to the blue chopper – the press called it Blue Thunder, some of the boys called it the T-Bird, but Alex always stuck with the abbreviation 'Heli'. The pilots made coffees for all of them, their flight plan already filed, and within an hour of Smithy parking the car they were all tucked into the back seats and heading for home. All four of the SAS team were asleep within ten minutes of take-off, totally exhausted.

Back in Stirling Lines, they'd been met by Mike Sanders who'd told them to go to their rooms, freshen up, then meet for a debrief and review of the op in an hour. It was better to do these things ASAP, to get it over with and move on, especially when there'd been casualties.

The sleep on the flight had rejuvenated Alex a little, and back in his room the first thing he'd needed to do was to call Andile, something he hadn't found time to do for several days.

"I thought that you'd gone off me," the girl answered, no opening greetings. Her voice was upbeat, happy to hear from him, perhaps a little sassy even.

"I'm sorry," he replied, already feeling a little jaded again. "Things got a little hot at this end. I'll tell you more one day soon," he added, not wanting to go into detail right now.

"I guessed that," the African woman responded. "And Nkosi speaks a lot to the people over there, so I always have a fair idea of what's happening. You're alright though?" she asked.

"I'm fine," he said, suddenly realising that he wasn't, his body aching a little from the crash into the lake and now hellishly tired, but no need to tell her all of that. He'd get the debrief out of the way, then probably sleep for a week.

"I need to see you Alex," Andile said, serious now. "We have things that we need to talk about."

"And I want to see you," he replied. "I'm meeting with Mike Sanders in the next hour, so I'll ask about a spot of leave. I think I must be due some." It was a long flight down to South Africa, a good chance to catch-up on that lost sleep.

Andile remained silent, not the reaction that he'd expected. He waited for her to say something, finally speaking himself, worried that something was wrong. "What's up Andile?" he asked.

The girl was quiet for about another ten seconds, deciding what words to use, how best to convey the message. In the end she just kept it simple. "I'm pregnant," she said softly.

It was Alex's turn to be quiet, lost for words. They'd made love once, and now... He knew he had to respond, just didn't quite know how to. "That must be about two months," he finally said, the only thing that he could think of. "You should have told me sooner," he added.

"It's only a little over six weeks and I wanted to be sure Alex, not to start some sort of false alarm. As a doctor I have the resources to do so, to make sure." She was quiet again, thinking, preparing the next question. "Now you can see why we really have to talk," she said in a small voice "Are you happy?"

At that very moment in time, Alex wasn't sure how he felt. The news was massive and just added to the hectic and stressful last few days, his brain now in an overload situation. Luckily, he realised that that was the wrong answer, that he had to be far more diplomatic. "Right now, babe, I just wish I was with you," he told her, hoping that the words were right, acceptable at least.

"We need to be together," she said, and he could hear the tears.

Alex sighed. He was again at that crossroads, his job or the woman that he loved. "I'll call back in a few hours. We have the debrief shortly, and then I'll sort out some time off, get down to you." He paused. "Just give me a little more time Andile. I'll call you soon."

They met in what a civilian company would call the boardroom, a long wooden table with seating for up to twenty people, though today it was just the four SAS men from the Irish operation and their leader. Bottled water was available in the corner of the room, flasks of coffee and tea next to it. It was self-service.

"First things first," Mike said taking the seat at the head of the table. "The PM sends his warmest regards, congratulates you all on a task well executed." He gave a short handclap of his own, a proud leader. "He's had an initial briefing from Colin Shankly, and also a short overview from myself. He thinks that you may have saved numerous lives, nipped this new organisation right in the bud. Well done."

The men nodded their appreciation, embarrassed by the praise. This was just their job, even if it was a strange one, another day at the office as they said.

"Grigorii will be released from hospital tomorrow, and I'll organise that our fly-boys pick him up and bring him here for a few days. I think it's important that you can all spend a little time together, and the President has agreed to it with the Prime Minister. I guess we'll be doing many more ops with Russian special forces in the future," he said with a grin.

"And now, down to the details." He pulled out his tablet, fired it up. "I have your initial report Alex, so let's start there."

An hour and a half later and the talking was just about done. The mission was a total success, the only thing on the downside was that it should have been faster, perhaps saving the life of Nicholas Thomas. "That's not a criticism," Sanders told them. "The terrorists controlled the pace, not us. We pushed where we could. I've explained all of this to the PM, but I think we all know how the political mind operates. Find a mole hill and turn it into a mountain as quickly as you can." That drew some wry smiles. "They're just wired different to us, accept it," he finalised.

"Apart from that, I think we can wrap-up the meeting and let you people get away to see your loved ones, or simply to get some rest. Any other comments? Anything that you want to add?"

Smithy looked to Alex, who drew a deep breath, turned to address the colonel. "There is one thing that I sort of brushed over sir," he said. Mike knew that it was important when Alex called him 'sir', so he sat back in his chair, waiting for the disclosure. "It's about the Jet Suit sir," the sergeant added.

"Yes, I gathered from your brief that it's pretty good, but we need our boffins to sort out a way to make it more 'weapons friendly' I think is the right term."

Alex hesitated, glanced at the smiling sniper across the table. "It's presently on the bottom of Carlingford Lough sir," he said. "I sort of had a crash landing."

The three SAS men left the room, Alex asked to stay back. He conceded that two hundred thousand pounds was a lot of money but was a little surprised that he was about to be getting a lecture for losing it. They had taken out a terrorist cell, in fact a whole new terrorist organisation. Perhaps the suit could be salvaged?

He was about to say something when the colonel cut in.

"I don't care about the Jet Suit, Alex," he said, reading Alex's mind again. "We have something much more important to discuss."

"What is that sir?" Alex asked, puzzled.

"I believe that the Green family is about to grow in size," Mike said, direct to the point. "Don't look so shocked, I'm the boss, I have to know everything." He smiled at that, put out his right hand, shook Alex's. "Your girlfriend is the sister of Nkosi's partner, and I talk to Nkosi almost every week about something. Do you really think that he can keep a secret from me?"

It was Alex's turn to smile, but his expression turned back to serious within a few seconds. He was back where he had been on his return from Africa only six weeks earlier, torn between the love of his work and his love of a woman. How could he keep the Regiment happy and give Andile and their child everything that they deserved? It seemed like an impossible maths problem, no way to come up with a right answer.

"I received a request from the new South African Defence Force just this morning," Mike Sanders said, his poker face showing little emotion, giving nothing at all away. "They are looking for an officer to establish and train their new special forces wing. Our help in re-establishing their military after COVID meant that we were high on their list of possible options."

Alex considered the words for a moment, looking for the catch. He spotted it. "You said 'an officer' boss," he said now sounding a little more confident, no longer referring to the colonel as a 'sir'. "I'm just a sergeant."

Mike Sanders nodded wisely. "And you'll recall our final discussion before you shipped out to Belfast?" he enquired. "The one where I said I could see you making a good officer?"

Alex nodded, blushing.

"Well this is your chance to prove it."

Please leave a review!

I love the feeling of finishing a book, completing a tale. For me it gives both negative and positive emotions: on the one hand, I can look forward to starting the next story, to dreaming up a whole new set of characters, new scenarios, trying to make all my new ideas sound believable.

The negative part comes because once you finish the fantasy side of writing, you need to take up the technical side – corrections, tidying the manuscript, cover design, book description, etc.

That's the hard bit. Making up the yarn is the fun bit!

I hope that you enjoyed *Irish Blood*, and I hope you can find time to give me some feedback by way of a review. Your words influence the books that us writers write, so please let me know what you want to read, what you enjoyed. Good, honest opinions are worth gold!

Thanks for reading and please try the next one!

Gordon Clark

January 2021

amazon.com/author/gordonclark

Other titles by Gordon:

No Gods, Future Virus, Vigilante, Syrian Shadow, Slasher, Beat the Clock, Arab Winter, South Africa – Our Land!

NO GODS

Southern Germany, 1945

The young soldier edged through the bright green trees, careful to make as little noise as possible, to keep visual contact with his comrades to his left and right. The war had been over for two days now, but this information hadn't reached some of the Germans it seemed, and the occasional fire-fight still broke out. He hadn't wanted to die during the numerous battles he'd been involved in, but to die now that the war was over… He didn't like to contemplate this.

His first combat action had been the infamous D-Day, arriving by landing craft on Sword Beach, fighting against the German 736th Infantry Regiment, a battle-hardened bunch of soldiers. He had seen half of his section killed on the first day, been re-assigned to another section, fought inland. Only three months before this he'd been a civilian, just a boy straight out of school. He remembered being terrified, bullets, mortars, bombs and body parts all around him. And a smell he would become accustomed to in the next two years: death.

Over the next month they had pushed on in to France, the boy becoming a man, a soldier. He ceased to freeze up when the crack of a bullet sounded, now reacting to the sound instantly by going to ground, searching for the source. By the time they reached the River Rhine he was a veteran. He didn't know how many men he had killed, how many bullets he had fired. Too many to think about, certainly not a thing to dwell on if a man wanted to stay sane.

His colleague to his right raised an arm and the line of troops all halted, dropping to one knee. A message was passed along the line. Something up ahead.

A lieutenant passed along the line, organizing the men. He stopped by the young soldier.

"I want you to come forward with me," the subaltern whispered in his ear. "We need to see what we have up there." He gestured to his front, where more light seemed to come through the trees, indicating some sort of clearing. He nodded his understanding: it was something he'd been selected for many times before. He was the platoon's lucky charm. He was their longest serving member.

Raising his Lee-Enfield 303 rifle to his shoulder and pointing it to his front, he moved silently forward, the lieutenant a yard back. He moved from the cover of each tree, looking for movement to his front, checking where the next tree and safety was. The half-light of the forest was brightening, the area to their front clear of trees. As he came to the last three or four trees, he could see there was a clearing, then a wire fence. He dropped to his knees, signalling the officer to join him.

"There's a fence sir," he reported. "Then a second fence. Could be one of those prison camps we heard rumour about."

"Any sign of the krauts?" the man asked, peering forward at the fence line.

"Nothing so far. Might have left."

"Let's carry on then."

He was up and moving, breaking the tree line. That's when the smell hit him. The smell of death, but even worse than he remembered it.

Then he saw it. The skeleton hanging on to the inner fence, about fifty yards to his right.

He pointed. "Sir."

*

The skeleton moved her head towards the movement at the edge of the forest. Soldiers, she registered. From her experiences, that was a bad thing.

Her name was Edya Friedman, and how long she had survived in this hell on earth she wasn't sure. At some point far off in the past she had been a junior accountant at a German law firm based in the beautiful city of Munich. She'd had a life, a fiancée and a future. But that was before the war, that was before a certain Mister Adolf Hitler had come along, changing the face of Europe forever.

She was stick thin, bones protruding out of her flesh, her hour-glass figure long gone. Sometimes she thought this a good thing: it meant that the

German soldiers raped her less than in her first year in the camp. It didn't stop them altogether though, nor did it stop her fellow inmates. Men needed sex.

She knew she was pregnant. Not because of her monthly cycle having stopped. That had become irregular a long-time back, mainly due to the effects of malnutrition. She just knew.

What she didn't know was whether the father was a German or a Jew. Not that she cared. She was going to die in the camp, and so would the child if it was ever born. There was no future for her or her unborn child.

As she watched, more soldiers emerged from the forest. She counted twenty, then gave up counting.

Turning, she started to walk back towards her wooden hut, wondering if the Germans would come back soon and give them some food. Even thin watery soup was better than no soup.

*

The whole platoon was now out of the forest, being organised in to sections by the non-commissioned officers and given tasks.

"And keep an eye out for booby traps," a sergeant warned a section as they approached the fence line with wire cutters. "Too easy to become complacent, then I have to send you back to the girlfriend in a coffin."

The men laughed. They'd heard all this stuff too often. It was the same crack since they'd landed in Normandy.

As they set about opening the fence, more emaciated bodies began to emerge from the huts, staring towards the working squaddies.

"Who the fuck are they Corps?" one young lad asked his Corporal.

"Don't know Nobby," the man told him. "But they bloody stink."

They started cutting out a section of the outer fence, amazed that people could be so thin yet still alive.

*

The men started moving nervously towards the fence where the activity was taking place, mindful that this could be something to catch them out, that the guards could rush around the corner at any time and give them a beating, or perhaps just release the German Shepherd dogs on to them, letting them bite chunks out of their bodies. They'd seen so much evil in the last years that nothing would shock them.

But while they were still alive they also had hope.

In the past months they had heard the sound of shelling in the distance, seen allied aircraft flying over the area. Rumour had it that the allied troops were making progress through Germany, that the German army was on the run. They had no radios, so no way to confirm or dismiss the rumours, and to ask a guard if it were true was to invite a severe beating, or a week in a pit in solitary. Better to just quietly hope.

The troops had breached the outer fence and were at work on the inner one. Only yards away, they could hear them taking.

"They're talking English!" one man exclaimed to his neighbour, eyes wide.

"How do you know?" the other asked.

"I worked in London for a while before the war," the first man told him. "They're English."

The word went around the group of bedraggled and bony bodies, some smiling at the news, some not really understanding what it meant, whether it was good or bad.

"Hey Tommy," one called out. "You killed the Germans?"

A young soldier looked up, horrified at the sight in front of him. "No Germans here mate," he told the half-naked bag of bones before him. "The war's over mate."

The man turned to the other Jews, astonishment on his face. "The war is over. We are free."

A hushed cheer came from the group. They were too weak to celebrate properly and some just made their way back towards the huts. A couple moved towards the hole in the fence, unable to wait any longer for the feeling of freedom.

"Where are you guys from?" a soldier asked them. "Which country?"

"We are Jewish," a man wearing only a pair of knee length shorts replied. "And now we are free."

*

In the next weeks the Jews were ordered to remain at the camp. There was nowhere else to put them, no transport to get them away from there. Doctors examined them, food was organised to try and build up their strength, they were allowed to come and go as they wished, so long as they slept within the barracks. No roll-calls were made, no beatings handed out.

Many still died, their condition too far gone for treatment to work.

The camp the English had found was part of the Kaufering string of camps, an offshoot of the larger Dachau concentration camp.

As the inmates gathered strength, the Allies found they had enough to do without playing nursemaid to them and tried to re-integrate them in to the local communities. Most of the Jewish inmates were too afraid to go back to where they had been before the troubles, fearing that the local people would turn on them. Stories of this kind of thing happening filtered in to the radio news, and the Jews faced more persecution after the war, especially in Poland.

Edya Friedman didn't want to go back to Munich. It was not far from the camp, and too close to too many horrible memories. She was registered as a 'Displaced Person' and moved to a camp in northern Germany, Bergen-Belsen. It had also been a concentration camp, but the British had burned it down on what they called 'health grounds.' They tried to rename the new camp Hohne, but the old Belsen title stuck.

Four months after arriving there Edya had her baby, a fine and heavy boy. She hoped he was of Jewish stock, but looking at his size and blond hair, she guessed he probably wasn't.

She called him Aviv, the word for Spring in Hebrew. She hoped it would signify a new start for both him and her.

There were hundreds of Jews in Belsen. Almost all had suffered dreadful losses during the war in the ghettos, or in the labour camps where the Germans had later housed them. Brothers, sisters, mothers, fathers, sons, daughters and lovers had all been lost, separated from one another, killed in front of other family members. They all had nothing, all of their worldly goods gone. It was a time to find a fresh start, and for Edya, that start had to come outside of Germany.

She met Adam, a middle aged man who had seen his wife hung before him for daring to try to keep her handbag. He had been made to watch, tied to a tree. They were united in their sorrow, but also in their hate and mistrust of the German people. They had to get away.

In early 1947 there was much talk about a Jewish homeland being set-up in Palestine in the Middle East. It was where their religion had its roots, a place with a lifestyle and climate different from the one they both knew.

And it was far away from Germany.

Palestine, 1947

"What the hell are we doing here?" a young British soldier asked after another night of guard duty. "It's bloody hot, and neither the Arabs nor the Jews want us here. We're getting killed for nothing!"

Though a simplistic view, his officer knew he was right. Since the end of the First World War the British government had sent out conflicting messages to the people of the region, on one hand promising the Jews a homeland, and on the other saying that they undertook to form an Arab State in Palestine. He also knew that following the Second Great War his nation was sick of fighting and close to bankrupt, and that supporting around 100,000 troops in Palestine was not high on the political agenda.

"You'll be fine lad," he told the boy. "Just think; you couldn't get a suntan like this in London."

It was the usual military fall-back position – humour. It worked again, and the private went off to his bunk to catch-up on a missed nights rest.

The officer looked out over the streets of Jerusalem, wondering where the situation was going. The Arabs had largely sided with the Axis forces during the war, hoping to be rewarded by them at the end of the affair by removing the Jewish settlers from their land. When the Axis lost, the Arabs were forced to take the bull by the horns and try and rid themselves of two sets of invaders: the British and the Jews. Most of the action was terrorist attacks on key installations; people dressed in long Arab robes hitting pipelines, check points and Jewish homes.

And the Jews were also unhappy he knew. They had been promised a land of their own for years, and now after two wars still didn't have it. They had been murdered in great numbers during the last war – people were calling it the holocaust, and the figures were still not at all clear – and their numbers were all over Europe without a safe haven to run to. The more extreme ones amongst them had also started attacking the British Army, so now they were getting it from two sides.

He watched the men and women pass the military base, wondering why they couldn't just live together peacefully. They even looked the same.

The boy came out screaming, letting everyone know that he was here on the earth, here in Palestine.

"He's got a good set of lungs," the female doctor said, cleaning the boy up a little before passing him to his exhausted mother. "One extremely healthy baby," she concluded, smiling at the woman before leaving the ward. The father watched her disappear.

"What do we call him?" he asked.

"I thought Ibrahim," the mother said, the shadows under her eyes deep. "After the Prophet."

The father paused, hoping his own name or the name of his father would have been the choice. He thought about arguing but could see that his wife was tired and knew that it wasn't worth the fight anyway. "Ibrahim it is then," he agreed.

His wife smiled back at him. "You want to hold him?" she asked, holding the baby up.

He took the child, walking to the open window of the room and staring out. His mind was on the raid he had planned for that very evening, and he stood staring blindly at the landscape before him for a whole minute. When he turned around his wife was fast asleep.

"Shit," he muttered to himself. He was now left holding the baby. He took a seat by the bed and soon nodded off himself.

*

Rashid Ghafour stood before the other five men that would be part of his strike against the British that evening, only three and a half hours after leaving his wife and new-born son at the hospital. His wife had pleaded that he kept away from the violence, that he gave her and his new child a chance to become a real family. He had of course agreed that he would. Any other answer would have led to a protracted argument, and he simply didn't have time for one.

He addressed his men. "The United Nations Council are again talking seriously about giving the Jews land, land that is presently called Palestine. In other words our land. You of course know this." He looked at the team, noting that three of them were probably less than eighteen. "Tonight we will try and disrupt things again."

One of the young fighters raised a clenched fist. "We will kill the foreigners."

Rashid hid a frown, knowing that once the bullets were flying this young boy would be less optimistic. "Keep calm my friend. The soldiers are not stupid, and they are well armed. We must be careful and be sure to achieve our goals."

One of the two older men spoke. "What are our goals tonight?" he asked, voice a little shaky.

Rashid faced him, knowing that the man was fearing for his own safety. It was a better attitude to the do-or-die one the youth had shown. At least this one had some combat experience, knew how bad it could get during a fire-fight.

"We are to wipe out a British check-point. They have four soldiers manning it, all with Lee-Enfield rifles, plus a machinegun post. It will not be easy, but once we have accomplished our own mission, our brothers will come through the check-point and wipe out a Jewish housing area, where three of their families dare to live by us."

The young man rose to his feet, eyes excited. "Can we join our brothers? Can we join them in the slaughter of the Jews?"

Rashid thought about an appropriate answer, not wanting to kill the spark in the man's heart, but also not wishing him dead on his first raid.

"We can see how our own work goes, then ask the main force commander if he should need us."

"Jews and bloody British in one night! That would be something."

The older man looked to Rashid, sadness in his eyes.

"If Allah wishes it, it will happen."

*

The British were next to the outskirts of Jerusalem, on the road leading to Bethlehem, two of the main spiritual locations for the two sides, the Arabs and the Jews. There was no barrier, just a camp fire by the road to light them up, and a sentry to stop anyone passing by vehicle, or on horse or foot. A mound of sandbags to one side housed a machinegun, their main fire power. Two of the men sat by the fire making a brew, the other two watched the road.

Rashid led his small party through the houses close to the post, keeping in the shadows, making as little noise as possible. Most people were already in bed at eleven in the evening, and the ones that saw them pass made their own way indoors. It was best to see nothing.

They had a mix of weapons left by invaders of their country over the last decades. Nothing new, but an old bullet is as deadly as a new one if it fires correctly.

Rashid had briefed them well. "We will get close to the sentry post and I will signal for us to stop." He raised an open hand. "There will be no words, nothing to warn them. I will then position each of you, give you your target." He looked from one man to the next. "You," he pointed to the youngest one, "will face away from the enemy, guard our backs."

"But I want to kill a soldier," the man complained.

"Shush," Rashid ordered. "You will get your chance when we carry on to get the Jews."

The young man smiled.

"When I think we are ready, I will give the order to fire. It should be easy." He added the last part as much for himself as for his team. "Six of us, four of them."

And now they were there, fifty yards from the unsuspecting soldiers. He halted them, went to set the first man in his place behind a wall.

BANG! The noise of the old rifle discharging scared him to death, sure that the soldiers were firing on them. He turned towards the target, trying to see what was going on, but the soldiers appeared equal surprised. BANG! A second shot.

He turned and saw that the over-enthusiastic youth had the rifle to his shoulder, firing at will.

"Stop it you stupid bastard!" he screamed.

It was too late. The British were also young, but all had seen some service in World War Two and reacted according to conditioned reflexes. They quickly picked out the group of Arab men to their right and the machinegun rattled loudly.

*

Ibrahim Ghafour had no memory of his father. His earliest recollections were of moving to a new house, of being refugees as his mother tried to find them a place to stay with friend after friend, relative after relative. The home his parents had lived in was long gone, part of a Palestine given away to the Jews.

The British soldiers had also gone before he had any recall of them, withdrawn when things got too tough and funding didn't cover keeping them there. The League of Nations British Mandate of Palestine was over, the British military fed-up with being the piggy-in-the-middle for the game of death played between the Arabs and Jews.

Ibrahim lived in a land divided, and the Arab population were the losers in the division. The State of Israel has been born.

State of Israel, 1967

Junior Deputy Aviv Friedman lowered himself in to the cockpit of his Dassault Mirage IIICJ jet, his pre-flight walk-around complete, blanks and safety devices removed. He stowed the various flags and pins in a storage area behind the seat, and slid in to the chair, positioning his four point safety harness around his shoulders and waist. It was a sequence of events he had carried out hundreds of times, something he could carry out in pitch darkness or bright sunshine. Today it was the latter.

He pushed back his fairly short black hair from a slightly whiter face than that of his colleagues, placing his flying helmet above his head and pulling it in to position on his scalp. He was twenty-one years of age and had qualified as a fighter pilot only two months earlier. He was nervous: this was to be his first real combat mission, his first time in a hostile sky.

It was warm in the cockpit, and he ran through the start-up checks, making switches and circuit breakers, checking that instruments ran-up correctly and setting his altimeter with today's air pressure. In his ear he could hear the radio chatter between the other pilots and the control tower, could hear the tension in each voice, the excitement that they all felt.

"Let's cut out the chat please," the voice of his Chief Commander demanded through the headsets of them all. "Focus on the start-up drills and remember you have live munitions on board. No fuck-ups."

A bead of sweat rolled down his back inside of the flying suit, another down the side of his face within the helmet. He reminded himself that this was for real.

A command came in his ear piece to start his engine. A final scan over the instruments and he pressed the starter button, heard the whirr of the motor turning over the compressor, hearing the increase in pitch as the speed ran up on the indicator, imagined the fuel mist filling the combustion chamber, then heard the whumph of the engine lighting up following the click of the torch ignitor. The temperatures indicated in different sections of the engine shot-up, the turbine speed increasing until the jet engine reached a self-sustaining rpm.

He looked out of the cockpit window at the jets around him, all going through the same start-up sequence. The noise was fantastic, something he treasured each time he heard it.

"Two-six Delta ready to roll," he reported in.

Other pilots began reporting their own readiness, the air thick with Avgas fumes and jet noise, a heady combination for a team of young aviators.

"Hold your positions and stay in the idle gate," the boss instructed them all.

They'd all been assigned targets in the pre-flight briefing, all knew who would be flying on their wing, who'd be providing top cover. They were a very fit, highly trained and motivated bunch of airmen, ready to die for their country if the need came. The only thing missing from the mix was experience, and in the next days they would get plenty of that or die trying.

"Two-six Delta. Make your way to the assembly point at the east end of runway nine-zero."

Aviv let out a long sigh as he released the brakes. It was time to go and put the training in to practice.

*

The tensions had been building for some time now. Egypt had sided with Jordan after an Israeli attack on the city of as-Samu in the West Bank, this in retaliation to terrorist activities from the area by the Palestinian Liberation Organisation, or PLO.

Aviv and his young aviators had waited for the next move, constantly on standby duty, watching reports of Egyptian troops massing along their country's borders in the Sinai Peninsula, and Syrian artillery shelling the country in the northern border regions.

When Egypt closed the Straits of Tiran to Israeli shipping, effectively closing the Port of Eilat, the Israeli government had declared the move an act of war.

The stage was set, and on June the 5th 1967, Israel reacted.

*

At five thousand feet Aviv levelled his fighter and looked to his left. A second Mirage floated about thirty yards away, so close it looked as if he could touch it by reaching out of the canopy. He remembered again why he had sweated his way through training to become a fighter pilot. His wingman gave him a thumbs-up, grinning below his visor.

They turned on to a south-westerly heading, their target an Egyptian airfield in the Sinai. The flight time would be measured in minutes, the computer showing corrections to their heading on the artificial horizon.

He adjusted the stick slightly to go to the indicated area. The desert ran out before him.

"Arming munitions," he told his comrade in arms, receiving a similar message in return.

The plan was to hit the Egyptian jets before they had a chance to get in to the air, to minimize their air superiority in a single solid strike. So far it appeared to be working, with no enemy jet returns on the radar.

"I can see the airfield about five miles ahead," he heard in his earphones.

"I'll take the first run," he told the man.

Pushing the stick forward, he dropped the aircraft to about two hundred feet above the sand, zooming in over the ground.

"All clear from up here," his wingman reported.

"Going in."

He raced over the sand and on to the edge of the enemy airfield. Ahead of him he could lines of MiG fighters lined up on either side of the live runway. He pulled the stick back, the nose lifting up, and pressed the release button for the high-explosive bomb under the aircraft's belly. As the ordinance flew free, the now lighter aircraft started to climb out, away from the late bursts of gunfire from the ground troops. A shock wave of air rocked the aircraft and he knew that the explosives had done as they promised and it was only whether or not he had been on target.

The voice of his colleague came through the intercom. "Going in."

He was now back-up at around five thousand feet and allowed himself the privilege of rolling his aircraft in order to see the ground. The second Mirage was streaking towards the plane hangars, smoke and flames already coming from some of the MiG fighters. He saw it jerk upwards as it started its climb, did not see the bombs but did see the explosions.

A hangar building disintegrated before his eyes, burning building parts raining down on the one next to it. Aircraft were in flames, and an explosion shook the airframe as something else on the ground exploded, perhaps an ammunition store.

"Return to base," he told the other pilot, looking from the carnage on the ground to the broad smile on the face of the other pilot.

*

His third mission of the day over, Aviv lay on his bed, dog-tired. He'd flown six hours, all of it at lower altitudes than usual, all under stress, and occasionally with bullets coming his way. He and his wingman had made it through the day's action, but three of his colleagues hadn't been so lucky. It had been an emotional rollercoaster.

He was just drifting off to sleep when a tannoy blared, calling the pilots to the Operations Room. The Chief Commander was at the front of the room.

"Well done today gentlemen, you performed as well as I could have hoped. We lost a few wonderful pilots and colleagues, but our nation also lost many good men, especially on the border with Syria. We will be heading that way tomorrow morning at first light. Your aircraft will be prepared tonight with for ground attack. First sortie will lift at oh-five-fifteen, then every fifteen minutes after that, another two aircraft will scramble. On return you will be re-armed and refuelled and go to next in line." He pointed to a board at the rear of the room. "You'll find your initial slot times back there. Now get some sleep."

*

Aviv had been given the five-forty-five slot, but was awake just after four, his head buzzing. He rolled over and tried to sleep, but images of his aircraft zooming over the desert kept him awake. He pulled himself from the bed and headed for the shower, then climbed in to his flying suit and walked down to the mess to get some breakfast.

On the wall of the mess were aerial photos of yesterday's targets, a variety of pictures of wrecked aircraft at different airfields between the Israeli and Egyptian borders.

He heard someone behind him and turned to see the boss.

"The Intelligence people believe we knocked out about three hundred of their planes in the first two hours of the war," he was told. "Gives us total air dominance."

The man then turned and headed to the hot plate.

"Shit," Aviv said to himself, then followed.

*

He knew he'd crossed the border and was in Syria. If he was shot down here, he'd be in deep shit. He glanced across at his wingman – a different one today, not someone from his own pilot's course. No thumbs-up today, just a minor nod of recognition.

They were passing over the Golan Heights now, looking for targets. The Intel was low, so they were tasked to 'search and destroy.' Aviv saw a column of armoured personnel carriers snaking down a mountain road and told the wingman.

"I'll take first strike," the man told him. "You watch out."

He watched as the Mirage rolled right, side-slipping down towards the road. Watched it roll back out to even keel and start strafing the convoy, the odd vehicle coughing out flames and smoke.

"Following you in," he told the other pilot.

He pressed the trigger, watching the rounds laced with tracer fly towards the target, altering his course to get the best hit rate. More flames, more smoke.

From above, his wingman passed comment. "I think that lot are done. Let's get back and replenish."

Aviv pulled up, rolled towards Israel and fell in by his companion.

*

The next day was more of the same. More bombs, more bullets, more smoke and flame, more young men dead. But the Israelis were winning, pushing their enemies back from the border areas, gaining ground that was not rightfully theirs.

On the 10th June it was all over. The Jewish State had gained ground in the Gaza Strip, the Golan Heights, the Sinai Peninsula and the West Bank. They had suffered terrible losses, especially in the ground offensive, but nothing compared to their enemies.

The battles became known as Milhemet Sheshet Ha Yamin in Hebrew - the Six Day War, referring to the days God needed to create the earth. In Arabic they were called an-Nakash. Translated to English, this roughly meant 'The Setback.'

In six days Aviv had flown thirty-two sorties, over twenty-eight flying hours. He could now consider himself blooded.

To read more, go to Amazon Books and google No Gods, Gordon Clark! Thanks for all of your support!

Printed in Great Britain
by Amazon

84591168R00139